A SOLITARY AWAKENING

BOOK ONE OF THE WARREN FILES

Hey, Nancy!
Thanks for giving my
book a chance! Happy reading!
-Kevin

KEVIN CADY

ISBN: 978-1-4834-4867-1 (sc)
ISBN: 978-1-4834-4866-4 (e)

Library of Congress Control Number: 2016904685

Because of the dynamic nature of the Internet, any web addresses or links contained in this book may have changed since publication and may no longer be valid. The views expressed in this work are solely those of the author and do not necessarily reflect the views of the publisher, and the publisher hereby disclaims any responsibility for them.

Any people depicted in stock imagery provided by Thinkstock are models, and such images are being used for illustrative purposes only.
Certain stock imagery © Thinkstock.

Lulu Publishing Services rev. date: 04/08/2016

For those who seek to understand why.

Solitude never bothered me. I suppose it's a good thing with how it all turned out. As a kid I remember not wanting to force relationships, a clever inclination that they would all most likely come to an end. I didn't justify it that way then. I was just OK being alone. It's interesting how the reason for something can stay the same yet age and experience changes its phrasing. What hasn't changed is this. I can't find much good in human nature, never have liked how people can transform, different company, different faces, versions of self for the moment at hand.

What happened wasn't the plan. Mom and Dad's hobby consumed our lives and was ultimately to blame for our splintering like irregular shards of glass. I was eight when we moved from a small town in the US to Son La, Vietnam. Mom and Dad worried more about the world's problems than they did our own.

April 30, 1975, the Vietnam War ended. On the first of May my family began planning our move. Their reasons are now clear to me, though, at the time, the change seemed unfathomable. My eight-year-old brain could only see reasons to stay, and like most eight-year-old brains, I wouldn't accept that which I couldn't understand. I remember hearing that the world needed help. Turns out it was us, and in the end me, that needed help. The freedom fighters and their son set off to fight their cause in the spring of '76.

When it came to education, "our situation" had always been different than that of other kids', and my home schooling trend from the States continued in Son La. I wasn't concerned with the social void, though I couldn't understand why my attending a normal school was out of the question. I wanted life to be normal. I wanted to be. Despite this disquiet, I'd always loved learning, and the silver lining was that Mom and Dad afforded world-class educators.

It took them a week or so to hire my in-house instructor, who doubled as my nanny; her name was Luna. I spent a wide ocean of time with Luna. She was middle aged and German, a lady that dressed as if recreating a battle from the First War of Scottish Independence. She'd the stature to be a participant. Our conversations remained practical.

Occasionally, when Mom and Dad were home early, we'd sit around the fireplace as a family. It was the one connection I longed for, maybe needed. It was one such night that all I knew changed. The fire bounced irregular shadows on our faces, a wineglass glistening in Mom's left hand, dark liquid sloshing this way and that in Dad's. An old Duke Ellington record spun on the player. My head bobbed and I fell in and out of sleep. Each partial lapse in consciousness brought a look left and right to make sure they were still beside me.

You never forget a sound if it spawns an absolute and irreversible change in your life. A crude bomb smashed through our front window. Mom swept me up while Dad moved toward it. I didn't know what he was doing, but he didn't seem surprised. The next thing I knew Mom was lifting open a hatch in our hallway floor, hitherto unbeknownst to me. She then rushed me down inside of it. I looked back and watched the flames devour her. I couldn't help it, though now it stands as the single regret I've borne. The split second that the door slammed shut still visits me while I sleep. I remember her face, helpless and tormented. Time stood for a long moment and I remember thinking that it would be the last time I'd see into her eyes, emerald green and blooming in the flames.

When you lose all you know you begin to discover what you really are.

As the ambivalence of what had become my reality soaked me, I cowered in a dark crease of the room that existed underneath our new home. I stayed there after the explosion until the walls stopped quaking, and I can't recall how long that was, but it seemed forever.

Then I tried to clear my head. Get back to the door. I pushed upward with all my tiny body. The door stayed fixed. As the idea of being stuck set in, so did my descent into absolute objectivity.

I gave up on the hatch, tried to rationalize. It was the darkest place I had ever been and I knew there had to be a light source. I needed to figure out where I was in relation to whatever else was down there. As I felt my way along the walls, they were cold and rough, the floor frigid on my naked feet.

I ran my hands along the walls and razor thin dashes were seared on the palms and tips of my hands, untreated concrete I guessed. A quarter of the way about this seemingly endless dark, I felt row after row of cans. The shelves organizing the cans wove like lines at an amusement park. I finally stumbled upon a flashlight and batteries, a lifetime's supply of candles, which revealed a lifetime's supply of books. Endless knowledge by candlelight, a tiny flickering flame in a sea of swallowing black.

I thought long and hard about why that place existed. Why had we come to Vietnam? Were we running from something? With no answers to be had, I settled into a tenuous and volatile balance of neutrality, objectivity. It wasn't until I was free that I began to understand the significance of my boyhood curse. The years that followed were twisted, a gnarled trail after my solitary awakening.

CHAPTER 1

*I*t's a bit of a shock I can live a semi-normal life.
With that said, is tracking down murderers normal?

The sun was yet to rise, and Elijah Warren drove toward yet another crime scene. A vicious New York whiteout was before him and made arriving unscathed less certain with evanescent moments. He couldn't help but notice the road was thinning, winding more tenuously. The Hudson River was far below, on the right, and a precipitous void led to it. Elijah was focused, well aware of, but unaffected by, the prospective violence before him.

Elijah Warren had thick black hair, which still lay messy from time on his pillow. The detective wore his usual outfit, dark pants, a white shirt, and a mid-width dark tie. Today, because of the weather, he wore a knee length overcoat to yield the cold, the wind. His tie hung lazily under a never-sealed top button. The outfit was an obscure combination of foreign yet comfortable. It fit him not, yet he'd worn it so perpetually that it'd become almost a part of him, cloth stitched with skin.

Days off from the bureau he found himself deep in Central Park, as far as he could get, loftily musing that he was beyond the city and away from concrete. He felt whole in those scarce moments, though it was work that satisfied, maybe occupied him, more wholly than that. He wore time-borne jeans and a tattered Alice In Chains T-shirt. Elijah stood almost six feet tall and both men and women at the office wondered how his naturally-formed arms—that shone through that same white dress shirt he wore—got there to begin with. He didn't seem to exercise, and often those at the FBI covetously mocked his "good genes."

The lucky bastard.

Elijah didn't spend much time with women but had more than enough opportunity. The deep blues of his eyes were piercing and looked out from under thick waves of black that dipped into his gaze. He had a thoughtful smile, though he rarely shared it.

He'd spent three years at the Federal Bureau of Investigation, recruited from a homicide task force on St. Louis' east side. Not many were there six months, but Elijah Warren fit in.

In St. Louis, he had a deep well of things to fix. Constant work took away from the time he could ponder, get caught in his head, and the violent nature of the supply chain didn't seem to trouble him. He'd made a name for himself being direct, calculated...somehow likable.

Elijah Warren will fight for you in the direst of moments. You will come to count on him.

His recommendation letter from the St. Louis PD was sadly written, with much pride.

The FBI came to count on Elijah in the following years.

Year one, Elijah was asked to find and capture a man named David Wills. In 1990 Wills began a series of drive-by shootings outside of Baltimore. The attacks were straightforward and lethal, neighborhood blocks left wet and thick with crimson and flesh, thick gore that painted bushes and settled in the creases of the curbs, ran into the sewers. Wills would choose a neighborhood and fire out the window. He never used the same type of weapon and it didn't matter race, religion, age or sex. Wills just killed for killin's sake.

Elijah was given the assignment after the eleventh attack.

David Wills was arrested after fourteen mass casualty incidents and Elijah Warren had made a name for himself with the two-hour shootout on I-83 to seal the deal. He was a valuable weapon. He was dedicated and intelligent. More importantly, he hadn't a personal life, a family. He really was the perfect asset, though at the present moment, he regretted such.

As his tires settled into the newly fallen snow, Detective Warren pulled tight his hood to brave the cold. He stepped out for only a moment before his fingertips began to sing.

It was January 13th, 1997, and the season was in full swing.

Fucking winters in New York.

Elijah was able to finish his thought just in time to receive an *equally* cold welcome from local law enforcement.

"Who the fuck are you?"

He stood and thought for a moment, wet snow sticking in his three-days-old five o'clock shadow and wind slamming him in the face. He decided he hadn't the patience.

"Elijah Warren. Here for the Bureau. Here to meet—"

"Oh! Detective Blanc! Yes. Of course. Yes-yes. Sorry about that. She's right this way." The kid couldn't have been more than twenty-two, and his beaming response met souring ears. Unfortunately the brain behind those ears knew why his response was so much brighter than the weather.

"Yes."

Elijah sighed into the frigid night.

"Her."

And a river of breath lingered.

It was a bitter night in New York, bitter and bloody at 854 Outcrop Drive. The house was in Grand View On Hudson Village, aptly named with its two hundred residents and the Hudson River trickling from there into Manhattan. There, thick groves of trees led up to the skies and houses were tucked below.

Elijah repeated an old phrase he'd heard and stepped after the young officer. It had something to do with surviving a New York winter.

Each minute the weather worsened.

His footsteps were swift and sure. Officer McMillan approached the front door and held it for Elijah to enter. Inside, a great atrium led to a hallway, mirrors on each wall, then into a vast room with soaring walls, the walls draped in paintings, enormous frames and bold colors. Sculptures sat frequently at eye level on white, engraved platforms, tangles of superfluous knick-knacks and priceless works, either internationally collected or exceptionally knocked off, though it could have been both. Elijah assumed it was just the former.

The weather outside had been a barrier to seeing just what type of home this was. The inside left nothing to the imagination. It was old money, sharp with a mark in each detail. Elijah talked quietly to himself, weaving through tall, leather furniture, over Persian rugs and past a statue that he couldn't pull his eyes from, dark stone, a hunched figure, eyes empty and a curled smile. He moved on towards the back of the house, craning his head to view the higher paintings, picture windows revealing sparse moonbeams and heaving gusts of snow.

"Wish the country's education budget was worth this."

Officer McMillan looked at him, a bit put-off. This mattered to Elijah about as much as it seemed. He continued, decisively. No detail of the home was overlooked. Nothing was ignored.

He followed McMillan to a bedroom on the second floor. An overwhelming staircase led their way, wide at the bottom and thinning with elevation. There, sat a thick burgundy carpet. They turned toward the northeast corner of the house and were met by Aurelia Blanc.

Detective Blanc's smile demanded attention; deep and wide brown eyes were enchanting, a suffocating magnet of sensuality that allowed you no air once locked in. They'd attracted Elijah incipiently, though her full ass didn't hurt. Plus she was smart. *Too* smart.

Aurelia was the best forensic pathologist in the Bureau, her undergraduate degree in abnormal psych from Harvard, where she doubled majored in law. She then earned her Ph.D. in neuropsychology from Yale, in Connecticut. Aurelia Blanc seemed to have it all.

Except personality, Elijah had thought on multiple occasions.

"Good morning, Detective Warren. I'm surprised you weren't here earlier."

Not anymore, he thought to himself.

"G-morning. And I feel like you *aren't* surprised that I wasn't here earlier. Either way, it's too early to be having *this* conversation. Whaddya know?"

She hated how mad he made her.

She hated that stupid, "G-morning," that she just knew was meant to piss her off.

"Well," she said, "I'm quite sure nothing you don't already *think* you know, Elijah Warren, but follow me."

He hated how mad she made him.

He followed her and admired her ass for a second longer than usual, out of spite.

A grand bedroom became their milieu and Elijah's mind focused. He looked about the room and listened to Aurelia's words, unaware that she would soon be his partner at the Bureau.

"At first glance it seemed typical enough, husband with a bullet in the rear of his skull on the floor, wife naked on the bed with one between the eyes. Two bullets. Two deaths. It's possible she shot him and turned the gun on herself, though the entry wound would make that a bit askance."

Elijah Warren listened. He paced, his chin in his fingers, which moved unknowingly on the scruff there. He archived what he was seeing—at the offset it'd been the overwhelming, uniformed white of the room, though it *was* pooled and splashed with crimson; rivulets ran through the thick, white carpet, spreading across the room in a circulatory system of liquid gore—then cross-referenced his thoughts with those of Detective Blanc, his methods precise.

She continued, "The woman's Teresa Randall, and that's her husband, Mike, local politician. Kind of a scum bag I think." She knelt down to Mike and gave him a thoughtful look, though Elijah couldn't tell quite *what* it was. "Not much relevant on either," she continued, sounding as if she was a bit bored. "After our initial walkthrough CSI found—"

"The bullets are both .45s but the entry wounds are different. One from a hollow point, the other a full met—"

"Yes… A full metal jacket. Don't pat yourself on the back yet, Holmes."

Had she just compared him to his fictitious idol? He hid a smirk, despite her aim to be quarrelsome, said nothing and looked at her a bit like she was an arduous math problem.

That moment lasted a bit.

"We have the wife shot with a hollow point, the husband a full metal jacket. The gun in the wife's hand doesn't match either bullet, and it's the only gun in the house. This means we're missing at least a person, and a gun or two, because neither bullet hole matches that tiny little gun."

She looked over toward the white-turned-red bed, the woman missing the top third of her face, now turned to a tilted mesh of whirling sponges and flesh and skull, thick, thick red saturated into the sheets.

"Setup? Horrible cover-up?" he asked.

"Thinking cover-up."

"Run her mobile phone?"

"Waiting on results. I think that'll be our best bet, at least to start."

Elijah nodded as she spoke, said nothing but was thinking the same. They worked silently after that. The blood splatter analyst had done her job, as had the CSI unit. What *they* were looking for was a different type of clue, one only accessible to people looking at the world a bit differently. Clint Adams, the FBI's director, had watched each detective excel and grow and baffle him with breakthroughs in seemingly innocuous cases, each as stubborn as the other, and knew that if they could put their overactive minds and egos aside, they'd be a great team.

Their movements through the bedroom appeared planned, their actions fluid and sure with no question of what to do next, working separately in an ostensibly choreographed dance, Beethoven's fifth for the noiseless soundtrack, each consumed by the task at hand.

Their focus was broken only when Officer McMillan burst excitedly into the room.

"Detective Blanc, I found out that Teresa Randall's last phone call was from Charles Larson! That's not her husband! You guys should check that out."

Elijah was pleased with the news, though the kid was starting to annoy him.

"They also found that Larson has a Smith and Wesson .45 registered to him," the kid continued.

The bullet would match the mess that was Teresa's head. Larson's call had come in at 8:05pm the night before, followed by a missed call from Mike at 9pm.

As the pair processed these details, their thoughts ran to the same thing.

"She met him at the door, invited him up, and was interrupted after missing a call from her husband," Aurelia said, not quite out loud.

Elijah was (unprofessionally) following the crest of her hair to her collarbone. He wished he wasn't so attracted to her. *If it wasn't for that personality.*

They were on their way out the door as the argument of "who's driving" to Larson's last known address ensued.

Aurelia's headlights cut through a furious sea of white as they spun a more specific web of what might have happened.

"There *is* a pretty logical line of thinking from affair to angry husband," Aurelia said.

"But why are both the wife and him dead?"

"Exactly. And why does neither bullet hole match the gun in the house? I follow why the husband could've had his gun ready. He comes home and finds his wife with another man, gets the gun and confronts them."

As they talked, Elijah wished he could actually commit to the idea that Mike Randall just happened upon his wife's affair. Luckily, it wasn't far to reach Larson's last known address. Twenty minutes and it looked like a different country. Detective Blanc's Subaru cautiously moved toward the house. She looked through the glass, a bit uneasy, squinting through the hurricanes of white. This part of town had been long since forgotten. Houses were standing, but not by much. If riots could change its ambiance, it may be for better. Doors hung loosely on hinges that were rusting into oblivion. Windows were frequently replaced with boards or another inadequate substitution. Trash blew about and cars sat up on blocks. Spray paint covered most everything.

On a morning as cold and unyielding as this, Elijah and Aurelia empathized greatly with the few remaining residents. The only redeeming quality of the Grand View suburb was the towering trees that lined the streets and filled the skies. In another time, it could be a beautiful place to live.

But not today.

Snow raged in cyclonic fashion and wind tore across the Outback. The only sound was the whirring and whooshing as the car was shaken by authoritative gusts. Elijah wished he wore warmer clothes, even before the bitter air reached him.

The shattering of the passenger window ripped him from a consumed reverie. Glass pierced Aurelia's cheek and the car careened over a ditch and into a yard diagonally across from Larson's house. The airbags deployed in an eruption of force, the lingering chemicals stinging their eyes.

"What the fuck!?" Aurelia was able to shout once her breath came back.

"Could be gunfire! Wouldn't have heard it with the wind!" Elijah said.

A second shot tore through Elijah's headrest and the question was answered. They instinctively fled the driver's side of the car and established themselves behind it for strategic view of Larson's house. Their ribs hurt. Their faces stung.

"This is weird right?" he said to Aurelia. "Can you see where the shots are coming from?"

"I obviously can't see, but I think I know which house."

He ignored her sarcastic, albeit amusing answer.

Aurelia glanced over the hood and through a glimpse in the blizzard spotted a figure looming in the far-left window of the teetering house.

"Shit," she said as a bullet forced her head back behind the car.

"McMillan, hurry up and get backup here. We didn't even get to the house and he's spraying bullets out his window like it's fucking Iraq."

The bittersweet news was that the weather was worsening, and so was visibility. They needed to separate and one to approach the house, one to provide cover. They needed to take Larson alive.

Aurelia slowly raised her .45, a Smith and Wesson as well, and shot five equally spaced shots above the window Larson loomed beyond. Elijah's feet moved as swiftly as they could in the fresh powder. He used the massive cottonwood trees as cover as he passed through the whirlwind.

He paused and pressed his back against the side of the house when he reached it. He then slowly moved towards the back. While passing windows he peered carefully inside. It was a wreck; trash covered the floor and furniture. No wonder he preferred time at the Randall's supercilious residence. The only item seemingly of any value was a television, of course. Elijah never understood the mixed up priorities of some people in financial turmoil. They could somehow afford a sports car and a TV, but not decent food for themselves or their children.

Aurelia carefully looked at the house, realizing she hadn't seen the figure since her cover fire rang out. She scanned the house; she began to worry. There were only three small windows and her tenuous ability to observe was yielding nothing. Just then she heard a crash at the back of the house.

Elijah crept around the back of the house; his pulse raced. His mind no longer worked on the pieces to the still abstract puzzle. He moved cautiously, with exactness and composure but didn't see the attack coming.

A man from inside came crashing through the window with a wild and tangled lurch, clobbered Elijah's head with what felt like the butt of a gun, an elbow, and a bit of his own head. Elijah collapsed. Snow billowed from his body as he landed in the thick powder. Blood warmed him and he looked up at his aggressor. His day had rapidly spiraled from being just a cold morning.

A threatening silhouette loomed over him and said nothing. A gun sat comfortably in his hand, begging to do its job. Elijah wondered if he would feel being shot. The cold had effectively numbed every nook of his body.

The all-too familiar feeling of staring into death's eyes tingled its way up his spine.

A gunshot broke the night's silence and he saw a hole tear through Charles Larson's hand. His gun fell to the ground.

Elijah grabbed his own pistol and pinned Charles to the ground, ignoring his screams and curses. Aurelia stood stoically, her pistol still fixed on the man she'd just shot. She slowly approached them as police cruisers arrived on the scene, light beams cutting the white-black swirls of night.

The officers walked Larson to the car and Aurelia helped Elijah from the ground.

The moment was silent and they stood still, light barely able to pass between their bodies.

Elijah quietly said, "thank you, Aurelia."

CHAPTER 2

As always, Elijah strolled into the FBI's New York City offices later than Detective Blanc. Aurelia watched him saunter through the door. His gaze covered the room like a blanket, and she saw him taking in each person, each off kilter stack of paper, the new hire that was walking aimlessly straightening them, the light that was flickering at the rear of the room, above Aurelia and to the side. She felt a small pang to the ego when she realized she hadn't seen it until she'd observed him doing so.

"What *I* don't understand," she said to him as he neared, "is how it takes someone so long to drink a cup of coffee."

"What *I* don't understand, is why you're in such a rush to hang out with either murderers or FBI tight-asses every day."

"Did you go to your little diner? Sit in your little spot?"

"I absolutely did. And I enjoyed *three* cups of coffee sitting there."

"I've heard that place is dirty. Like, they don't wash things."

"That… does not bother me," he said with a wink.

She glowered a little.

"That… does not *shock* me. Just know that we live in New York and there are other places that serve shitty coffee and have little corners for you to sit in," she replied. "Ya don't need to go to a dirty one." She turned away. A coquettish grin crept across her face. Elijah's likewise, unbeknownst to her.

The two walked to the interrogation room where Charles Larson sat waiting. They looked through the glass. Charles wasn't particularly memorable looking. He was tall, average build, average looking. His shoulder's slouched heavily, his eyes remained downturned. His hands were in his lap. His right foot was twisting in little pendulums, heel off the ground.

"Who gets first try?" Aurelia said.

"Go get him, doc. Show me the way. I'll have another coffee."

She hated when he called her doc, like it was a bad thing that she had her doctorate. She doubted he could even read. One of those prodigy recruits for the Feds. Probably tested so well or was so highly recommended that he got the "pass," like the asshole football players she sat beside in her freshman microbiology course, attended rarely, maybe put their name on exams, didn't buy the books, passed anyway. Her mind's eye showed her Elijah at that age, aloof and naturally gifted with no sense of empathy, she fathomed, skating through courses with either his smile or his tongue. Even still, it was well known for being silver.

The room that held Charles Larson echoed Aurelia's high-heeled steps in an ominous clicking.

"Mr. Larson," she said coolly. "Good morning. My name is Aurelia Blanc." He looked up after seeing her fit legs come into view, intrigued, until he saw her face, and realized who she was. She read his expression.

"I do apologize about your hand. Though, I assume you understand the options you gave me. Can I sit?" He looked back at the floor, but nodded. She thanked him.

"Charles, can you explain why you opened fire on my partner and I yesterday?"

"You were going to arrest me."

"Well, at least you're honest. That's a start. Do you plan to continue being this cooperative?"

"There's not really a point in not cooperating."

"That's true, though I don't hear that often. I guess in the spirit of it, what happened to Teresa and Mike Randall?"

An enormous silence filled the room, and she looked at him. His discomfort emanated from his non-verbals. Aurelia tried to know the shifting emotions on his face, though couldn't. They were askew from typical murderers. He was maybe confused, repulsed by what he'd done?

His eyes were wide, then shut, open again almost in tears, cheeks pulling in, letting out, mouth-corners shivering, eyes into the ceiling then down to the table with a slow shake of his head. He finally spoke.

"Teresa and I," he snorted back phlegm and the proclivity to cry, "were lovers. Had been for a year. Mike treated her like shi-" A tiny glob of spittle wavered from his bottom lip with another snort. "Mr. Local Politician." He looked up, then at Aurelia. "That's why the FBI was called in for this, I assume? Anyway, six months ago she came to me with this idea. She said she loved me, wanted to be with me. But—" He'd now given up on harboring tears. They fell like spring rain upon the metal table. "But she knew he'd kill her if she left him. She *knew* he would."

Aurelia said nothing, but kept his gaze, unwavering.

"She…" His voice lowered. "She said that we could kill him. If she was able to plead self-defense, all the money could stay hers, and mine."

Aurelia continued her silence, her unflinching regard.

"We planned to make him suspicious. Nothing much, just so he started to wonder. Then, after a while, we set it up so that he came home to a stranger's car, Teresa in bed. Like I said, we knew he'd try to kill her. So when he was about to, I'd shoot him. She lives, and he dies trying to kill her. She says it was self-defense."

"Were you late, Charles?" It was the first thing she'd said. Now he was blubbering madly, an obscure hiccup seemed to arise every few seconds.

"No," he said, almost a whisper.

"He comes home early, finds her in bed and fires a shot?"

"I came running when I heard it. And I sh-sh-shot him. I was too late. I— She had a gun, j-just in case. She should have been safe. She said she'd be safe."

"Well, Charles, like I said earlier, at least you're honest." She stood and exited while his gaze went back to the floor. Her high heels back to clicking.

"Wow, Doc," Elijah said. "Really impressive stuff. He made you work for it."

"Nope he's soft as a kitten. How's your head by the way?"

"Fine. Thanks for being so thoughtful. So, think that's the whole story?" He already knew her answer, as did he his own, but needed to change the subject. Her unspoken insult was better than his.

"Yea I do. Teresa gets him to go along with it, then is killed in front of him while he still commits murder. Lots of bad choices but I don't think he's happy about 'em."

Shortly after, they went to separate offices. Neither knew that the following few minutes would change the trajectory of their entire lives, permanently.

"Warren! Blanc! Get the shit down here!" The booming voice of the FBI's director echoed down the hallways. He was abrasive, a little crass, and at five foot seven not real intimidating, until you met him. He spoke directly, in statements and not questions. An oversized cigar always hung from his mouth or his fingers. Small lightning bolts crashed upwards from his temples to his vacant hairline when he was upset. His shoulders would swell (but not much), and his head would lower. His jaw would clench. They'd seen this more often than they'd have preferred.

Clint Adams was ruthlessly good at his job, fair and loyal, with a father figure's ability to induce guilt. He was probably a little old fashioned for the 1997 FBI, but he was pushing sixty and not close to retirement.

"Get on in here," he said dryly as they entered. "You two did well on the Larson case. Warren, I was sorry to hear about yesterday. Glad your head's still attached. I brought you all in to tell you you're working together from this point on. Any issues?"

It took a bit longer than it should have, but they both said, "No, sir," in unison, quietly. No matter the words or circumstance, it was like Clint was scolding.

"Oh, and your next assignment. You're not gonna like it... Or where you have to go... Or really any part of it... But have a look at the file this afternoon. You leave tomorrow."

"To?" Elijah asked.

"Enjoy the next few hours not knowing," Adams replied.

CHAPTER 3

A ll you find in a file is information, and most people don't kill for what's quantifiable. What's real is more than what's quantifiable. Emotions follow no code, no rationale based in science. Emotion is what swims in the blood of murderers, and it's why sitting and looking at stupid files all night is a waste of time! Elijah always felt that reading files was a bit of a waste of time, and he'd been trying to convince Detective Blanc of such for several minutes.

Crimes make sense when you look at the why. Murder is personal, and despite it not being as valuable as seeing it in person, being there to investigate, we'll be able to start figuring it out. Understanding a motive lets you connect with the murder, feel that emotion.

Elijah was pretty sure she was patronizing him in her responses. Their argument was descriptive, and a bit off topic...

Charles Larson fired a bullet into Mike Randall's head. That bullet split into the back of his skull along the superior temporal line, then tore through the hemispheres of his brain, exited through the nerve endings above his right eye. That all too real *bullet* was fired because of passion, because of emotion, and because he'd seen his lover gunned down in her bed. In a few short months, those names would just be letters, sitting in a dusty file. No one would care anymore. Friends would have moved on and families will make their peace...

At some point, Elijah said something about the resonance of murder surpassing words, or something like that. He babbled about seeing murder, cold-blooded murder, and it sticking with you like an ache in an old catcher's knees.

The conversation wandered on until Aurelia got them focused, and she grabbed his hand, moved it to a file that she'd shoved at him.

"Go on now," she said.

They were in an all too familiar room, though never with each other, case files for the "Indiana Killing" laid equidistant between them. The daylight hours were waning, and they'd put it off as long as possible. They each poured another cup of black coffee, bitter and charred from the morning's final brew.

They sat silently for quite some time, turning photographs and reading bits here and there. Finally Aurelia said a name, Claude Beauchene.

"So who is Claude Boosheen," Elijah said. "And why do you think he's relevant?"

"Claude Boo-*shane*," she said, emphasizing his mispronunciation, "was a French anatomist in the 1800's. He was erroneously credited for the 'exploded skull technique' of skull display!"

Elijah looked at her with childish petulance. She continued and pretended not to notice.

"It cuts the human skull into a grid of three-dimensional cubes, then shifts them away from each other by about an inch, showing how they all fit together."

"OK. So Boosheen?"

"Elijah Warren, I'm getting back to it. How is this not interesting to you? So, the credit really belongs to DaVinci. One of his early sketches theorizes the exact same technique. It just hadn't been done. Edme Francois *Beauchene* came and developed the real world application of it in the 1800's!" She paused a moment before she continued, looking down at the photographs, now scattered around piled like an ant hill, her face open in interest and her eyes wide, her mouth pursed a bit like she was lightly blowing out a candle. "I've never heard of an entire skeleton done this way though."

"Neat."

She sighed his name and kept reading.

They went on into the evening. One picture, an abandoned farmhouse, kept catching Elijah's gaze. The Polaroid house teetered on its foundation, the sides yawned. The paint was chipped and the chimney had lost most of its bricks. The victim had been found inside, just a couple days prior.

Bicycle wheels had been whirring on uneven pavement. The kids came skidding to a stop. The smell of death thick in the air and a forgotten driveway was on their left. It disappeared into a looming horizon. Led by young boys' prurience, they investigated. They rode their bicycles slowly, along the worn path toward the smell. Old oak trees lined their way. They climbed the final heave of earth and coasted down, down toward the house. They drew nearer and the smell became tangible. It seemed to thicken in their noses and throats. They stood in a line for a moment in front of the house. The sun was beaming in piercing rays from the west, sending long shadows across the rolling fields. Oranges and purples splashed the sky above. Their silhouettes crept, hunched, along one corner, to another.

It took one boy leaning down on all fours, one precariously atop, to see through the window. The balanced boy had a leg down and one stuck out to the side to make himself taller. His nose peeked over the sill and a shriek filled the air. He wavered, kicked down into his friend, who crumbled, dropped the other boy to the floor. They looked back with an upside-down gaze to find their friends running wildly, back to the house's front and back to their bikes. The boys had never pedaled so violently. The bicycle's frames wailed horrific moans into the fading Midwest colors.

Inside the window, a skeleton had hung horizontally, four feet from the floor. Thin metal wires held it together, and it had been cubed into perfect little bone cubes, then pulled apart with a vicious exactitude. Each end of the skeleton had a fixture, fastened to a wire suspension system that hung from the ceiling, a Halloween marionette above liquid horror.

Underneath this "exploded" skeleton, lay the additional remains of the victim. It was thick, oozing, exhaling wafts of dank blood, thick veins of churning black and swirling eddies of crusting gore. Another part had a thick curl of tendons, sitting half-covered in blood and liquefied flesh like a nest of lock ness monsters. Elijah and Aurelia ruminated on the near surgical precision it'd require to pull off the skeletal cubing, the instruments.

The killer had constructed a crude fire pit below the body and below the floor of the living space. They'd dug down and walls were built up with stone. The victim was torched to death above. Tissue dripped from bone.

"Look how clean the skeleton is." Aurelia spoke into the silence in the room. Darkness had now long since covered the city.

"So first this guy was melted, then his skeleton was diced, and separated?" Elijah exhaled loudly, apparently with not much else to say.

He thought for another minute. "Guarantee he isn't known for practicing this, whatever, 'Boosheen technique.'"

"It's pronounced Beauchene, but that isn't important. I agree. If he can *do* this, he's too smart to crucify himself," she said.

The words eloquent and intricate were displaying in Elijah's mind. The words ruthless, calculated, followed. A sudden wave of heat fell over him and he set down the images. He was at once overwhelmed with the idea that this was the beginning of something not soon realized.

He gazed at Detective Blanc for a long moment. She was leafing through another report, her face relaxed, her hair sweeping in front of her neck and chin, bobbing in front of her eyes, which popped up to meet Elijah's with a startling awkwardness. They talked only to plan a time to meet for the following day.

As Elijah stepped through the door of his New York City apartment, he couldn't help but feel exhilarated. Swirling prospects and potential filled his mind and forced the corners of his mouth to twinge just slightly upward. Where would a case that begins so obscurely take him? He was happy not knowing, just musing.

He moved sinuously, without the lights. He knew his way to the liquor cabinet. The small light above the sink was all he needed to cut his lime and pour his gin.

The dead of night approached precipitously and Elijah perched on the corner of a cement partition that encased his 35th floor balcony, a stoic, yet swaying gargoyle. His vibrant blue eyes looked thoughtfully into the sea of lights as one-by-one, they were extinguished. He went to bed long after.

CHAPTER 4

Nashville, Indiana, is a town of around five hundred. Strangers are friends and friends are family. A man melted and cut into pieces sent a shockwave through town, a domino effect of incredulity and gloom. It'd been a silent few days with interactions tired and scarce.

The Indiana winter had allowed a few days of cold sunshine, a fine gift in January, but ironically, the days following the boys' discovery of Marcus Felway brought a blanket of darkness that intoxicated the blue like oil to the sea. The clouds sat low on the horizon and filled the vast skies, billowing upwards in layers of decay. Lightning ruminating within them and lit menacing silhouettes in the pillowed black.

Akin to many places in the rural Midwest, Nashville is isolated and oceans of farmland separate it from towns in congruence. It's surrounded by Brown County State Park to the south and Yellowwood State Forest to the west.

The geography of the Midwest is optimal for keeping to yourself, and for the same reasons, it's a great place to commit murder. Roads go days void of travelers and the space between towns becomes a tangle of back roads and hilled forests, ravines and rivers.

It was morning, January 15th, and they were meeting to catch their flight.

"G-morning, Doc," Elijah said, finishing his slow walk to the cab, Aurelia, waiting beside, impatiently, tap-tap-tapping her right foot, arms crossed, jaw cocked to the side, eyes digging.

"Is it?" she said.

"Well—."

"Shut up. Shut up again, then get in," she said, fanning her arm toward the door in a *here you go little princess kind of way.*

"Well… I was *going* to say, more pleasant than the time I spent with you yesterday. No offense."

"It wasn't a choice evening. Though I feel none with you would be." She smiled at him a little.

Elijah didn't really know what to say to this, so he said something that was more like a sound, a half hiccup half questioning *hehhh*.

The doors closed and the cabbie sped off.

It was a quiet ride to the airport. The partners sat in silence, each in their own thoughts. Elijah peered from the window, watched concrete blur together in a kaleidoscope of bubble letter graffiti.

In a way, he'd always felt trapped by the city. New York didn't much fit him. Nor did people in general, and there were likewise plenty of those. Thanks to the gin his head was heavy. It was lolling with the turns of the cab. Not that he was a stranger to it.

They hadn't talked of the case yet, an unspoken understanding that it was too early to discuss what they'd read and seen the previous night. There would be plenty of time.

New York is three hundred square miles of sprawling concrete, and it did so, impetuously around the yellow dot that was the cab. Birds and planes above see the mass, organized chaos that defines its existence, allows it. The sidewalks were filled with routine, hurried people and blank-to-angry gazes, dark suits and white shirts. The traffic carried on its own life, the pulsing veins of the city.

The cabbie slammed into the brake pedal at unspeakable intervals, lurching and heaving like New Year's morning. Elijah was losing patience. Aurelia was pretending not to notice because she could tell Elijah was wearing thin on patience. Each swift brake caused them to heave forward, lock into their seatbelts and slam back against the dirty, rubber seat lining.

Their flight was set to leave at 8am. They settled for 8:30am. It was a short flight to Indianapolis and Elijah slept while Aurelia buried her head in their work. They each had a copy of the "Indiana Killing." She studied intensely, tried to find something she couldn't define. She wondered what it would be like, feel like, to burn a man alive, what it would feel like to cut someone's skull and skeleton into exacted blocks, piece them together.

It'd take patience.

It'd take passion.

Maybe a lack of empathy? She didn't know.

The victim's name was Marcus Felway, a wealthy engineer from Bloomington, thirty minutes west of the farmhouse. He was a modest spender, had a home of average size and value. He was married to his first and only wife of almost ten years. No kids. No criminal record. Marcus had been missing three weeks. His wife, Sherry, an attractive woman older than Marcus with drawn out Minnesota O's, gave a near-hysterical report of his disappearance.

To Aurelia, the crime seemed personal, and as Elijah mentioned the night prior, it was an intricate murder. She couldn't help feeling that the killer picked Marcus, plucked him from the world after exhaustive research. Maybe it was a part of something bigger, the first little glance at a complex work of art.

The coroner had had only the left-behind wallet to prove the man's identity. His fingerprints were gone, his teeth removed. This led Aurelia to another question, why torch someone beyond recognition but leave a wallet behind?

She caught herself in a naïve thought. A popular musing about some monster responsible, lurking in the shadows of the world, a creature not human but something she could hate, feel distanced from. The unfortunate truth she already knew. This person would not be a monster. They would simply be human, one that breathes, walks, loves and hates, is scared, feels triumph. Each new case began with Aurelia—incredulously—hoping to find a monster responsible for the current atrocity, an unrealized hopefulness stifled by the reality of experience.

She'd swam down dark channels, through seething waters of scorn, into life, twisted by experience. She'd heard too many excuses for murder, for rape, for whatever. It affected her more than she led on. Humans somehow could justify horrific examples of conduct, unspeakable violence or other derisions of society.

The question that sneakily ruminated beneath her consciousness was if humankind had a limit, a cut off point for what would not become mundane? Could we finally arrive at a place of peace through realization of evil? Could the world really be as peaceful as the hopes in her head?

Elijah woke abruptly as the aircraft touched back down to earth. He rubbed the sleep from his eyes and looked sideways to Aurelia. She had fallen asleep with papers strewn all around. He gathered the images, the pages of text, and tucked them into the manila folder, put the folder back in her briefcase. He then woke her gently.

Detective Blanc led them to the private aviation area on the north side of the Indianapolis Airport. Due to Nashville's location they had another short flight on a private, government jet to complete their journey. They'd land next on a tiny airstrip just outside of town.

Few places differ more than Nashville, Indiana, and New York City. The obvious would soon glare the detectives in the face. They would soon experience fresh air, clean and crisp, vast farmlands and sparse lights that littered the dark of the rolling countryside in the evenings. The cramp and hurry of the city was now miles behind. The weekly forecast, however, was straightforward and consistent across the country. It was bitter, cold and unyielding with winds that would whirr and whip, low grumblings of thunder and vicious knife blade slashes that cut the skies of the world.

The aircraft touched down on time, despite the palpable tension during flight. Not long after leaving Indy the trip turned into a re-creation of the picture book train trying to make it up the hill. Elijah spent a good part weighing their odds.

"The good news," he felt, was that "there's a much better chance of survival than most people think! Really! There's actually a survival rate of almost ninety-five percent in plane crashes!" Aurelia didn't seem to appreciate the conversation.

The air outside was blistering, a harsh and real force against their skin. The detectives stepped onto a spiderwebbing tarmac.

"We'd prolly be safe!" he said, trying to catch up with her as she strode away. "I mean, my chances are worse than that when I see a matinee in Queens." In two successive stages they opened a door to an FBI-arranged Explorer. "And also, think about how much more dangerous being in a car is. We're in those all the time and car crashes kill more people per year than—"

"OK. Thank you. You know strange things. And listen. Can the plane/car crash conversation be saved until we're not traveling in a plane, and car?"

"I tried to make the plane crash conversation positive."

"I do suppose that's true."

"So where in the hell are we going?"

"Well…" She let her words linger as well as her gaze out the windshield, intentionally blank and disbelieving as it fell upon the fields of corn, the single road that led away and into some distant trees.

Nashville is six blocks north to south, three east-west.

A handful of people own the majority of the real estate.

The black Explorer pulled up to the police station six minutes after leaving the tarmac. In the town of five hundred, the full time police staff amassed to three, a chief and two officers. One man, who looked to be fifteen, was named Ben Thomas. Ben was a first year, but local to Nashville. He stood average height but slouched to a more realistic height of five foot five. The second was a woman, Jane. Jane had a last name but Elijah had forgotten it almost immediately, Longifer or something. Jane seemed to be in her thirties and had giraffe-like features. She had thin and yellow hair.

The chief was an oversized man named Jarred Blane. His face was round with several days' worth of hair on his face. He appeared to be forty and looked like a lineman that let himself go. Chief Blane greeted them with a nod and a half-cocked smile. "Welcome to Nashville. Thanks for makin' the trip." He spat a thick stream of brown into a plastic water bottle. "We've never seen anything like this."

"Thank you. We've had a warm welcome aside from the weather, which is cold, quite cold," Aurelia said with warmth that opposed the topic. "And believe us, we've never seen anything like this either."

"We can get right to it. The memorandum of understanding gives you anything you need from us." He spat again. "What can we help with?"

Elijah quickly suggested the farmhouse. The Chief spat again.

"Of course. You all need to check into the motel? Food first? Hoosiers is right—"

"Later is fine. We're already fixated on this. I think we'd prefer to go and have a look." Elijah spoke what Aurelia thought.

They drove gradually through the quaint downtown and observed carefully their surroundings.

"Grew up in a place like this," Aurelia commented as her eyes sinuously moved over single story buildings, handmade wooden signs above doors.

"Where?" Elijah said quietly.

"Little place in Wisconsin, called Adrian. It was only for a few years, but I loved it. We moved when I was eleven. My favorite thing was the forest. Seeing the trees change in fall, all those colors. My imagination went to cool places 'cause of it I think. I can exactly picture our woods. Do you have memories like that?" she asked him.

All consuming darkness filled Elijah's mind and he said softly said that he did.

"What are—"

"He's turning." Elijah had cut her off.

Two taillights were the only things alerting Elijah Warren of the change in route. Snow had begun chasing the carpool halfway into the drive. A troubling thought was unspoken but in the car. It was only mid-January; the whole country was being transformed into tundra and winter was far from over.

The already feeble road turned into something less substantial when they met the driveway. They crept along. Crunching was beneath the tires and snow beat down on the windshield. The old farmhouse came into view. The ground beneath it had eroded. Roots from nearby trees sprung from along its cracking foundation and gave the odd appearance that the house was in a nest. Bowing steps led to the door, a tattered awning swung and clamored in the wind. The paint was a stale yellow.

Once the house was beautiful, prototypical for the time and place it was built. That appealed to Elijah. He always felt that if you built a mountain cabin on the beach or a beach home in the mountains, it wouldn't make sense.

The farmhouse fit.

Chief Blane stepped out of the car first and led the way. Aurelia followed behind him with Elijah trailing after. Elijah noticed the windows were intact and was both thankful for it and surprised by it.

"What have you guys done? Standard protocol so far?" Aurelia asked.

"The initial stuff. We checked for prints, searched the grounds. State police was in charge though so I don't really know what *they* did," the Chief spoke in a back and forth manner, each sentence a slightly different speed, like someone was controlling him from a record player. "All they found was in the report. CSI was here and stuff," he added with a spit into the bottle attached to his hand.

The inside of the dwelling looked like the out. An ample layer of dust was protecting the entirety of the house. It had been a long time since someone lived here. The front door led to a tight foyer. You could go straight and upstairs, or straight and past the stairs along a thin hallway to the living area and kitchen.

The three walked past the stairs and steadily down the hallway, the boards blearily singing and groaning. They covered the thin hall in twelve paces.

A door was propped up on its side, along the wall and on their right. They stood within the frame of the door for a moment and peered into the kitchen. Sections of cabinets were attached to the wall. The countertops hung limply above sparse lower cabinets. They turned the corner to the living room and the images from the file became real.

"The county coroner's office has the skeleton I assume," Elijah said. Chief Blane nodded.

Aurelia talked out loud for a moment, but to herself. She wanted to find something out of place, something added to the scene. She couldn't fight the feeling that the killer wanted to be pursued. He'd left the dead man's wallet behind, but nothing to give CSI any inclination of who he or she was. Nothing to go on but too much to ignore. She felt they'd find something more if they could find the right perspective.

Aurelia did her part of their symphonic dance. She first walked to the fire pit, lonely in the room besides a beautiful rocking chair that sat in the corner. They squirmed a bit as they looked curiously at the ornate chair. It was clearly old, but out of place in the home. It was obtuse in the utter nothingness that existed otherwise.

"This has got to be his," she said aloud, still quietly to herself.

"Hey now. Don't just assume it's a him," Elijah said with a sarcastically curt finger jabbed her way through the air.

"OK. Let's say… the statistics would suggest that our killer is a white male, between thirty and fifty. Probably abused or neglected by his parents."

"Whatever." He knew she was right.

Aside from the obscure chair, all that remained to examine was the stone structure built to contain the fire that consumed Marcus Felway. The area had since been cleaned, the forensic evidence already collected by state police. As they learned in the file, nothing was found, but Aurelia and Elijah were there to look for something different.

"Chief, do you know if the staties looked much into this chair?" Aurelia said.

"They said it was the only thing in the house. Dunno about anything else."

She observed the fine detailing, small animals carved into the arms and legs, a bear that wrapped its claws around the base of the seat, a peacock on one of the legs, an elegant mountain landscape scrawled on the backrest. The work was exquisite, careful and deliberate with a sense of balance and completeness. She made a mental note that no one would leave this chair behind when vacating a house. Especially if all else was taken.

"Who does the house belong to now?" she said.

"Technically nobody, ma'am," chief responded. "The last owners were named Beth and Martin Cullen. They passed away almost twenty years ago with their son and didn't leave the property to anyone. Out here, when that type of thing happens, the house sits like an old puddle. People aren't fightin' for the rights if you know what I mean, government included."

As Aurelia and Blane talked, Elijah was moving around the room with keen articulation, the other half of the collaborative tango. He listened intently to their conversation while scrutinizing the room for himself. Every minute or so he'd look back at the rocker, silently taunting him. Elijah listened for changes in the sound of the floor as he walked. The perpetually singing floorboards didn't allow much insight. He then analyzed each of the stones used in the construction of the pit. When nothing else piqued his attention, he returned to the rocking chair. "What did they do for a living?" he finally said.

"I heard they had money and kept to themselves. Prolly artists or whatever. Normal for here. Not real sure to be honest with ya. I know they traveled a lot and had real estate elsewhere," the Chief said.

Elijah wasn't exactly satisfied with the answer but had nothing to say. Aurelia and Blane kept talking.

Warren went back to the chair, knelt down on one knee before laying his back against the floor. His head was toward the rocker. He used his feet to push himself under. He froze when his eyes scanned the text, opulently carved in the bottom. He read it aloud.

"Run, run 'til the blazin' sun
So much to hide…a tumultuous ride
Truth will be found upon warmer ground
So run, run 'til the blazin' sun"

The ambiguous words filled the room, filled their minds. They recognized with certainty that something atypical was on the horizon.

CHAPTER 5

Welcome to *Colorful Colorado.* An assuming state motto, in some cases an overwhelming exaggeration. Despite uncompromising beauty, to say it is altogether "colorful" is a misleading notion. The brown expanse of the eastern plains coalesces mundanely into Kansas. The alpine tundra becomes a sea of white, flowing clouds and swirling snow in a menacing tangle.

Though, in summer the pearled aspens bend and loom in familial patches, individuals but part of one root system, leaves all shimmering green-to-golden in afternoon sun and breeze. The rivers are clear and swift and roaring in the canyons. Jagged, granite peaks loom overhead, and the sky beyond is a vivid expanse of bold sapphire.

While heading west, the man wearing black stopped in Limon in the central east plains. It'd be his last stop before Ouray. The prior leg of journey had been eyes-pried-open long. He needed gas and a full tank at that. Previous supplies had come from Kansas City.

It was half past nine and although fall had just come to an end, the sun had been down for more than two hours. The man wearing black pulled up to the pump. The door opened and his left foot crept from beneath the brake pedal. It lifted and moved in a slow hover through the door's frame. It made contact with the ground and slowly turned perpendicular to the car. When the turn was complete, that same leg shifted toward the edge of the seat. It settled, then his right leg followed scrupulously behind. Finally his torso, arms and head followed. As if his batteries were running low, he was in slow motion, meticulous and sure. His exit might have turned heads if there had been any to turn. The lone attendant didn't even bother to look up from the cheap porn he'd slid off the shelf and from its plastic.

The man wearing black turned his head toward the pump and took a step forward, then another. His hand reached out just enough to open the gas tank cover, followed by the gas cap. His other hand eased to the side and lifted the pump's handle. It stayed at pump height and moved to the tank like the open air had a track for it. His eyes telegraphed his movements.

Gas began into the car.

The man lingered in a curled, dark mass and stared at the screen. He looked at the numbers attentively, always calculating. A subtle noise stirred at the rear of the vehicle, enough to make him turn in that direction. Nothing continued and he ignored it, knowing his plan could have no setbacks. Seasonal change is never an exact science.

The abrupt *CLANK* of the pump shutting off didn't startle the man; he pulled the handle from the car and gently placed it back down. He turned to walk and pay. Several minutes later he returned with water and a receipt for what he spent in cash.

park...reverse...neutral...drive

He crept back onto highway 24, heading south in the direction of Colorado Springs. Although he'd no intention of stopping there, he reveled in its beauty. As a youth he'd studied pictures of massive red and white fins of rock that seemed to crash upwards from the ground and into the sky, the Garden of the Gods. In his mind was a distant but affecting picture of his childhood, himself, hovering above a picture of North Gateway Rock. It must have been hours. He scrutinized each crack and ripple in its soaring wall, each pocket and every angle change. He felt it the most majestic in the park. The man wearing black had always been perpetually amazed by the earth's ability to craft the profound, the beyond belief or understanding. He grew up living in books, as far away from other kids as possible. At eleven he began memorizing them.

The lights of Colorado Springs came over the distant and empty horizon shortly after 11pm. After west 24 merged into north 25, he drove a few short miles before turning back onto west 24. He pondered and cursed the city planner's motivations in developing the city, its half connected streets and indirect routes of travel. He wasn't sure, but fathomed it could be the very same planner that created the ever-confusing non-grid in the city of Denver.

He passed Pikes Peak, a huge lingering mass of black distinguishable because of the tiny light atop its summit, 14,115 feet. He drove, and he thought about the people that *first* discovered the Rockies, those that lived there before others took it, brave men and women that he might have been able to respect, men and women forging new paths and thinking and seeing the world with open eyes, accepting eyes, eyes that sought truth. He wondered what it would feel like to forge the path he was traveling with only his body as a motor. He'd revel in the opportunity.

He shook his head slowly at the thought of Christopher Columbus, that tall tale.

The man wearing black had a piercing gaze, fixed and robotic. The car moved steadily. The high country passed in shadows and a sliver of moon lit the world from behind thick clouds.

Not quite six hours later, the green hatchback passed the un-illuminated sign for Ouray, Colorado. The driver knew it well and smiled at its silhouetted shape in the night.

He drove a steady seventy-five and kept a crack in the window. Winter's bite swam in.

In Ouray, the snow began to fall. The man stared longingly at it floating down through the beams of his headlights.

He drove, picking the most efficient streets, and exited town heading south onto the Million Dollar Highway, US 550. A pristine lake sat six-and-a-half miles further. Time moved quickly in the man's head and he was suddenly turning onto the old forest road that circled Crystal Lake. He was on autopilot.

As the road became less traveled, thickening trees held the snow in their branches. The man's headlights were cutting through blackness in vivid yellow beams. Turns sent them tumbling across the lake in rippled streaks. The road took him, them, west then back south. Halfway around the lake, the tires eased.

Slowly… the man put it in park, moved his way out of the driver's seat and to the right side of the road. A forest service gate blocked their way, forgotten dirt just beyond. He unlocked the padlock with a key from his pocket and gradually pulled the gate toward him. He swung it open and a whispering creak rode up the length of the metal. He then pulled the car through, got back out, and closed the gate behind him. They continued to the end of the old, dry wash.

The man grew a wry smile as he adjusted his rearview mirror. The gate, he felt, was brilliant. Authentic, down to the materials. No ranger would have blinked twice if they'd come upon it, and if they had, the Forest Service's funding would be to blame for someone not taking the time to check into it: some rogue gate. Who'd care?

The man in the vehicle, the woman in the trunk, traveled another eight miles before stopping at the end of the wash, a small pullout. They were a tiny dot in a massive forest, miles of black surrounding them.

A cleanse of heavy ease came over the man and he step... step... stepped across a light layer of snow. His hand met the tailgate and slowly it rose. He grabbed a sled, then two spools of pencil-thin cable, twisted layers of crude metal, then locking carabiners. The other half of the rear was filled with an oversized, brown suitcase. Inside that was a woman named Serena Miller. After unzipping each side in long pulls, pulling open the flap, he stood for an extended moment, looking.

Serena's hair was matted, her eyes far away. She looked out from somewhere that wasn't quite at the surface of consciousness, like an animal waking from an afternoon nap a bit too early. She had deep red lines etched into yesterday's immaculate skin, and broken fingernails. Her feet were bound and snarls of the metal dug with her each subtle shift. She was alive, but being home in Kansas seemed eons ago. Her body was starting to shut down. She could feel it.

Little pictures and blurbs of a walk through the financial district of Kansas City came easing back to her. It was 3am and downtown, and she was a little drunk to be by herself. There had been a potluck, which meant uncomfortable conversations and a lot of fake laughing; of course she was a little drunk. The memory shards stopped coming. She fought, felt a little ripple somewhere in her mind, focused on it and grabbed the image of the bar located two blocks from her apartment. The shards disintegrated again and she fought to get them back. She remembered walking up to the door, then nothing. Then she heard noises. It was the ease of acceleration and brake of a pedal. She then had heard the pavement whirring just beneath her. That sound was unmistakable. She had tried to open her eyes, then pried at them. They stayed closed behind what seemed like tiny dentist jackets. She had tried until she could no longer.

An unknown time later her eyes burst open, a long gasp-cry-exhale and twisting knots in her neck and back, elbows and wrists. Her ankles were curled and pressed into corners, her knees bent to her chest. She had a pounding headache. It pinched from behind her temples.

She had heard not a sound from the front of the car. She listened for what felt like hours and couldn't sense a bit of human nature, a rustle against the door or a sigh induced by long hours driving through the night. She had felt a terrific discomfort and knew the night would not end well. Her once complex life had become simple and terrifying.

She was torn out of her reverie when strong hands wrapped beneath her, scooped her from the trunk and dropped her abruptly onto the sled. The man wearing black took off with his things into the dark forest. The woman's gagged mouth could say nothing, but her eyes were no longer distant. They were now those of a *wild* animal, cornered or fighting for its last breath.

A thick gash—from something dense and blunt the evening prior—leaked blood from her head and kept bouncing off the sled, which was knocking into icy roots and rocks as he dragged her across the uneven snow. Blood splashed down in splotches. She began to cry, but not because of pain. She was suddenly at ease, elsewhere because of a sure understanding that she would soon die. She pictured her dad's face, his off-kilter smile, Mom's hands-on-hips lean. She could hear her brother in a distant corner of her head, his gentle and rolling laugh. She'd probably taken them for granted. Most people seem to.

Her head took another sharp zing off the sled. Her teeth came crashing down into each other.

Serena Miller's existence had spiraled in a direction she could have never predicted. She'd always been aware that individual moments can come to define your life, though the phrase was taking on new meaning. A drunken turn before or after, one more drink at the party or a second longer finding her coat would have left her life unscathed, intact. The sled continued on.

She heard the faint sound of water splattering into rock.

The noise got louder… louder…

Serena's thoughts were becoming less euphoric. She now thought about her last meal, her last conversation with her best friend. She thought about the last guy she had sex with, some nobody who shook violently for a few short moments before graciously falling asleep. He'd also sweated a lot. She thought about the last time she talked with her mom, an asinine argument that she—at that time—just couldn't let go of. The sled collided again with a rock in the trail and sent a shock down her spine, down her legs and into her toes. She felt the warmth of fresh blood drip from her fingers. She'd been digging again, gnarled flesh caked under her nails.

The sled stopped moving.

The water was now upon them, massive and booming its voice. Serena could tilt just enough to see it heaving from the top of a cliff line, twenty feet above.

The man grabbed her by the hair and pulled her onto the bitter earth. She writhed and shook sadistically, her body blue from bruises and cold. The man noticed. He let the moment linger. He then dragged her several feet to the cliff base and to the left behind the waterfall. Liquid daggers began to sear her skin, a thousand pinpricking needles.

Between the waterfall and the stone was a space of eight feet. Each length of metal cable spanned six and a half feet. The man wearing black grabbed the cables then bound Serena's wrists. Two echoing clangs bounced from the wall to the water as the carabiners at the other end of the cables slammed shut onto two I-bolts, drilled into the stone.

Before lowering her to the cables' full potential, he ungagged her mouth. He listened to her scream and inched her into the excruciating rush of power. The cables suspended her where the water met the earth, a descending ramp of granite, and over a sharp precipice where her feet dangled.

The cables dug deeper into her wrists as the violent rush of water pushed and shoved at her, a marionette with a hurricane for a master. She'd forgotten about her fingernails, the tears and scrapes in her skin. She shook violently for as long as her body would allow, and the man kept watching.

It took quite a pleasant while, but Serena finally stopped quaking, arching her back and kicking at the stone ledge with her heels. She died in two abrupt convulsions. After that her body slipped back and forth in the current. The bolts creaked and the carabiners shifted. The man wearing black headed back to the car.

park...reverse...neutral...drive

He could see the splintering of dawn through a patch in the trees, his eyes full of wonder as he relocked the gate. It wasn't long before he was back to Ouray, unlocking a motel door and reflecting on the day's radiant brilliance.

CHAPTER 6

"What's it mean?" Aurelia said, speaking quietly as they drove back towards Nashville.

"Not one idea. Maybe the chair just had a poem on the bottom."

She looked over at him incredulously.

"But *you* think otherwise." She of course wouldn't admit it, but thought Elijah was more impressive than anyone she'd ever worked with. He saw things in the world that others didn't. Plus, he was freakin' hot. She'd read his files, St. Louis SWAT turned esoteric detective. His assignments for the bureau had been twisted with obscure complexities, each with its own enigmatic lock. Elijah always found a way to turn the key. Each case's success hinged upon some recondite insight that it seemed only he could unearth. Adams sent him attempted cases, thought to be unsolvable.

"With this much effort," he said. "Mastery of a skill. *At least* money enough to finance it. Time to make it all happen." Elijah wasn't really speaking in sentences, but in blurbs of thought. "Bet he's not done. Burning someone alive's fuckin' sick. What if we're finding what he *wants* us to find?"

"He *or* she, right?" Aurelia said.

"He *or* she. Right. Shut up. Aurelia, I think we're gonna be in the dark a while. He, I mean, whoever they are, I think is not in a hurry." He paused for a moment and stared out at the darkness of the Midwest. "I hope I'm full of shit."

"Me too," she said. "Let's grab drinks and food, nothing more to do tonight. I'm buyin'. By the way, good idea to check with local businesses tomorrow. In a town this small, someone may recognize the craftsmanship of the chair."

Elijah pulled the car into the local bar and grill, Hoosiers, and parked around back.

"Of course it's called Hoosiers," she said. "How does this state still take pride in high school basketball from the fifties? Something's gotta be wrong."

"Don't say that. Winning a high school championship is like winning a Nobel Prize around here."

They laughed out loud together for the first time.

The word "downtown" had different meaning than it had earlier that morning in New York. To the north was a small bank, a convenient store, a diner and a liquor store. The other direction was less animated. It had a small hardware shop.

The sun had set earlier in the day, but the full moon was generous enough to light the whole state. Pausing briefly as he opened the door for Aurelia, Elijah looked beyond the reaches of town and out two directions, south and west. He remembered reading in the file about state parks in those directions, and formed an idea to pursue the following day. He shelved it with spirits of forgetting about work for the night.

Elijah walked in and his eyes met Aurelia's ass as she leaned on the hostess' podium. He shook away the accident (this time) and hoped she didn't notice. He awkwardly glanced in a couple different directions. "Still serving food?" he said, a little too loudly when he arrived beside her.

"Yep. Right this way," replied the hostess, in a voice that was spoken through drywall.

"People are so much quieter here," Aurelia said.

"Small town, less people to talk over. Basic math."

She shook her head and followed behind the waitress through low and crude tables, uneven wooden chairs and a jukebox. They sat down facing each other with the window by their sides. "We definitely earned a drink. Poison?" she said.

"Gin. I don't reinvent wheels." Elijah's order hadn't changed since he was fifteen, barring the occasional whiskey bender.

She looked at him with squeezing eyebrows and he said…

"People think too much about things they've already decided. If you know what you like, why not stick with it? One good thing just isn't enough to satisfy people." He stopped, looked at her looking back at him.

She was relentlessly beautiful in that moment. The idea snuck up on him then sank in, and he felt her gaze wash over him like rainfall in the tropics. It softened him into the coarse, wooden bench.

"I think having a perpetual order is shortsighted," she said. "Just because you're fixated on something doesn't mean you really want it. You've never had a relationship last too long because you were comfortable, concerned with how hard it'd be to start a new one? That's what sticking with one drink is like."

"I don't know if it's healthy to compare your drinking to your relationships. *Especially* when you're comparing the ways you manage them similarly."

"I should deduce that you've had *many* longstanding and healthy relationships?"

"Indubitably," he said, and looked at her with eyes a little wider than usual. She hated how blue they were. He sat up a little taller and his chin tilted down a bit.

"I doubt that."

"Are you saying that I *haven't* had many longstanding and healthy relationships?" he said.

"I would never."

"Our person needs to hurry and end this dreadfulness. I'm sick of filling this void."

In reality, Elijah had just never enjoyed conversation. He'd never been a talker and felt like most people talked either to hear themselves, or to appease those they're talking to.

Neither of *them* were putting on a show, catering to the other person.

They were being themselves, and somehow that worked.

The waitress approached the unfamiliar couple in a bounce of naivety. Her ponytail flipped with each step and she wore a smile un-jaded. In a sweet southern accent, she quickly spoke her name and asked about food and drinks and beamed out some specials that weren't very special.

"Gin and tonic, please," Aurelia said. Elijah glowered at her.

"Same," he said.

"Bartender's quick, so be ready! Thanks ya'll." She bounced away like she'd moved to town for the job.

"I thought you had something against my gin?" Elijah said, now a sour face.

"I never said I had a problem with gin. I said I have a problem with being too set in your ways. Gin sounded good tonight though," she added.

"I bet your child version was a pain in the ass. Wisconsin happy to see ya go?"

"How did you know I grew up in Wisconsin?"

"You mentioned it earlier," he said. She smiled, on the inside.

"Good memory, Detective. Though you seem to have more of a reputation for that than I do. And by the way, am I a suspect here?" She liked that he actually listened to her.

"I can't possibly see what you're saying, and when it comes to the case, you can't be too careful. I'm suspicious of everyone, especially you." The corners of his mouth pulled in.

The waitress bounced-skipped their drinks back to them and shortly after, took their orders. Elijah got his usual: a burger, medium rare, fries extra crispy. Aurelia requested the chef's choice, which wasn't on the menu. She said she liked to be surprised and generally liked all food.

They spent the following minutes talking about nothing. They talked a bit about their favorite places in New York. They talked about the Cold War. They talked about fries and how people absurdly got worked up about whether or not to call them "French."

Neither detective had words for what made the other so suddenly accessible. It didn't make sense, but that didn't matter. Their food arrived followed by their second and third round of drinks. Aurelia didn't ask what she was sent to eat, but noticed the waitress' name on her nametag as she thanked her. It was Annie.

"I think this is elk!" Aurelia said, taking a huge bite around thick toppings and a glistening bun.

"No way they have elk burgers."

"You wait, when Annie comes back here we're gonna ask her. How's your *boring* burger?"

"It's better than what is probably raccoon. I bet you'll get tapeworms from that," he said.

"Oh yea! Good idea. Let's bet. Elk or Raccoon. We'll request one room and one bed at the ol' Moonbeam Motel, and the loser sleeps on the floor?"

She said the last couple words from behind her glass before bringing it to her lips.

"I think we can charge the feds for two rooms, but I *would* enjoy watching you sleep on the floor. I'll sleep like a king on my mattress of clouds."

They found themselves laughing, eating and drinking, and going back and forth like this for some time.

Less smoke was lingering around the ceiling of the bar. It was late and the detectives stood up askance and near-shouted goodnight to Annie on the way out the door. The hotel was close so they walked after grabbing their suitcases from the car. Their tilted jaunt home was short, but cold, despite the liquid jackets they wore. Elijah ignored his good judgment and put his free arm around Aurelia. She didn't mind. Despite the cold, she thought to herself that she wanted the walk to last longer. They arrived only minutes since leaving. The motel attendant looked to be asleep, but was coherent enough to point them down the singular hallway that accounted for the entirety of the place. "See you in the morn…" the attendant said, trailing off as they pulled their bags down the hallway. It didn't take long to reach their rooms, separate ones.

"Goodnight. Sorry about your loss. Elk sure was good," she said. "I'll figure out a new punishment since you wouldn't get one room." She smiled at him.

"Rub it in. I'm gonna figure out some way to be punished, and get you back way worse."

They parted ways for the night with an abnormal sense of ease. The feeling was finite, because the case had a whole different plan for them.

Elijah surveyed the room. To his right, toward Aurelia's room, was a small desk tucked against stale wallpaper and a bed, ripped agonizingly from the 1970s.

"Floral patterns on vomit-hued cloth." He spoke out loud to the dated room. To his left was a small television and dresser with drawers that hung open. The carpet was shag.

The 70's were still very much alive at the Moonbeam Motel.

Detective Warren cared little about aesthetics though did wonder about the Moonbeam's sanitation standards. The dated décor had him thinking about numbers, statistics and probabilities. He looked at the bed, the phone, kicked off his shoes and pushed disease from his consciousness.

Turning the corner to the bathroom didn't do much to change his rumination. He looked at the faucets, the toilet bowl and its lever, the thick runs of black where grout should show about the room.

He stood for a moment in the gaze of the mirror, staring at himself. Elijah would turn thirty in the upcoming year and his work had taken its toll. He was obviously still young, but the wrinkles in his face were making parallels—especially when he smiled—and his thick head of black showed gray in its recesses.

"At least I'm not balding," he muttered to no one.

He reached down and turned the faucet… No avail. He stood still for a second longer, doing nothing but existing in a still semi-twisted state. He bent forward to examine the underside of the faucet head, though Elijah was far from a handyman. He could have fixed it had some foreign object been obtusely plugging the pipe.

Maybe.

Living in the city didn't augur much in home repair skills, especially for those working long hours and with an aversion to mundane tasks. He stood defeated and stared at the faucet. The look on his face read anger, annoyance and a slight amusement. He thought to himself how ill-fated events, significant or otherwise, could be amusing after the passing of initial emotions. He sat down on the side of the tub and turned the handle. Success.

His toothbrush moved underneath questionable water and began its task. Elijah then stripped down to only black boxer briefs, then climbed into bed and pushed the flowered comforter to the floor. He sprawled on his stomach for fleeting seconds before being consuming by quiescence.

Aurelia stood with her bag still in her hands. She looked down at the carpet. Her face was pursed like she'd sucked the juice out of a lemon. The room screamed, but nothing nice came out, sickening colors and stains and battered furnishings. The overhead fixture omitted an unsavory glow; it was dim and yellow and casting a veil of depression over the room. She went to the teetering dresser to unload her clothes. One suitcase made it hard to pack for a trip of unknown length, but she'd done her best.

Everything had its spot, cosmetics minimized into smaller containers, everything rolled into little torpedoes, socks tucked in shoes.

She fought off her milieu and tried to focus on how nice her evening had been. It really *had* been nice, despite the circumstances.

After organizing, Aurelia discovered that the faucet wouldn't turn on. She tried the shower. She sat and brushed on the side of the greening tub, and she thought about Elijah.

They'd been working indirectly for about a year. Neither had been particularly pleasant to the other, due probably to the vast sea of differences that separated them. She did know that the most fun she'd had in years had been sitting at Hoosiers with Elijah that evening, drinking cheap gin and laughing about—

Hell, it didn't matter *what* they were laughing about. They were laughing.

And the way he looked at her…

That was impressive, like his complete attention was absorbed in only her. She didn't think that existed in men. He actually listened, responded to things.

She spat toothpaste into the tub and rinsed her mouth with the only running water. It was just after 1am when the last light went out.

CHAPTER 7

The following day was a pleasant surprise, at least in terms of the weather. Aurelia stepped two quick steps out into the morning air and found herself uncomfortable in her winter dress. The sun beat down with heavy warmth. The air lacked its usual bite. Outside the motel entrance was a small bench that looked south in the direction of Brown County State Park. She found herself in a consumed reverie of nostalgia. She could picture rolling hills, the coalescence of reds and oranges and yellows, lingering greens. She could hear whimsical chick-a-dee-dee-dee-dee-dees in her consciousness. She mused about what life would be living back in a small town, what life would be if she left the FBI to forge a new path, a path with fewer murders and less concrete.

She fantasized about waking up with the sun, making coffee and breakfast in a little house that she'd picked out and decorated, jazz musicians in paintings on the walls and a thick, high wooden table to sit at with friends, laughing into the night about past mistakes or future plans. She could imagine herself sitting on her porch, reading a book and listening to the sounds of the world. Her house would be on a little street with no traffic. It'd be one story and would be blue with tan shutters. No one would bother her there. She'd be far from gunshots and sirens. She'd be far from the phone calls that woke her in the night, the atrocities that followed her home, the dead faces, the equivocal stories that haunted her with their ambiguity, the blood-splashed photographs that each case brought, then swept away like leaves come fall.

Life would be simpler in her little blue house.

She'd never recognized these thoughts before and maybe would never again, but for the moment, they affected her. She felt her spine softening and her posture deflate. She felt, but didn't realize, her eyes gazing off toward the barren trees of winter. She settled back into reality after a moment's lingering.

Elijah strolled out the door of the Moonbeam and met Aurelia's gaze. He greeted her with a, "G-morning, doc," and asked if they should be on their way to breakfast. She laughed, though couldn't pinpoint exactly why.

"I hear that diner is top notch," he said, tilting his head a bit and prolonging his gaze.

She laughed again, knowing obviously that he'd request the diner.

"How many options do we *really* have?" she said, swooping her hands side-to-side and letting her eyes follow, pouring over the sparse downtown. "So I suppose it'll do." She said this and harbored all but a thin twitch of a smile.

"Perfect. Now keep in mind that you owe me. I chose the diner because I knew *you* wanted to go," he said back.

The partners walked toward Estelle's Diner at 8:15am. Doing so, Elijah realized that he too was pleased and a bit shocked by the formidable weather. It was the first time in a while that he didn't wince as the outside air touched his skin. Estelle's was four blocks to the north, and they were silent for the stretch. It was a silence born from comfort, silence they were OK with. There was no pressure to make conversation for the sake of it. Separately they reflected on how the feeling was calming. Elijah opened the door for her as they approached the old diner. "Openin' doors," she said. "Chivalry must not be dead."

"Not really. I just know I'm a dick, so I try to make up for it with little insignificant things," he said.

"Those little things are sometimes what matter most."

She smiled and told the hostess it was only the two of them. The diner was quiet and cozy. *Just as it should be,* in Elijah's eyes.

"So..." Aurelia spoke with her arms on the table. "Why do you spend every morning by yourself in a place like this?"

"It delays going to work."

"I won't believe that. Maybe it's a *residual* perk, but it's not why it's a priority." She looked upon Elijah and tried to read his face. It was stuck somewhere between a first date's discomfort and a child's reluctance to tell on himself. She watched his ideas flow until he'd settled on something. His lips eased apart, an idea's incipience, then shut again.

As his lips began again the waitress came crashing in. She was probably sixteen with tight bundles of blond curled about her chin and rosy cheeks. She smiled like Annie from Hoosiers, like there was no evil in the world.

Kelly Lynn received an, in-unison "black coffee" order and went skipping back to the kitchen.

The vast ocean void between Elijah and Aurelia was beginning to dry up. For a lasting moment, their eyes said everything and their mouths said nothing. Then, Elijah finally answered her.

"Home's never had much appeal because there's never been a family in the picture. I was fifteen when I started coming to places like this. It was just to be around people. Foster homes aren't always affable and I'd just go to sit, drink coffee. It felt normal, and I wanted to be."

They didn't speak again for several minutes.

"Thank you for such an honest answer, Elijah. I'm not sure what I expected." She paused, met his gaze. "Did something happen to your parents?"

"Not exactly. And it was a long time ago. It's OK now. Just a part of me. Ya know?"

She did know, and he continued.

"I think *now* the diner thing is still about comfort, trying to be normal. If I go somewhere familiar and have a few good interactions, it's a nice start to the day. And when I know what most days bring, those interactions, albeit mostly meaningless, can mean a lot. It still helps me feel normal, even if the rest of my day is anything but."

Aurelia listened and couldn't help but feel connected to his words. She knew well the toll the Bureau could take, the shadows it could cast on your soul, your outlook.

She knew well the weight of forgotten memories. She repressed a stir from deep in the recesses of her mind.

She wondered if Elijah Warren was more than he'd seemed over the past year.

"Well, Elijah Warren. That makes a lot of sense to me."

"More than you'd have thought? You seem to have low standards for my reasonability."

"You don't share much about yourself, Elijah. It's hard to make a judgment."

"Maybe there isn't much to know."

She knew that wasn't the case.

A half hour passed and they drank their coffee and ate their breakfast. Elijah ordered eggs, over-easy, with bacon and toast. Aurelia ordered biscuits and gravy. Estelle's was making a diner fan out of Aurelia.

At nine they paid the bill and walked to the police station. The chief met them at the door and teetered forward to hand over the list for which they'd come. This list consisted of six names, six addresses. They were all members of the local art community, collectors and creators. Maybe someone would recognize the craftsmanship of the chair.

The chief lingered with nothing to tell so Aurelia and Elijah turned to leave. It was a short walk back to Hoosiers, where the car stayed parked for the evening.

Prior to leaving NY, Clint Adams had given them a new camera to aid in their work. He'd passed it on and said something about *wasted resources* and *convenience for the sake of laziness.* Apparently something called digital photography was on the brink of making film cameras obsolete, though Elijah *couldn't* believe that it would. Sure, they'd been able to take pictures of the farmhouse. And sure, they could now share those pictures using a little screen on its back. But a thousand dollars? Who in the hell (other than the FBI) would buy one of those?

The first name on the list was Pearl Borning.

After only a few minutes of driving, the Explorer pulled into a small parking area allotted for Pearl's Antique Shop. Elijah stepped out the passenger door and looked at his surroundings, more of the same, barren fields, lush during the growing season, in every direction. No other buildings were visible, except the petite box of a shop amid blue skies and the brown expanse of earth. He and Aurelia met at the front of the vehicle and headed towards the entryway of the shop.

A high-pitched bell rang as they opened the door. "Good morning," came a cheerful greeting from the rear of the shop. The woman, who the detectives assumed was Pearl, came lumbering out from where they had heard the voice. She was probably sixty and close to two hundred pounds. The woman squeezed through the small aisles inherent in most antique shops to greet them face-to-face.

"Good morning, ma'am. My name's Aurelia and this is my partner, Elijah. We work for the FBI and have been investigating the farmhouse murder. We were wondering, could you have a look at some pictures for us?" Pearl looked concerned.

"Of course. Though, these photos aren't gruesome are they? I heard what happened out there; the work of someone truly evil and I don't have a real strong stomach."

"No ma'am," Elijah replied. "We actually came to you because of your line of work. You've been in Nashville's antique scene for a while now?"

"Yes, sir. Twenty-five years this March. I love this town and hate to see bad things happen in it. I'll help all I can."

"Thanks in advance for your cooperation," said Aurelia. She briefly talked on what they'd found the day prior, and showed Pearl the photographs. Unfortunately, neither the chair nor the poem had any significance to her.

She looked intently at the photos on the camera before finally saying, "Detectives, I'm sorry. All I can tell you about this chair is that the craftsmanship is divine. Whoever made it has either been practicing a lifetime or is a young prodigy. The detail's staggering and *whoever* created this piece *must* have been proud of it." Pearl obviously loved her chosen business; the sight of the chair brought her to the brink of tears.

"Any chance of someone leaving this behind during a move?" Elijah asked.

Pearl looked back down at the photographs one last time.

"I can't imagine a person leaving this chair *anywhere. Especially* if they're into antiques. Something like this can easily cost hundreds of dollars, up to thousands. This isn't just something generic you overlook on your way out the door."

"Well, Mrs. Borning, thanks for your time. You've been a great help," Aurelia said, though didn't mean.

While he drove, Elijah looked at their list of people to question about the chair and poem. The next candidate was named Dane Forney, who lived only five miles from Pearl's shop. Dane was a carpenter who focused on wood-based novelty items. He worked out of his barn, a converted shop.

Dane's house was different than the rest around Nashville. It was modern, both in terms of date built and architectural style. It was a dome with windows spread consistently around the roof's spherical circumference, spaced off and on like a single color on a chessboard.

The detectives approached the front door to find a note instructing visitors to, *Join me in the workshop*! They walked around the circular house and found a more traditional structure behind it. The barn that held Dane's workshop was just that. They knocked on the old wooden door at around 10am.

"Good morning and welcome, ya'll! I'm Dane. What can I do ya for?"

"Good morning, sir; this is Aurelia and my name's Elijah. We're detectives with the FBI, here to investigate the farmhouse murder from a few days ago. Wanted to see if you could have a look at some pictures for us?"

Dane amenably (almost too much so) beckoned them inside.

He bounced away like he'd been wound up and set loose. He careened through the center of the shop, dichotomizing the room both figuratively and literally. To one side were sprawling layers of shelves that reached up towards the ceiling, completed works, a grouping of animals carved from thick wooden blocks, one per project, a section for dining room tables, one just for ornate clocks, a section of suns and moons. Looking around, the detectives saw a proclivity for precision in Dane.

The other half of the room was a rambling amalgamation of woodworking tools and current projects, tons of them, a head-height bear with carved legs and an abdomen and arms, but an untarnished chunk for a head, an enormous tea kettle with decorative carvings (a bit like a sea of snowflakes) upon its top half and handle, a great hawk with piercing eyes and talons that (on one foot thus far) grasped a fish.

They followed through the shop, heading for a door at the rear of the building. Elijah was mostly thinking about how painstaking the work would be. He shuddered a bit thinking on how much patience it'd require to carve and craft so meticulously, a feeling akin to that which he'd felt examining Marcus Felway's "exploded" skeleton.

Through the door at the back of the shop was a room with four small chairs. They looked rigid with time-borne fabric but were more comfortable that they'd appeared. A loveseat remained empty as three of four chairs were filled. Covering the walls were pictures of the Seven Wonders of the World. "Your photographs?" Aurelia questioned.

"Yes ma'am. I wanted to shoot 'em all before I turned forty. Accomplished it last August, a year before my deadline."

"You've got an eye for it. And quite an achievement to visit them all," she said.

After a quick introduction, Dane examined the pictures *they'd* taken.

"'Run, run 'til the blazin' sun,' " he said aloud. "Interesting. Very interesting."

"What is?" said Elijah.

"Just the words, interesting idea. Kind of epitomizes winter here. HA! Everybody runs inside 'til the sun comes out, brings some rain and the growth of a new spring. Magical time of year," he said and his voice faded with it.

Aurelia and Elijah shot each other subtle glances.

"Anyone around here write poetry?" said Aurelia.

"Well, I'm ashamed to say it, but I try. Not well mind you. HA! Don't think anyone here makes their livelihood like that. Not much money in writing."

The man had a point.

They spent another few minutes talking, asking questions and listening to answers, but left—as before—with a void in their understanding and an emerging disquietude about Dane. They couldn't pinpoint the genesis of this unease, but it was there.

The next four listed names produced results that sang neutrality. Each member of Nashville's art community was struck by the eloquence in the chair's creation but couldn't fathom who'd made it or brought it to town.

The final name on the list was Mark Tulane; they left him at his door shortly after knocking on it. Mark's house was the furthest from town, not a day's drive, but thirty minutes farther than anyone wants to drive after spending a day so fruitlessly.

Elijah was behind the wheel, and the two were silent as the Explorer chased west after the setting sun and the town of Nashville. "Maybe it *was* just left there," Aurelia said as the sun was consumed by the horizon.

"Yea, maybe."

"I don't really think so."

"I don't either, but coincidence can't be ruled out. Maybe it's as simple as that, poem and all," he said.

They didn't speak to each other for the following miles, a dismal statistic spinning a simple record in their heads. No lead after forty-eight hours meant their chances fell to less than ten percent. It had been days since the body was found, longer since Marcus Felway was burned alive. They threw their hopes in a pool of tumultuous doubt.

Aurelia called Director Adams to arrange a helicopter to fly over the forests the following morning before a quick dinner at Hoosiers. Then, they both turned in. They said goodnight and opened the doors to their separate rooms.

Not a minute later they came crashing back into the hall with small scraps of paper bunched in their hands.

Run run 'til the blazin' sun
So much to hide…a tumultuous ride
Truth will be found upon warmer ground
So run run 'til the blazin' sun

They looked at each other, silent, knowing too well what the notes meant. They were being watched, and the case was far from over.

CHAPTER 8

M ario Arnold worked in real estate. His days were typical for a man in his mid-twenties, and analogous with the *rest* of his life. He fit in with the ranks at work. He had a small amount of debt from community college. He grew up in a family that ate together, took local vacations and paid their taxes on time. He worked a regular amount of hours and drank, but not to excess. To almost anyone looking in, Mario wasn't a perfect candidate for anything. On this day however, he had been noticed.

He was perfect.

It was just past 8am when he said goodbye to his cat, Wally, and walked out of his modest Boston town house. He'd pulled on his worn sport coat, buttoned it around his premature gut, and tied his generic dress shoes. His light brown hair, which had begun to run from his forehead, was combed neatly to the side. Mario always felt belittled by the *top* real estate agents, their expensive suits, shiny cars and big-boobed women beside them at Christmas parties. He envied them entirely.

He lived in the community of Winchester, north of Boston, so he could save some money. Sadly, this meant a thirty-six-minute commute stood between him and the office.

His walk was quick to board the Lowell Line, and summertime in Boston was blooming in layers of grandeur; lush trees lined the streets long before shedding their colors for fall, the day hot with rippling waves emanating from the blacktop. It made him reminisce and think longingly about college. It wasn't that many years past since summers consisted of drinking watery beer and boating on Lake Waramaug. When had real life turned him into an adult? He'd been thinking about how suddenly it seemed to happen.

On a normal day it took six minutes for Mario to walk to the train station. At minute three, Mario was right on schedule, turning left at the Peruvian Deli and moving past the pawnshop, his plodding steps in no hurry.

He turned the corner to begin covering the last block. As his steps brought him across the mouth of an alleyway that existed on his right, he felt something unforeseen, a dagger of pain that first stung, then seemed to paralyze his leg.

Looking in the direction of the pain, his vision began to scatter. Moments were suddenly elastic and as he began slowly (in his mind) crashing to the cement, a terrific force ripped him down the lonely passage. His attention and memory were at odds with one another, each hostile in their losing battle. His head and body suddenly hurt and throbbed. He opened his eyes and looked up to find a man wearing black dragging him down the alley by his wrists, bound by a length of metal cable. The back of his old sport coat tore as it dragged along the cement.

Mario superfluously thought about what he should do, not considering what he *could* do. He would race after an idea only to be outrun, left in the wavering distance and disconnected from his goal at starting line. Mario ran and chased, he darted and ducked and spun and turned circles, idea after idea becoming the same jumbled coalescence.

Still being dragged, Mario's upside down gaze saw a black-hooded figure, and when it turned, a macabre void of darkness where a face should be. Mario couldn't remember having been so scared.

His consciousness lost its fight.

He awoke with a screaming voice in his head. It was his. At first when he heard it, it was far away, then it crept like ominous footsteps. The sound began to steamroll, picking up speed like an avalanche and with the hiss of a train whistle, still deep in his skull but coming closer.

When he reached consciousness, he gasped back his scream, horrified by the noise but *more* horrified that it had been coming out of him.

He realized his hands were bound behind him, ankles bound as well, and was lying on a floor he fathomed as tile; small grout squares pushed into his naked body. He craned his head to see what he could, then pulled his eyes closed. They were heavy, a startling heaviness that he'd never experienced. He opened them again, a deep red and pulsing heat at their corners, and determined the room was an old basement, maybe an old bathroom? Yes! It must have been. Mario looked more carefully upon some rusted piping protruding from the drywall.

Mario kept scanning, writhing and rolling to see both sides of the space. Panic drove his breathing, which he was losing grasp of. There was a door. The door was newer than the rest of the space, a keypad to its side. At that moment, the drug swimming in his bloodstream came back over him. His mind careened into shadowy oblivion, and he lay helpless, a squirming coil on the tile.

Images of life in Winchester were filling, floating across the sky, fading in, out, coalescing with others. Mario could see his house, his bedroom and Wally, stretching in a beam of sunshine from the window. The pictures were all so beautiful. As Mario walked down the radiantly marooned street, he couldn't help but stare up at the images and the bright sky beyond them. He walked slowly and didn't think about where he might end up or really from where he'd come. On his right were stone statues, all different, but all leaning toward him from above as if to tell him something.

They inched closer by the minute, though he didn't notice, because on the left now the earth began to shake. Granite walls began breaking through the concrete, violent, stone rockets careening into the heavens.

The walls, Mario could now see, had jagged stone teeth and were moving towards him. He turned to run in the direction of the statues, but saw they too had bested him, their expressions all the same gnarled smile, the same dead eyes. He knew in that moment that he was going to die.

He took one last look to the images in the sky, now fleeting, as menacing clouds overtook the blue, then ran in the single direction his setting allowed. He watched the tower of light before him—between the walls and the statues—shrink down to a pencil-thin gap. He pushed harder not to be caught, smashed, but his feet seemed to sink, to stick or gain mass. How was he moving so damn slowly?

The light then filled the space, washed over Mario and filled his vision, surrounded him. He didn't know how or why at first. He just allowed himself to exist, to bath in the warmth of that light.

It took a moment, but he noticed an overhead light had been turned on. The man wearing black entered the damp room slowly, allowing the door to shut behind him. His movements looked almost robotic, but weren't unnatural, just prolonged. He crossed the small room and sat down in a corner. A single chair now existed. Whether or not it had before, Mario couldn't remember.

"Good morning," said the man. His words came so slowly that Mario felt he'd never get them out of his head.

"How long have I been here?" Mario asked.

"Three days. But it took a full day to drive here, so it has been four days since you were home in Boston. I assume *that* is the information you truly wanted."

"Why am I here?"

"I am going to kill you to help prove a point," the man wearing black said calmly.

The man's voice echoed in his head, or was it the room? "Did you say," he gulped, "that you're going to kill me?"

"Yes. I did. Do not worry. You've had good rest, so trust your senses."

"I feel horrible. Am I drugged?" he asked. He already knew the answer but didn't really know what else to say.

"Well, my ability to accomplish what I want is made significantly easier when you haven't any conscious understanding of where you are or how you got there. And when you are unable to assault me physically, I don't have it worry about. Now do I?"

"I have a family. I love them. Please, isn't there anyone else? I mean, can't you choose someone else? Someone with less to lose?"

"I suppose, yes. I could have chosen someone with less to lose. Though," he scoffed, "I could have *easily* chosen someone with more to lose. I regress. The word 'chosen' indicates that this has happened in the past, and thus, is not something we can change now. Do you see the predicament that puts us in?"

"Yes."

"Terrific, Mario. You understand. You must be more precocious than I initially thought. To be honest though, you're missing the point entirely. I didn't choose you because you *do* have a family, nor would I have chosen someone else specifically because they didn't. I chose you because it made sense in that particular time and place. It just worked out, if you are more comfortable with that phrasing." The man wearing black sat without moving, frozen in the position he'd initially settled into. Despite Mario's best effort, he still could not make out his face within the hood.

Mario began again to panic. His consciousness fell away from him and he remained quivering on the floor in inconsequential jerks. The man wearing black sat still and watched with the same empty eyes and twisted smile as the statues in the dream.

CHAPTER 9

A lot can change in two weeks.

Wars have been fought.

Lives have been destroyed and mended, and the moon completes half a cycle.

Two weeks had passed since Elijah and Aurelia found poems on their pillows; the date was now February first, and *absolutely nothing* had happened in Nashville. They'd checked the forests, followed up with the art community and re-questioned the victims' friends and families. They'd poked around further at the farmhouse property, found nothing but a taunting frustration, a taunting frustration born from being close, from being toyed with and left in an enormous void of obscurity. Would the killer return? Had they left at all? The killer could walk a free man's walk and the detectives kept this in the forefront of their ideas.

The winter's bitterness had stalked after them through the month, continued to hound in tearing gusts that shrieked up and down the streets like freight train banshees. With each day that passed, the howling felt more a part of them, a constant presence that filled their dreams and their waking days.

Their thoughts had spiraled, tumbled and turned. Why had the killer carried on so abstrusely? Why bluntly lead on the feds but leave nothing more? Things still didn't add up, and a sick frustration had settled wholly into them like a child's disappointment. It seemed as if the whole town was laughing at them, and although friends were "made" quickly, the goodbyes were fast (but felt?) and Elijah and Aurelia had made their way to the airstrip. Two short flights later, they were back to the concrete jungle. They gave quiet goodbyes and took disparate taxis from JFK. Neither of them quite had direction in their words, young feelings in stubborn adults.

Director Adams had instructed them to go straight home, to take a few days. He knew of their frustration and empathized with it, and even sensed a different kind of confusion in them both, an odd sensation Clint couldn't quite put a pin in. He *too* felt that the "Indiana Killing" was the start of something novel, was troubled by it, but the askew nature of the murder and its investigation *wasn't* most troubling his detectives, and for the moment, it wasn't his place to ask.

Elijah walked through his doorway after spending over two weeks away.

Nothing had changed. The decor bore a striking resemblance to what most might consider transitional living. Through the door stood a small kitchen, paper plates strewn about. Then a living area existed, khaki tones coloring decent furniture and a few end tables beside. The living space opened up onto a balcony, facing east over the bay toward Roosevelt Island, and *that* was beautiful, a terrific feature that cast light onto how nice the space was *meant* to be, despite its size. After all, it *was* New York.

Through the living area, opposite the door and past the kitchen was a shoebox bedroom that fit little more than his double bed. The thing that made Elijah Warren's home most distinctive was its complete lack of character. Void space hung on the walls; nothing but fallen gin soldiers sat on the end tables, long since forgotten on the battlefield and crusting at the bottoms with curls of lime. No magazines sat on the sparse shelving, no books. He didn't even appear to get mail. The truth was, Elijah never saw much need for any of that.

He knew of a home's fragility, its temporary nature, and though his perspective was different than most, it could be explained. Elijah Warren felt most things could be explained, even the unexplainable, if one was inclined to try. History, he felt, explained this best.

When it came to home, comfort was Elijah's lone concern. He occasionally thought about someday having a home that suited him. It would *not* be in New York. Maybe somewhere like Wisconsin. Maybe Minnesota? Who knew? He was home for the moment, and that would do. The door had barely closed and a lime was cut. Gin was poured.

The trip from the airport lasted half an hour for Aurelia, speedy considering what it could have been. She hated nothing more than sitting in traffic within miles of home.

She walked up the stairs to her apartment, turned the key and went in. As she stood in her hollow doorway, she realized it was the most sad she'd felt in a very long time. She needed to get back to work, and soon.

The next morning, she woke early with the sun and a renewed sense of calm. It wasn't quite the same as what she felt—occasionally—in Nashville, the serenity of countryside, but the simple act of waking up with the morning light made her feel good. As her eyes were still nearly closed, she wasn't sure what to do with the day, so she sprawled across her bed, stretching her arms and legs to graze the corners of it. Half an hour later, she dragged herself from the coziness of a down comforter, plush pillows. It was a Tuesday and she actively decided to do nothing. She walked from bed to the kitchen wearing only a pair of small, black briefs to make coffee. They showed off her legs and curvaceous ass.

Her bare feet pressed easily across the cool hardwood and her nipples stiffened. She caught a glimpse of herself in the stainless reflection of the fridge and felt a bit like she was doing something wrong. Maybe it was because she spent so little time there. Maybe it was because she barely ever saw herself naked. She was *unconscious* during sleep and *hurrying* in and out of the shower. When was she really to look?

She wondered if *Elijah* slept naked.

Once her coffee was made, she sat down in her living room and read the morning paper, which was two weeks old. February's incipience was bringing nicer days, which were aberrant for the time of year. This one was the nicest in a while, cold mornings and warm near-hot afternoons.

Aurelia loved that.

The high was to be fifty, and the expanse of sky out her window was blue-blue with gleaming sun. Maybe some time off *would* be a good thing. She turned the final page of the paper and flashed a look at the clock on the wall, 8:30am. She decided to dress and head out. She thought she might visit a diner up the way.

Elijah woke bearishly that same morning with a sudden need for cool air. He burst up from beneath a blanket on his couch, where the east-facing window allowed sun through in stone-hearted beams. He crowed with discontent and rolled from the couch. With a smack, he remembered how hard his floor was. He stood then stretched and pulled his sweatshirt up and over his head. Still not content, his shirt followed, exposing his chiseled upper body. He had been still in his travel clothes, including his jeans, wool socks and boots.

He teetered his way to the kitchen and his socked feet slipped about the floor. After locating an (of course) old jug of orange juice from the depths of the fridge, he stood with it turned up, downing it quickly.

He wiped a bit from his chin with the back of the hand he held the jug in.

Returning back through the kitchen, Elijah flipped on the TV, closed the sprawling shades with the press of a button and collapsed back onto the couch. Productivity was about as far down his list as jumping off the balcony and onto a bicycle with no seat. Seinfeld episodes seemed to always be on, and he was fully OK with that.

A while later, he stood stagnant in the shower and realized (painfully) how much he wanted to see Aurelia. Prior to the Nashville trip he hadn't thought much about her at all, let alone anything positive. For him, something had happened on the trip, and he couldn't quite explain it. He knew that her presence changed the way he stood, the way he felt about himself, about life and how maybe his could look. He was, around her, the best version of himself.

What he *didn't* know was what *she* was thinking.

His head was bowed forward underneath near-cold water. It ran off his shoulders, down ripples on his sides and down his V-lines and ass. It spiraled in the drain like the thoughts in his head.

Aurelia sat with a stubbornly neutral look on her face at the Sunflower Diner. A short four blocks through the decent air had brought her to the corner of 3rd and 26th and a tucked away table that suited her. She felt great sitting there, watching General Worth Park through the window, across 3rd, looming willows that hung and swung in the breeze and some grass that sat with buildings for a canopy, the charging back and forth of humans before all that and the mostly yellow-black blur of the street roaring. She showed just a trace of a smile, the remnants of which could not be suppressed, and thought uncharacteristically about what she might want *her* story to look like. All *those* people had one, things they wanted, passions, chosen ways to spend time.

Right? She hadn't wrapped her head around *what* exactly she was thinking. What was it that *she* wanted? She finished a third cup of coffee and blueberry pancakes a short while after that. She laughed to herself because she couldn't help but enjoy sitting there and thought about how maybe Elijah wasn't crazy, a mindset for each day with a clear and planned starting point.

She thought about this still and thanked the kid for her fourth coffee. Then she thought about Elijah some more. She wondered how he felt about their trip, about her. She knew she felt something, but couldn't (wouldn't?) see quite what it meant. Time continued to pass as she gazed out at the willows. She imaged her little blue house sitting there. She subtracted the buildings and the people and the roar of the city.

It was March 15, 1997. Elijah woke at his usual time and headed to Madison Restaurant. It hadn't quite been two months since they'd returned home, but it felt like it. The "Indiana Killing" might as well have been a closed case. The question of why was still the fraying string that dangled in their minds.

Work had been slow and Elijah was bored.

His return brought endless paperwork. How was there no fieldwork for him to do?

That had started the week after returning from Nashville.

That was five weeks ago.

As Elijah sat facing 53rd street, he thought about Aurelia. Without having anyone of which to admit it, Elijah missed sitting across from her. It was a small thing, but he fixated on it. They'd not talked.

At the office they passed like ships in the night, but whatever it was keeping them apart, who could blame them? They were relationship illiterate.

Just then, she came bursting through the door of Madison Restaurant.

"I'd make a rude joke about knowing where to find you, but I don't have time because I need to show you this. A woman's body was found in Ouray, Colorado. It's him," she said, her hair trailing behind her as she handed him a picture. He took it, but for a moment just looked at her as she talked. He missed a couple sentences and then said...

"Wait. Colorado? Why do we think it's him? It's been more than a month."

"Just look at this. She was tied up late last fall at the bottom of the still flowing waterfall. The waterfall obviously froze during the winter and since it's so far into the backcountry, she wasn't found. The waterfall's just now beginning to thaw."

"How'd they find her?"

"He *had* to have planned it this way. There was an authentic forest service gate, apparently installed last year, and no one looked into it until a couple days ago. It was left open so a ranger saw it, followed it back, hiked around and found her. This was carved into the cliff."

She handed him a piece of paper that had Director Adams' chicken scratch on it.

Open your eyes, feast on the prize
I'm out of hiding, prepare for inviting
Truth is now found upon warmer ground
So open your eyes and feast on the prize.

Elijah's eyes blazed over the words. He then thought back to the original poem.

"'Run, run 'til the blazin' sun. Truth will be found upon warmer ground.' Holy shit! He literally told us what to expect. He told us we'd have to wait until spring. Aurelia, this was at least six months ago. He's more calculated than we thought. If he put the girl there last fall..." he said, his voice trailing off.

"Exactly. Who else is out there? Who knows how long he's been planning this. The poem was sent to the office this morning and Adams called me in. He's expecting us."

"We need to get to Ouray," Elijah said.

As she walked the direction of the door, Aurelia turned her head back toward him.

"Flight this afternoon," she said, and gave him a smile and a wink. Her bangs grazed her gaze and she tossed them away. The most honest part of him wanted to chase after her, to grab her and kiss her, to tell her how being with her was what he wanted and how he didn't care about some insane murderer.

Instead he said nothing and watched the door close behind her.

CHAPTER 10

T he Telluride Regional Airport in southwest Colorado doesn't warrant much traffic.

Unlucky for the bureau, lucky for us, Elijah thought, as he waited on the tarmac. He took a step onto their government appointed jet and swam in the feeling like a warm pool come summer. Elijah *loathed* flying commercial and *hated* airports. So today, he enjoyed himself. He got to forego the incessant badgering, the hoops you jumped through simply to board the plane. Were the minutiae precautions really achieving anything? Was the speech about how to put on a seatbelt really all that pertinent? Maybe so, but what was coming next? Not being able to meet family at the gate?

Aurelia boarded behind him, carrying her usual confidence. She looked elegant. What Elijah had always thought of as pompousness, was now a lucid portrayal of being faultless, and although Elijah figured *she* didn't see herself as such, *he* did. He'd always noticed her negatively and it was strange for that to change. It was strange to desire company, but he did. He desired hers, and was often cursing himself and his dreadful ability to form and sustain relationships.

The plane, a Beechjet 400A, could seat seven including a pilot. Today though, it held three. The pilot was a man Elijah knew only as "Captain Riff" or "The Captain." The Captain was a private contractor who piloted the majority of the bureau's high-profile flights. Today he wore his usual uniform, an oversized Hawaiian shirt, plaid golf shorts and flip-flops. He had a kind face that bore a too-handsome smile and eyes that were old but young and would be still striking through a haze of smoke. He walked and talked and stood with placid swagger. He wasn't exactly professional, at least in the traditional sense, but he worked at a moment's notice and got you there fast and safe. And generally, he was good for a laugh.

From back to front, the Beechjet had four, forward-facing seats, two facing backward and a cockpit. Elijah and Aurelia sat opposing one another on the passenger side of the plane.

"Ah yes," Elijah said. "The perks of government travel." He was rifling through the mini fridge.

"Jesus, it's only noon," she replied.

"Well, we have a pretty substantial flight, and the only part *I* want to remember is the final half hour. Even the *east* of Colorado is boring as shit."

She shook her head in his direction and reached around him to snag two small bottles of whiskey from the fridge. "That's reasonable," she said. "Although, your justification is horseshit. When people like drinking they fabricate reasons for it. Like, it's five o'clock somewhere, or we *have* to drink at the zoo! Bad excuses… But hey, I'm joining you, so my judgment is clearly hypothetical."

Captain Riff came over the plane's intercom after the detectives were seated and informed them of the departure. He was sure to include customary, tasteless humor. "Lady and gent, I assume you know we're all heading west. You don't need to know much else, but we *are* leaving now. Just keep it R rated and leave some whiskey in the fridge for me, because I'm already low up here." Then he belched, turned off the speaker, and began down the runway. The FBI's hiring priorities were unclear. Fashion or function?

The detectives looked out the window as the plane left the ground. Prior to meeting that morning, they'd wondered if their interactions would be uncomfortable, jaded or awkward. It was the first time they'd be forced to interact since Indiana.

Luckily, prior to falling asleep, they'd both laughed quietly at Riff's speech. They'd picked right back up where they'd left off during January's closing days. They'd finished their adult beverages and talked like no time had passed, each with that same sense of comfort they'd felt before. It was kept professional, each understanding (individually) that they were ignoring something, but would have to for the time being. It was the potential for something, and they each protected that at any vast cost. They fell asleep as the plane crossed into Pennsylvanian airspace.

Aurelia awoke an unknown time later and looked down onto what could only be Kansas. She went back to sleep.

Colossal cumulus clouds situated themselves amid the small airplane in a confounding mass. The acrid clouds, rotting and oversized cotton balls, foreshadowed the following days.

The Beechjet propelled into the state of Colorado. Geographically speaking, not much changed. The eastern plains of Colorado are not only sans mountains, they're entirely flat with unbearable cold in the winter and unyielding heat in the summer. Combine that with a lack of most else and you understand Elijah's theory that gives that space to Kansas, cordons it all off, and sends inmates there to roam free and maintain the windmills. "Free energy!" he'd said.

Aurelia had calmly pointed out why that idea wasn't realistic.

As the Front Range approached, Aurelia was roused by some mild turbulence. She woke Elijah when she saw the mountains ahead. He revealed the blues behind his lids in a bleary shake, and his gaze made its way out the window.

The Front Range of Colorado spans from Fort Collins, at the north, to Colorado Springs, in the south. The region interested Elijah for a myriad of reasons. One thing he could not ignore was that the mountains inspired him. They whispered into him a charge of energy, a feeling of grandeur, a sensation of being large and small in the same moment with purpose in being lost (which he never really was physically). Somehow or another the mountains represented a sense of calm that came from being wholly satisfied, a sentiment he attained scarcely. He gazed longingly out the window and down towards the earth and wasn't concerned with how he looked. He stared and gawked like a child waiting for the circus. If Aurelia had stayed awake, she would have been moved by the childlike fascination.

Sooner than Elijah would have liked, the wheels touched down onto the runway of Telluride. He gently woke her when it was time to alight.

CHAPTER 11

The regional airport outside of Telluride, Colorado was perfect. It was a short drive to Ouray and it was, "nice and tight like a yoga instructor," Captain Riff had said via intercom.

During flight Elijah and Aurelia read about the thousand Ouray residents, the demographics, the median income, the crime rates and the town's sources of revenue. They found out that Ouray was the "Switzerland of America," and home to world-class ice climbing, endless towers of ice, frozen in time for the winter and simple-yet-novel as the killer's selected backdrop.

It was just after six when Elijah and Aurelia met fresh Colorado air. The sun was slipping elegantly behind the mountain skyline. Streaks of purple, orange and yellow radiated in bold streaks through a vivid blue expanse. Elijah knew that Montana was "Big Sky Country," but the Centennial State couldn't have been far behind for the title.

Aurelia stood at the stairs' summit, an ellipsoid void where the plane's door once was. She shared Elijah's view and thought to herself that she'd been missing out having never been to Colorado. She took in the horizontal rock veins in the San Miguel Mountain Range, white and red bands, hundreds of feet high and alternating, the stripes accented by layers of evergreen. She pondered the patterns' creation, and she loved the colors, like back in Wisconsin. The mountains, with their staggering presence, dwarfed her in an internal battle she'd not yet settled. They made her feel relevant, though obtusely inconsequential.

The partners walked toward a waiting Ford Explorer. The temperature wasn't a degree over forty, but Aurelia's light jacket kept her warm, and Elijah was too involved in the view to notice if *he* was cold.

Elijah swung the SUV toward the exit, and the sky lingered behind and above them, slowly fading into a star-filled dreamscape. A roaring river tangled with the road until twenty minutes later, they reached town.

The night required nothing, thanks to the murder's remote locale.

Local authorities were to be prepared at 8am the following morning.

Driving through downtown they found the old west, modest buildings and hand-carved signs, then came upon The Victorian shortly after. The inn sat facing southwest with yet another stunning view, jagged crests of rock hanging in the twilight.

Check in was fast, and they hoped they'd have running water. An outside staircase led them to the second floor. They dropped off small suitcases and headed back out for dinner. Aurelia, of course, grabbed the file on the way. They both had a craving for Mexican food and Buen Tiempo had been passed on the ride in. They tracked back to it.

Buen Tiempo was an explosion of colors and noise inside, piñatas lingering above and music fast with horns.

"Does everyone look happy to you?" Aurelia said, sitting down across from Elijah.

"Thinking the same. I guess New Yorkers are always rushing. Even out drinking they're in a hurry."

They looked around. People sat and not only talked, but listened to each other. It seemed the world did less and less of that. There was a drunken young couple to their side having a very different type of night. Elijah and Aurelia were lost in envy.

Aurelia pulled the file from her purse not long after they'd sat. The waterfall murder was different from Indiana, but a sick familiarity was felt. There was calculation and foresight. There was a blunt disregard for humankind. The Ouray victim's name was Serena Miller, and she had been seen the evening before her death at a work party. Reports from the party were inconspicuous. The most curious bit of information was that it was in Kansas City, 859 miles from where she was found dead, that she'd been seen. How the hell had she gotten to Ouray?

Back in Nashville, Aurelia thought the killing was personal. The torture and the time it took, the brutality. Now, she wasn't so sure. She stared down at Serena's face, an arctic mask of horror, and felt guilty for having no answers.

"How do you think he's choosing them?" she asked.

"No idea. But I think we need to ask a different question." He paused long enough to take a long pull from his G&T. "How many has he *already* chosen?" Aurelia looked at him and waited. "This girl, Serena, was found in the thawing waterfall, left there last fall before it began to freeze. Then, several months later, the killer torches and cubes Marcus Felway. He allows us to find Marcus, waits for us to investigate, then taunts us where we're sleeping. Pretty personal. Then, we're kept in the dark for almost two months until Serena thaws, 'Upon warmer ground.' The time frame *must* be relevant."

Elijah was talking faster with each sentence. Aurelia was getting lost in the blues of his eyes, but keeping focused on the point…to the best of her ability.

"So who knows how many more bodies we're set up to find? Who knows how many people he killed and hid last fall or winter?" He took another drink. The horns played in the background over crackling speakers. The piñatas swung overhead and the world continued. "Who knows about last summer? *Who knows* how far back he's been doing this?"

Aurelia reached out and put her hand on his for a second. She simply told him that they'd find him, and that made him feel better.

It would have been strange to eavesdrop on them. One minute they were discussing a woman who'd been kidnapped, dragged through the woods and left to die in the alpine of Colorado, and the next they were eating, arguing amenably over how best to order food and whether or not Nirvana would have been as successful had Kurt Cobain not killed himself. To them, it was something beautiful.

Aurelia and Elijah teetered back to the Victorian, not thinking about the altitude and how it affected the booze and their bloodstream. The town of Ouray was allowing them to pretend they weren't tracking a murderer. Having not to do with the cold, Elijah had his arm around Aurelia. She felt how her cheek could rest on his chest, the way she fit right under that arm, his smell and the way he made her feel, like they were far away from the world and its problems. They approached the stairs leading up to their rooms without speaking, a powerful silence that seemed filled with anticipation, a comfortable yet anxious unknown.

They reached their rooms but stopped there and stood facing each other in the nighttime air. Neither could explain why they couldn't turn away. Elijah pored over her, found himself lingering in her eyes. They told a story, which he still didn't know, but he finally said goodnight.

"I'm sorry," she said after, and leaned in and pressed her lips to his.

Elijah said nothing, and a minute later he found himself still standing, now alone in the hallway.

While falling asleep that night, his mind raced, and for once, it wasn't about someone being killed.

CHAPTER 12

T he man wearing black had neurons firing as if solving Fermat's Last Theorem. He spoke indolently, (half out loud, half not) though his thoughts were anything but.

He thought/spoke about how he pitied them, these people, existing in their quite repulsive imaginariums. They don't think for themselves. People follow. They mold. People kowtow, and if the man wearing black had learned one thing, it was that time was priceless, and he would waste not a second of it conforming. His task was monumental, and now that he'd found Elijah and Aurelia, time would soon bring the swell of completion he so longed for.

The man deliberated with only himself as he looked around the train's car.

The rails were leading to Portland, Oregon, and he knew precisely where he'd debark. The man wearing black had been a passenger for many hours, having started the trip in Missouri. A stolen vehicle had been torched and dumped, its final resting place outside a town called Columbia, at the bottom of a river on the town's west side. The man doubted greatly that it'd be recovered, though, if it were, the fire that began inside and ate its way out incinerated that which could incriminate him. The car burned high and hard before settling into a watery tomb.

The man wearing black left nothing to chance. In life, he'd grown tall with no reason for hurry, a babe walking and talking and growing in a world whose demands meant nothing to him. Meticulously, he developed his existence, made his own way, a master moving his chess pieces.

Hitherto time had been short for his *malicious* intentions. Youth had found him bright and well thought, questioning but not sinister. *Life* had taught him that.

The train rocked in an easing dance as it charged toward Portland. It was halfway through the state, and the man wearing black was closer than ever to the next piece in his grandiose puzzle. It was thrilling for him, having *finally* found people to solve it.

The man wearing black rose like a phantom from his dining car's seat, folded his napkin and placed it on the table beside a sub-par tip, then turned toward the sleepers, matchbox cells with a slight bed and thin covers and a window with the world going by. As he walked, a middle-aged couple was arguing loudly about keeping track of the tickets. The man felt his feet settle, a sick and silent affliction that kept him equidistant in the aisle between them and a sleeping hippie with feathers in her hair and hemp in her clothing. The man said nothing, and was about to begin again his walk to end the day.

But the husband looked up from his seat and blurted, "mind your own fuckin' business, creep." The man's wife looked at him, clearly with something to say but unwilling to do so.

The man wearing black responded after a moment filled with only the rocking clatter of the wheels on the tracks.

"When you speak rudely to your wife, loudly enough for others to hear, it can become another's business." He paused, and looked then at the woman. "Though, her snide retort proved her equally miserable." He looked back to the husband. "This aside, once you make it another's business, you may find you don't like their business, the jibs and the jabs, the dirt of it." He looked back and forth between the both of them, and then said, "what if someone's business was murder?"

The married couple listened to his unhurried words, almost a whisper, and felt an overwhelming dread fall over them. The husband wished he'd never opened his mouth. The man wearing black continued and their insides sickened with fear.

"You just can't know if someone nearby is willing to slash open your stomach and behead your picturesque wife." He paused a final time and the rocking train clickety-clacked below them. "Crazy world out there," the man wearing black said, and turned towards the sleeping car. He eased forward a right foot, eased the left, until he reached the door. His hand hovered out and grasped the knob.

He didn't bother to turn back to the married couple, though it wasn't to prove a point.

That, would be proven later, and would require a smaller audience.

Behind him, sitting and quivering in a way they'd not before done, the woman suggested notifying train security, but her husband shot that down tersely.

"Really want to make this worse, Brenda? Are you an idiot?"

She reconsidered and thought it best to drop the subject.

The husband tried to push that face from his mind, the subtle shape haloed by the darkness of a hood. He couldn't.

He chose *not* to notice however, that he'd deflected his own anger at himself onto his wife. A distant piece of his consciousness made him wonder if the man wearing black had a point back there, but only for a moment.

The clickety-clacking was still beneath the man wearing black, and his head lay on an inadequate (for most people) pillow. His mouth was a narrow slit with perked corners, and neutrality lay on the rest of his face. It was the same neutral satisfaction from when he'd been talking to the old squares, the same as when he dragged Serena Miller and her wilting body through the mountains of Colorado, the same as when he burned Marcus Felway alive. He was fast and deep asleep in moments.

Not so many hours later, with half that many hours' worth of sleep, he stepped off the train in time to see a beautiful Portland sunrise. East of the city, the man wearing black watched the aura of fire ease over Mt. Hood. A smile crept across his face and lit him up like a Christmas tree.

The train whistle blew and pulled away behind him.

It was a typical morning for Terry, the train's security officer or, "attack man," as he self-proclaimed. He was making rounds. Terry's job was less dangerous than, well, most things, but he carried himself like he was an agent in the Secret Service; the most notorious criminals he dealt with were unruly high schoolers smokin' joints or bangin' too loud in the rooms.

Terry had already checked the front half of the train in quick patterns of movement, the result of many years of monotony, with three separate sleeping cars left to cover.

The first car was normal, people snoring and grunting, horizontal bodies rocking with the train. A few over-achievers were awake drinking coffee, reading, probably the stock section of the paper. He walked in a leisurely jaunt to the second car, swinging some keys and humming a tune he couldn't separate from for the life of him.

In the second car, the first passenger's doorway came into view, and he noticed it was cracked, a splinter of vertical lighting crossing the hallway and painting the opposite wall. He (of course) went to investigate.

The compartment had a bed on the left, two small chairs on the right. The void between them was minimal, and the red aura of morning filled the space. A man in his fifties, (Terry's best guess) lay across the bed, his stomach slashed open, snarls of intestine, stomach, and spleen spilling from the cavernous void. It was a simple matter of time before gravity finished pulling it all to the floor.

A woman of unknown age (at first) sat in one of the chairs; her head sat upright on the floor, face leaning against the wall beside her. The space where it once met her neck was a bubbling mess of crimson with a bone for its core. Terry gasped and stumbled backward, crash-knocking into the other side of the train car's hall with a fumble of the radio. He stumbled down the hallway and sputtered sentence fragments to the people in charge.

The train came to a halt.

CHAPTER 13

I f there was one thing both Elijah and Aurelia could manage, it was making the best of situations that had no business in the realm of normal life. The kiss from the night before would (should?) be a cakewalk to ignore, to not think about.

Elijah was (for the moment) just staring at Aurelia, and they'd been doing a good job of letting things be. They were talking about the stale continental breakfast, the nasty layer of grime under the cappuccino machine, the bagels that you could break in half. They made jokes about the local weather forecasters on the old TV in the upper corner of the room, the trite wallpaper. Their hands touched as they each went for coffee at one point, and they both noticed it, excitedly.

Their Explorer made it to the police station at 8am. Elijah was wearing his typical detective outfit and Aurelia had on grey dress pants, a black sweater and grey jacket.

The sun existed behind menacing clouds, the day's shot at salvation, veiled. They stepped out of the car and were assaulted by what they couldn't see. The wind whipped and tore, bit with cruel, slamming gusts. The prior day's feeling of spring had been replaced by what felt exactly like winter. Aurelia pulled the collar of her knee-length coat up to her ears. She then pulled the knit hat she didn't expect to need from her pocket. Elijah noticed the wind, but was too consumed by the mountains' allure to fix the problem. He just looked on.

Since Ouray had only a thousand residents, their police force was just slightly larger than Nashville's. Their collective staff totaled eight. The chief was a woman named Cheryl, who had long, blond, hair with natural highlights. She looked out from eyes with no makeup and spoke in a firm, patient voice.

"Good morning, Detective Blanc, Detective Warren. We sure are glad you could make it. We've never seen anything like this."

"We actually had almost an identical conversation the last time we were chasing this guy around," Elijah replied.

"We're glad you sent us the poem," Aurelia said. "Shall we get going?"

"Sure thing. You can follow me. The roads are a little rough but not too bad if you have four wheel drive," Cheryl added.

Cheryl led the caravan in her police-tagged SUV down the Million Dollar Highway, toward where the body was found. Elijah and Aurelia followed behind. The road wound southbound toward Crystal Lake and with picturesque views ubiquitously around them, their breath was taken. After ten minutes, the cars reached the forest road's turnoff. They then traveled west, just as the killer had done six months prior, just before he dragged Serena through the woods.

The dirt road was well established, but not well maintained. Deep grooves riddled it like splintering veins. The two vehicles tossed haphazardly, this way and that.

As they moved west around the lake, the view of the lake tumbled from the driver's window, snow-capped mountain peaks and evergreen trees surrounding them.

When they made it to the forged gate, they opened it, turned right and headed down the road it protected. The gate looked professional, the same as the *sanctioned* gates in the forest. The killer had done his homework. He'd taken the time on the details, and obviously knew the forest service wouldn't do much to investigate.

They parked at the end of the old wash and began their hike.

Their feet followed the path Serena's head had bounced along almost a half year earlier. To their left, the terrain fell sharply downslope fifty feet; to their right, it rose for a few hundred before reaching a mountain summit. The faint trail they were following cut across the mountain horizontally, slowly gaining elevation. They hiked for a mile before finding what they'd set out for.

They approached the cliff line on their right side. The granite rock wall began only as high as their shins and slowly climbed to an impressive fifty-foot amphitheater. They could see the waterfall and that it was still frozen from the top of the cliff down to a slim void at the bottom where water was drip-dropping onto slanting rock from the bottom of two raw toes, icy, barely melting and peaking from the bottom of the ice pillar. The detectives' eyes followed the contour of her body up the vertical ice column until they'd seen all of her. She was naked with twisted limbs and a face wretched in pain, still-framed in arctic horror.

Suddenly, a past moment became real and Elijah could see Serena in the water, wrists wrapped in metal cord and torn and bleeding, her body a wicked marionette in the rushing force, water sounding off the rock like the roar of a raceway.

Then it was silent again, and for himself, he read the words carved into the wall.

Open your eyes, feast on the prize
I'm out of hiding, prepare for inviting
Truth is now found upon warmer ground
So open your eyes and feast on the prize.

"What's here? What else did he leave for us?" Elijah said out loud to himself.

He walked patiently around the waterfall, isolated like a Roman column, eight feet from the wall.

Aurelia moved about the obscure crime scene. Reexamining the bolts that held Serena's wrist cables and the words in the stone, she felt more lost. The materials were common, and though the poem may prove useful, intellectual exhaustion would be the route traveled to find out.

They left empty handed after many hours. Another piece to the puzzle was not fitting where they hoped it would. Maybe something would turn up in the high country of Colorado, but it seemed they were chasing another dead end.

They arrived back in town and went straight to the hotel, unfed and sick with the day's disappointment, but a message was waiting.

CHAPTER 14

Few Ouray, Colorado, residents were awake when Aurelia and Elijah went to sleep that night. One of the few was Mick Ferlong, still wide-awake. Mick managed the local newspaper, The Ouray Tribune, and was in charge of printing the following day's edition. He cringed looking down at the front page coming through the press. The article's headline read, "Kansas Girl Found Dead," and had a picture of a smiling girl beside it.

March 18, 1997.

A grizzly murder has plagued our beautiful town. Serena Miller, a young woman from Kansas, was found dead, west of Crystal Lake at the bottom of a waterfall. Local rangers discovered her body as the ice started to thaw for spring, apparently having been left there last fall. Little has been released, but according to local authorities, the girl sustained head wounds and bruising before being left. A chilling poem was found carved into the stone behind the body.

There may be details missing, but what we already know is enough to generate concern. It's rumored that detectives from New York have been flown in to investigate, but no official word yet. However you look at it, this Poetic Murderer has struck fear in our hearts and town. Please everyone. Be safe out there.

t was September 15, 1996. The weather was beginning to cool. Beauty was upon the Great Smoky Mountains with arcane winds. A man *not yet* declared the "Poetic Murderer" drove a Mustang from Asheville, North Carolina, to a small town called Townsend, in Tennessee; the man wearing black was enjoying himself; he loved the montage of just-blooming colors that littered the rolling of the hills. The drive was to take just over two hours, though since his driving imitated his walking, it'd take three.

No hurry.

No hurry.

The car rocked forward, the nose tipping down after a steady climb to the crest of a rounded mountain peak. The Smokies weren't as grand as the Rockies, but the man wearing black felt differences, not comparisons, were paramount. The tumbling hills of the Southeast brought him a sense of lolling calm, like a hammock or a swift ocean breeze off the coast of Rio. The tumbling of the rivers and the caves made him feel dangerous, exotic, like the National Geographic stories he read as a child, the tales of adventure and discovery in parts of the world he felt he'd never see. He drove and noticed and re-noticed each bird that fluttered wings beside the car, each splinter in the street and the changing of the clouds in the sky. He noticed the people walking on the sidewalks and each one's gate, their posture and stance. Ironically, it was darkness that taught him to examine the world so closely.

The man wearing black arrived in Townsend at 10am and drove through town to a small cabin to the south. The cabin was located on the border of The Great Smoky Mountains National Park. Sitting atop a high peak, it overlooked steadily fading horizon lines, distant mountains rolling like the sea, layers of blue fog settling into and flowing through them, quintessential in the park's name.

After parking the Mustang in the gravel driveway, the man wearing black stood and gazed out over the landscape. He took it in, allowing the smells to fill him, the sights to soak him. He stood and basked in that moment and found himself still there a few minutes later, ruminating on the entity of time.

He opened the door to the cabin, walked through, and closed it behind him. The man didn't move, but scanned the cabin with a hawk's precision. He noticed the (askew) entryway rug, whose color he found repugnant, exactly where he'd left it. He noticed the blinds, a few degrees downturned and an oblique seven inches from the windowsill. Just as they should be.

The cabin was six hundred square feet with plain furnishings and run-of-the-mill wall hangings, wooden spoons and forks in the kitchen with a rooster above the sink, a countryside landscape in the living space, a wrought iron rack for knick-knacks by the front door.

This is where the man wearing black still stood. He turned and gazed upon the view outside once more before closing himself in.

It'd been twenty-one minutes since he'd parked the car.

He made his way through to the kitchen.

He scanned.

He made his way up the stairs to a bedroom and laundry nook.

He scanned.

When he'd adequately scrutinized the house's existence, he walked to the stairs that lead to the basement. He descended the thirteen steps, a number he (of course) remembered from his last visit. His heart was a slow bass drum of anticipation.

At the bottom lay a man named Tyler Bromville, motionless, equidistant between four walls. A dark void filled the room around Tyler, and though he couldn't notice, two exits existed down there. An IV was plunged into his left arm, and he lay still, thinning incipiently, dark rings under closed eyes and an erratic, full-body tremor that occurred every few minutes. He was very alone in that swallowing dark. Rough cables bound his arms by his sides to a standard hospital bed, his ankles the same, and the cable had made red-razor tears in halos around all four. Blood ran and painted the stale bed in droplets of agony.

The dark clothed man switched a switch, and light filled the room. Tyler pulled his eyelids back and looked toward the stairs. He screamed and wretched and echoes bounced maddeningly in his head. He pleaded and cursed and squirmed in his restraints. To the outside world, Tyler's panic was a thin murmur of discontent, a passive groaning that showed not his inner rage. He looked almost calm, placid, a gently rippled lake at dawn with tumultuous waters beneath.

The man wearing black walked over to him and looked down. He spoke after a minute of staring. "Your body is deteriorating. It's shutting down. Your mind will cease to produce conscious thought, and being in this basement, in total darkness, is a perfect metaphor for your final days. Your subconscious will take over, and in this room, you will only dream. If you become self-aware, only blackness will be there, and there you will stay, tumbling in a world of acrid dreams and unseen reality."

The man wearing black was still standing above Tyler, a dark-shadowed arch silhouetted on the wall. He continued his slow and steady rant.

"Unless I turn on that light, you'll see nothing, and your brain will fill that void." He leaned in closer, and spoke quieter. "You'll feel my breath before you'll know I'm here, and you'll spend your remaining days stuck in a maze of your past nightmares." The man wearing black stood with an unforgettable force of presence.

The man then walked past Tyler and to a void doorway that led to another room. Tyler kept his eyes fixed on that space, but saw naught, and fell back into darkness before the light was extinguished. The man left a short while later after connecting and running some wires, setting apart some metal teeth, and hoping the upcoming winter would be heavy. He *had* picked a house with its back facing north. He drove away thinking about Tyler.

The IV would keep Tyler tenuously alive, but it also contained a mystery blend of ingredients to help form his morose dream world. His unfocused mind would be surely racing already, confused, his stomach hurting, like it was all being twisted in a barbwire blender of what made him human. Tyler couldn't understand it, but could feel each sensation, mind and body.

The man wearing black had taken everything from him, and would systematically continue to do so.

CHAPTER 16

March. 1997. Present day.

"And now he leaves us a fucking address?" Aurelia said, loudly.

After returning back from the waterfall, the front desk manager at the Ouray Motel gave the detectives a fax that had shown up earlier in the day, addressed to them. Earl looked uncomfortable and told them that he didn't even look at it. They walked away from the counter and entered Elijah's room to read it together. It was written in immaculate cursive, the same as the poem on the chair in Nashville. With the address was one ambiguous line of text.

14 Peak Ln.

Townsend, Tennessee, 37882

When is man capable of being in uncertainties, mysteries, or doubts, without any irritable reaching for fact & reason?

Clint Adams was on the phone moments later.

"For the love of hell, can you two not find something that he hasn't *left* for you to find? I mean, you've basically done nothing! Any asshole can call and read me a fax."

The partners sat on the bed and stared at the note, the Director on speaker, filling the room with his cigar rasped voice. They didn't say much else, but by the time the conversation ended it was clear that Clint Adams was concerned for his two detectives.

After they said goodbye Captain Riff was pulling on his clothes, taking one last look at the flight attendant by his side, easing out of his crash pad in New York and fueling up the plane. He was on his way within fifteen minutes of getting the call.

It was three times that long before Aurelia struck an idea. "I think this is John Keats."

"John Keats?" Elijah said.

Aurelia had learned about him during college, and she explained her thoughts to Elijah as patiently as she could.

"John Keats was a British poet who only lived to be twenty-five. He was a romantic and thought beauty was intimately individual, and that finding that for yourself was critical. He died in 1821 after only having his work published for four years."

Elijah nodded.

"And now he's more studied than almost any other English Poet!"

She was getting excited, her voice speeding up a bit and her chest puffing out, her big, doe eyes moving quicker. Elijah liked it.

"So why would our killer be quoting a romantic who sought beauty?" Elijah said.

"Maybe he thinks this is beautiful."

"Maybe so," he said. "I feel like *there's gotta* be some purpose for it all."

"Let's see if we can find it. Ouray must have a library."

Cheryl, the local chief, opened the door for them a short time later.

The library was small, but beautiful. It belonged in the mountains. It was a log cabin, and snow piled up on its sides and roof. Large windows let moonlight shine through.

Inside, a large, rustic desk met them. A few tables sat beyond in a cozy space; many rows of shelves surrounded them on the walls. The library had ceilings that rose fifteen feet and stood supported by large, wooden beams, meeting in the middle of the room. A mural was painted on one wall, the majestic San Miguel Mountain Range. A computer sat on the desk and shined a bit too bright to be old. They logged in and found Keats' work.

Elijah whistled as they walked the aisles, picking up different books and spiraled bundles of text. Aurelia passed him once and Elijah followed her around the corner with his eyes. They met back in the middle of the room with a modest stack to search through. It wasn't as much as Aurelia had hoped for, but it would at least occupy them until Captain Riff landed.

Shadows sat higher on the wall when Aurelia spotted what she was looking for. It was the quote from the note, and she found it in a letter Keats wrote to his brothers George and Tom in December of 1818. The letter explained Keats's theory of "negative capability." She spent quiet moments thinking and rethinking the esoteric content before explaining her ideas to Elijah.

"If I look over and you're spacing out again, I get to smack you," she said, a minute or two later.

"Agreed," he replied.

She began again.

"Negative capability is a way of thinking focused on unobstructed openness to ideas. It's connected with his idea that the search for what is beautiful is superior to the search for what is true. His idea was that experiencing beauty could be completely objective, personally, whereas even fact can have deceit at its core." They sat across from one another, the books stacked between them. Light softly lit Aurelia's face as she talked to him.

"It's basically emphasizing subjective openness?" Elijah said.

"Pretty much! It's about not referencing your past experiences when experiencing new ones, because each time you do, you limit your ability to encounter the new one with true openness. Look at this." Aurelia picked up a text outlining Keats' antithesis to help prove the point, and paraphrased it. "Keats' way of thinking was in response to a man named Samuel Coleridge. Coleridge was a philosopher who believed that thought and reason could always explain what is true more than something beautiful. Beauty was surface level to Coleridge, and he spent his life searching for absolute fact.

"Coleridge was as much a scientist as he was a philosopher. Keats on the other hand saw no value in explaining or categorizing. He thought unobstructed experience was the only thing that really mattered. Experiencing what someone truly finds beautiful, he felt, could teach more about the world than the ways human society has decided to classify things. Their philosophical ideologies are in complete opposition of one another."

"Then is the Poetic Murderer supporting Keats' work, or chastising it?" Elijah asked.

"I don't really know. I guess I could argue that maybe he's trying to explain, or teach some kind of truth. I can also rationalize that he's doing something 'beautiful.'"

"I wouldn't let him decorate *my* house."

"Although, I feel like you might need it," Aurelia said.

Elijah ignored her and continued. "I think you're right though. It could be either one."

"What do you think we'll find in Tenne—"

She was interrupted by her mobile phone. It still amazed her that she could have a phone as small as her cordless with her anywhere. "Detective Blanc," she answered. "Yes sir. We'll be right there." They copied the pages they thought would prove relevant and replaced the books they'd removed from the shelves. A short drive later, they arrived back at the Telluride airport.

CHAPTER 17

At 4am there isn't much option when it comes to air travel. Elijah and Aurelia were thankful for this as they were swallowed up by the plush chairs, the fridge minibar and the entity of sleep. Captain Riff flew toward Tennessee.

Elijah walked down the street he once lived on. His house was just ahead on the right, or so he initially thought. After his first look around, he noticed though all familiar, nothing was recognizable. Had the structures changed? Had he? The obscure sensation that maybe it was *he* that was changing, wouldn't fade too far from his conscious horizon.

The gnarled street brought him to a small strip of shops, a grocery first. It looked akin to something distant inside him, but the walls were alive; they were crawling, and although he still couldn't see exactly, that organic mess made his skin crawl.

Nameless storefronts continued down the street, and Elijah turned to look at the houses behind him. They had disappeared. Replacing them was fifteen feet of earth that ended in open sky. He was walking atop a massive plateau; tall rock walls supported it in the sky.

He stood still, torn between options, investigate the walls breathing life, or find out what existed beyond the cliff boundary? He moved to his right, toward the cliff. He could see water below; a vast expanse of ocean and skies lingered directly before Elijah. With passing seconds the blue in the sky was diluting with the grey of cloud cover, its shadow a morose veil upon the water. Then the clouds sped up, hurried bursts across the blue, hazing sky. Staring off into the vastness, he felt angry, like the fleeting time was a death sentence, a thinning void of hope that if he lost sight of, just for a second, would kill him. He turned back to investigate the storefronts but stopped stark still. He was startled by the intense sensation that someone was in front of him, and suddenly he knew it wasn't himself he was scared for.

A searing pain then filled his chest, and when he looked down, he saw razor lacerations begin across him in immaculate cursive. He wanted to fight the invisible blade, but his hands were frozen, lifeless and helpless. The first letter was finished,

S

and rails of blood fell with gravity down his stomach. He turned back toward the ocean cliffs, as if retreating was an option. No way he'd jump. The second letter was done,

H

and he writhed in a sick distress, but couldn't move.

E

After the third letter, Elijah lost consciousness. He fell to his knees before his phantom attacker. The ground was cold, and his knees hurt when they crashed into it. He toppled to the side, then onto his back. His eyes were closed tight so he could only feel the final letters etched into him, but he knew what they said.

SHE

WILL

DIE

Elijah's perspective fled to the sky, a bird's eye view revealing all around him.

His mind lingered in that dreadful moment, looking down on himself with the lines of red horror on his chest.

"Wake up! What in the hell is wrong with you?" Aurelia said.

Aurelia had spent a minute or two trying to rouse him. He'd been twisting and turning in his seat, his face scrunching and his arms and legs grappling with one another.

"Are you OK?" she said.

"I'm good. Yea. Sorry. Guess it was a crazy dream. I assume we're in Tennessee?" He had lied to her, and the dream had planted the seed of an idea that he couldn't come to terms with. The only "she" in his life was Aurelia, and though he knew it was a dream, the thought of losing her made him squirm.

The captain stepped into the cockpit door to bid them farewell in typical fashion. "Elijah, always a pleasure. And when did Clint assign you such a hot partner?"

Aurelia gave the captain a narrow gaze as they exited, and he returned it with a smile that you couldn't be angry with. She laughed, and so did Elijah.

Just after sunrise, the partners stepped off the small airplane. They found themselves in Knoxville, Tennessee, sixteen miles from Townsend, their final destination. Aurelia was mumbling about another rented Ford Explorer.

"What were you expecting? A Ferrari?" Elijah joked, trying to shake off his nightmare.

Aurelia slowly cocked her head toward him and smiled sweetly. "I like you," she said, and got into the car.

"I like you too," he thought to himself. His thought was accompanied by the harsh understanding that he'd never really *liked* anyone.

The two of them drove toward 14 Peak Lane.

CHAPTER 18

They found a quaint cabin atop 14 Peak Lane, owned by an elderly couple with the last name of Generro, who visited rarely, according to full-time residents of Townsend. The FBI had found it difficult to track down someone who knew the Mr. and Mrs. Generro, let alone someone who'd *seen* them lately. The most recent reports were of their car, a Ford Mustang, passing through town on (what looked like) its way to the cabin. The report was from the prior year, September of '96. They'd not been back for supplies, and there wasn't another sighting of the vehicle.

The Poetic Murderer had gained access to the Generro's car, their vacation home. He'd taken control of the Cullen's house in Indiana. He seemed to be targeting property owners with a non-existent list of relatives, but killing individuals that would be immediately noticed. His victims had had families, immediate relatives to report them missing. The property owners hadn't. Were *they* dead as well? Were they yet to be found? Were they somehow involved? Nothing added up and it seemed overcomplicated.

As the tires eased higher in elevation, the detectives considered the familiarity of the cases, and the conflictions in their conception.

Tall trees surrounded the car as it climbed a macabre climb. Snow was falling and bare branches wrapped the vehicle like a skeleton's bony fingers. Winter wouldn't quite let go, but further into spring, the natural tunnel would have been beautiful.

On both sides of the Explorer, a steep drop existed, ending in more barren trees, naked from the winter's months. The rolling Smoky Mountains extended as far as their eyes could see, and white covered them gently. The morning light was vivid, though the clouds were thick, and it lit up the hills and falling snow in magnificent beams through the dark.

Arrival at the cabin showed them no signs of life. There wasn't a car in the driveway (which they'd have assumed), and shades covered most of each window. The house was small, and it sat at the end of a hilltop peninsula. All around the cabin were the sprawling Smokies. Just as in Colorado, Elijah wished they were there under different circumstances.

He stepped out of the car. His feet crunched as they met snow-covered earth. Hot breath poured from his mouth. Aurelia stepped out with her eyes fixed on the door. Her usual confidence and focus glowed on her. *Damn,* Elijah thought, but shook away upon its incipience. It wasn't the time to be thinking about her *that* way.

Each pulled out a pistol and moved toward the door. In Elijah's right hand sat a .40 caliber Glock 23. The FBI had created the .40-cal. bullet just a few years earlier, and he began carrying it because of its near-non-existent recoil. It was deadly accurate. The new bullets also induced hydrostatic shock, which not only affected the point of entry, but neural processing as well. Brain hemorrhaging can begin not long after it breaks the skin.

Aurelia held a Smith and Wesson 1911, which shot massive .45 ACP rounds. It was first created in 1911, and had proven reliable since. It had been used in both World Wars and would probably make an appearance in the next. Aurelia understood exactly what it was meant for, and she had it fixed on the door.

The two detectives approached the cabin with safeties off. They moved past oversized flowerbeds that framed the walkway to the door. The beds were newly dug but lay barren and hardened from the winter. Elijah slid to the left of the door and placed his back against the wall. He looked back at Aurelia, who stood facing him. With the wave of a hand, she signaled Elijah to search and surround clockwise; they would close a collective loop at the rear of the cabin.

Their dance had begun again, and the stakes were higher than when they'd searched the dead politician's house. They moved as one.

They each turned opposing corners, moving toward the back of the cabin. They scanned the slim void at the bottom of each window on the way by it. Their eyes met as they arrived at back corners of the house. They saw together the door heading into the basement. The mountain earth fell away from the house and allowed for the basement entrance to exist. A thick layer of snow still covered the ground, the house's north-facing angle preventing the sun's touch. Aurelia began toward the basement door as Elijah looked back to the front of the cabin. His eyes made it back to her and his adrenaline began to surge in a feverish burst. In that split second he recognized what was happening, and the world seemed to go into a slow crawl. A small ring of metal points stuck out of the snow directly under Aurelia's foot.

She stepped into fresh snow and heard a snap; she knew she was in trouble. Jagged teeth sprang closed tearing bloody gashes in the bottom of her leg, crushing her tibia and fibula. Her gun fell into the snow and she buckled earthward toward a now-maimed ankle. She could feel teeth scraping flesh, pinching the fractured bones.

Elijah's eyes moved over his side of the yard, scanning for more waiting traps. His feet then closed the distance between them.

"Fuck. Elijah, I'm sorry. I didn't see it," she gasped. Her eyes squinted in agony.

"You're gonna be OK, Aurelia. This'll hurt but I've gotta get this thing off of you." He pulled out his phone just long enough to send a message to Clint, then turned back toward Aurelia. Blood was arcing in little pulsing spasms and dyeing the snow.

Back in New York City, Director Adams paced around his smoke-filled office and looked out the window toward the Brooklyn skyline. He was working on his second cup of coffee and had already pondered what challenges, or opportunities, as he always put it, the day would bring. His pager began to vibrate just after 8am. He looked down and saw Elijah's message, picked up his phone and made the order for a rescue helicopter for 14 Peak Lane. His heart began to rend, and he lit another cigar.

A local law enforcement task force assembled in Nashville, Tennessee, two hundred miles west of the remote cabin, and in forty-five minutes, they'd arrive. The S.W.A.T. and medical personnel would spend the first part of the trip on a plane, the second on a helicopter to land near the cabin.

Elijah threw his phone down and focused his attention back on Aurelia. Her face was a portrait of pain. Her eyes squeezed shut and her breathing was heavy. She knew she needed to control herself, but the rusting teeth sent shockwaves of pain up her leg.

"Aurelia, look at me. I'm gonna pull it open. When I do, ease your leg out. I may only be able to loosen it a little." He knew he was asking a lot; bear traps weren't made to be released easily.

"OK. I'm ready." At first her voice shook, but it strengthened just after. Her eyes were focused once again. Elijah knew she was ready. They looked at each other for a long second before he began, his vibrant blue eyes glimmering in the sparse sunbeams. She stared at the rusted trap when she saw him start.

Elijah pulled at the teeth of the trap and the corners of his fingers tore. Little daggers of pain cut and bled. The trap began to move, insignificantly at first, then slightly more. "Now!" he shouted to Aurelia. The teeth opened just enough for her leg to ease from the trap. It snapped shut and he felt a harsh slice on his left hand. He heard ticking begin at the inside of the back door, just a few feet from where the trap had been set, and he forgot his hand. Flames began to devour the door's edges, and a blast blew the door into a thousand splintering shards. Wooden daggers rocketed across the yard and the detectives' bodies tumbled down the mountain.

CHAPTER 19

B efore the door shattered to pieces, light broke the threshold of the frame and Elijah dove toward Aurelia. They cleared the blast and rolled in tumbling bounces to a stop. Still flaming splinters were lodged into trees surrounding them. Smoldering pieces of door stuck up from the snow like flaming icebergs. Aurelia now laid still, Elijah next to her. Her eyes were calmly opened, refusing to retreat from reality. Blood pumped through her veins and her heart pounded in her chest. Burgundy paint splatter created a myriad of patterns on the snow from the different holes in her mangled leg.

Elijah looked over at her with relief after finding her conscious. "Aurelia, are you OK!?"

"I fucking loathe this guy."

Elijah laughed. How could she make him laugh at a time like this?

"Me too. Don't worry. We're killing him."

He stood and said that he'd be back, and she knew where he needed to go. The house was a complete question mark. Once again he was readied with his Glock. He moved toward the door, blood spots appearing in the snow from his hands, and prepared himself to breach the basement. He gave himself only a moment to notice that a small chunk was missing from his left ring finger.

The entryway where the bomb sat appeared to be a mudroom. Inside sat the remnants of the explosive set to kill them. Small wires led in two directions from the bottom of the explosive's casing, one further into the basement, disappearing into the next room, the other toward the outside wall and underneath. Elijah assumed it led to the bear trap. The bomb must have been triggered when he released it from Aurelia's leg. He moved inside without a sound. He then looked further into the basement. It was empty, except for a hospital bed in the middle; a man made of bones stretched the length of it. At first Elijah couldn't see if he was dead, but his chest was rising and falling in tiny heaves.

He looked like calculated starvation. His arms and legs were strapped to the hospital bed, and an IV was attached to his arm. He *had* to have been there for months. He looked toward some stairs before moving to the bed. The man couldn't speak and didn't register Elijah's presence. His heart was barely beating, at only thirty beats per minute. Elijah moved toward the stairs.

"Two minutes, boys." Ian Powell was the team leader for the S.W.A.T. unit. Their job was simple: kill any hostiles in the cabin atop 14 Peak Lane. EMS would be right behind them. Director Adams had called Ian just forty minutes earlier. Now, he and his team were assembled, armed, and ready to kill anything needing to be killed. They'd arrive three minutes earlier than expected.

Elijah reached the top of the stairs. The first floor was simple and unsuspecting. A few pieces of old furniture were set around the living room. It definitely belonged to an older couple. He moved cautiously to the kitchen, checking each corner. He finally moved up the last flight of stairs to a bedroom and laundry space.

The house was vacant, except for the man in the basement.

When he deemed the house safe, Elijah brought Aurelia inside to be more comfortable. She sat with her leg propped up on a ground floor couch, and Elijah wrapped her leg the best he could. She could see two choppers come into view off in the distance over his shoulder.

Two helicopters touched down and S.W.A.T. moved toward the front door in a tight unit as the medical team awaited word on Aurelia's location. Ian had time to kick in the front door and found Elijah inside with his hands up.

"FBI! I called Clint Adams." Without a word, Ian approached, his gun fixed on Elijah's head. He checked his credentials then instructed his team to stand down. Elijah said what he knew and medics hurried in. Some set Aurelia in a litter for transport to the chopper, and several headed to the basement to examine the man in the bed.

Once inside the helicopter, Aurelia's pant leg was pulled up and cut. They began work on the crimson gashes, and pain echoed in her temples. Apparently there was no time for painkillers. The helicopter began to rise.

Aurelia lay with her eyes closed. She daydreamed about a life with Elijah. The minor details were missing, but those didn't matter. She just wanted him.

Elijah moved back down to the basement after seeing Aurelia off. Ian followed after radioing for a crime scene unit and medical examiner. The sight at the bottom of the stairs sank into Elijah for the second time in a few minutes. He walked over to the bed feeling a sick sense of hate in his veins. Whoever the kid was, he'd suffered.

To Elijah's surprise, his heartbeat had expired since first passing through the basement. He laid the same as before, but his chest was still. Elijah noticed that the IV bag had stopped dripping, and that the wire from the explosive casing led to the bedside IV. *Possibly a shut off switch*, he thought to himself. Ian was standing near the stairway; his team had retreated back outside.

Elijah then turned his attention to the room around him. He went into investigative mode. He went through a half-complete dance. Mentally, he found it more challenging than usual. He wanted to know exactly how Aurelia was. He wanted to be with her. He paced the desolate space. Per usual, there was little to find, but in one corner, near the stairs, he spotted a single hair. It was jet black and a few inches long. He dared not touch it, but grabbed a glass from upstairs to place overtop for CSI to find. This was an opportunity that could not be missed. From the bottom of the stairs, he turned and took one long look at the room. His eyes squeezed half shut; the hair could be a start, but he wanted more. What was he *supposed* to find?

Fuck it. At least they'd found something. After another moment, he left.

Once outside Elijah rhetorically asked if he could borrow the S.W.A.T. helicopter and its pilot. He needed to get back to Aurelia. Besides, S.W.A.T. could stay and keep the house secure. They could hitch a ride back.

CHAPTER 20

Priscilla was a waitress at a small cafe overlooking the Willamette River, which traversed the east of Portland. She leaned on her elbows with her chin in her hands, staring at a man seated at one of her tables. Heads bobbed between them and she mused what he might do to her. He seemed unique, and *damn* he was handsome, though he *dressed* like a fucking murderer. There was something that couldn't stop her thinking about the man dressed in all black. She figured he had a huge cock, knew how to use it, unlike those twinks back in Wyoming. She'd heard him ask for a table and his voice eased like a phantom to pull her to him. He spoke like he'd never been in a hurry. Whatever it was, it was intriguing.

The man wearing black ordered his morning coffee, black also. He'd been taken aback by the waitress, her beauty, the raw sexuality that seemed to radiate from her. He forgot all about how it'd taken her too long to show up at the table. Two minutes or less for table service. He'd read all about it.

He watched her all the way back to the wait station after she accepted his coffee order. The girl stood average height with curvaceous features and dark hair. She looked all Italian. She walked freely, swinging her arms in seductive tosses. Her hair fell several inches past her shoulders.

Spontaneity was paramount in his big picture, but this fixation was strong and sweet and stirred a dangerous lust within him.

She brought back his coffee and took his order of toast and jelly.

The Poetic Murderer smiled wide but with no teeth and spoke her name, which he'd read on her nametag.

"Priscilla. That, is a captivating name. Did you know that its origins are Latin?"

Priscilla shook her head.

"It means ancient and admired."

She smiled, barely. "It's just what my parents called me."

"You aren't from here, Priscilla."

How did he know? "I just moved from Wyoming."

"Getting away from something?"

"Everything," she responded, with a little hint of surprise in herself. Why did she actually answer him? "Excuse me," she said, and walked back to the kitchen.

This was a problem. His process needed to stay serendipitous to be true to his purpose, but one deliberate act of reason couldn't throw it all off. Could it? He rationalized with himself for a few moments and looked out the window toward Mt. Hood. Their meeting *was* coincidence. Walking into the café *had* been random.

It seemed to follow his rules, even if he was choosing her selfishly. His jaw tightened and he looked back to Priscilla, across the room now and leaning across a table to set down orders. He took a long, slow gulp and allowed the warm liquid to slide down his throat. His hand inched back to the table and set the mug down.

He looked again at Mt. Hood through the window and allowed himself a full smile. It seemed Portland would be even more enjoyable than he expected. He reflected back on the old squares from the train and thought to himself how beautiful their deaths had been. It was a shame that they wouldn't be connected to his masterpiece.

CHAPTER 21

Elijah knew that the University of Tennessee's hospital was the nearest one with a level-one trauma center. It'd be necessary for Aurelia's wounds. The memorandum of understanding gave the FBI access to local resources, but this instance of its use may not have qualified. Elijah ordered the pilot to take him there and disregard prior orders, and they lifted away from 14 Peak Lane. The pilot had seen panic in Elijah Warren's eyes and granted his request.

The hospital was twenty miles north of the cabin in Townsend. Aurelia was rushed to the emergency room after landing atop it.

"Hurry!" said the doc, as a long needle entered the fleshy soft tissue beneath one of the wounds. She cringed, but looked straight at it. She thrashed in little jerks. What followed wasn't better, and it wasn't uncommon for bear trap victims to lose the affected limb. Two doctors worked simultaneously. One doctor stitched up her wounds. One put her leg in a traction splint. The traction fastened the bones and slowly pulled to help realign them. When they were done, more than a hundred stitches crisscrossed her ankle like a trashy tattoo.

Elijah jumped from the helicopter before it touched down on the UT hospital in Knoxville. He took the stairs two at a time. He was a bit brash at the desk, flashing his badge and babbling Aurelia Blanc's name. Soon after, he stood at the glass of the operating room, a stare making its way through, blood easing down in streaks from his gnarled finger. It'd need to be repaired, but not now. He kept his eyes fixed on the heart rate monitor.

The Poetic Murderer had made his game personal.

CHAPTER 22

At the county coroner's office a man named Gerard began his inspection of the body found on Peak Lane. The body was transported from the house after being officially declared dead by the medical examiner. The still nameless young man lay ice-cold on butcher paper in front of Gerard.

Gerard's job was to determine a cause of death and gather details to help with the case. The start of the autopsy was typical, recording height, weight, scars, birthmarks and tattoos. After an hour, the report was finished, but it didn't take long for Gerard to find something worth passing on. He phoned Adams in New York, as he'd been brashly instructed to do.

When Gerard had flipped the dead man to inspect his back, he pulled down his own eyelids and jerked his head off at an angle. He needed a moment. Markings had been carved...deep, at least a half-inch into the skin's surface. The name *Mario Arnold* began at the top of the spine and ended in the crease of the lower back, a vertical column of gore-lettered flesh. The markings were done with precision; someone had taken their time, but the skin along the top layer was withering and wilting, fading away like rotting gums from teeth. Even still, each letter had been clearly written, perfectly rounded curves, like a child's template for cursive.

Gerard also discovered that the man had been drugged over the past half year, kept alive with a cocktail of basic nutrients and twisted with some aggressive illegals. Through the IV in his arm, he'd been allowed to exist in a dark and futile nightmare, a horrific existence that made Gerard shutter at its thought. To keep someone this way was *beyond* sick; it was maniacal.

Meanwhile, the crime scene investigation unit was examining the basement's particulars. They were focusing on the explosive rig, which wholly consisted of the bear trap, the explosive device and the IV system. As Elijah had recognized, small wires connected the three components. With CSI's hands on it, they could document that the bear trap being released from Aurelia's leg had set off the bomb. The bomb had shut down the IV, and the man's heart finally got to expire just after.

After Gerard called Clint, the name Mario Arnold was being run through local police databases. It was being run through national and international databases. The local police records came back with two hands empty, and after a few hours of waiting, Director Adams had found nothing in the vast chronicles of the FBI. It didn't mean it was hopeless, but Adams cursed and buried his head in his hands. He lit another cigar and kicked his feet up on his desk, a darkening city beyond the vast window behind him.

Back at the crime scene, the single hair had been collected for evidence and sent back to the lab in Nashville, Tennessee. Would it belong to the killer? The dead man with the sanguine letters in his back? The analyst began a search for usable strands of DNA. As a bit of good luck, he was able to extract nuclear DNA, which could potentially lead to more conclusive results than basic strands of DNA. The difference is in the quality of the hair sample, and this one's root had still been attached.

It wasn't long after that Clint found Mario Arnold in an unsuspecting file from when the man was sixteen. Mario had been tried and convicted for vehicular homicide but given a soft punishment due to surrounding circumstances and his young age. A man had walked—illegally and with a blood alcohol level of .18—across a main road in Mario's hometown of Nahant. Mario's sweet-sixteen car was totaled and the man came through the windshield, curled up on Mario and trapped him under his seatbelt.

The jury fought and argued, came back for days and slept little in between, but finally decided Mario couldn't be given the full sentence. Blame was shared with an adult that should have known better than to walk blindly across the busiest street in town. Since then, Mario's record was vanilla. Not even a parking ticket.

Clint thought it was as substantial as a fart in a hurricane's winds, but Mario's last known address was labeled Boston. He moved quickly putting people to work, a hunt for all that could be found about Mario Arnold. It seemed unlikely that the dead man had been labeled for them, but who the fuck cared? It was the best news Clint had heard in quite some time, and he was sick with rage and fear that Aurelia and Elijah might not make it through the case of the Poetic Murderer.

CHAPTER 23

A urelia was a still frame in the hospital bed. A close eye showed her chest rising and falling, but she looked a corpse, her eyes closed and her arms beside her. She'd been out of the operating room for a few hours and spent that time chasing after her consciousness. For no particular reason, she ripped her eyelids back and found Elijah sipping coffee in the chair next to her bed.

"Do you know," he said, "that you look at me angrily even when you're sleeping?" He had that stupid, handsome smirk on his face.

She fought to smile, but did.

"You are *quite* aggravating, Elijah Warren. It's a damn good thing you're so attractive." She stretched aching limbs and felt as though some large vehicle had plowed her at full speed. Everything hurt, even though her injuries were specific to her leg. She tugged the cup of coffee from Elijah when she saw his hands start to bloom into conversation. He *always* talked with his hands.

"Hey! Eh. Fine." He knew the coffee was damaged goods. "Doctor says you're gonna be fine. As a bit of positivity, the bottom of your leg isn't void space, and I was told you'd make a full recovery. The traction splint will stay on for at least a week, and you'll have to stay 'til then. You've got a hundred stitches in your leg, some in, some out. They also said you were pigheaded and a lot irritating, but they couldn't do anything about those things. They *also* mentioned that you were wrong about Kurt Cobain." She glared at him. "I stood up for you!" he said with a raised expression and of course, raised hands to match.

"I'm *quite* sure you did, Detective Warren. Maybe someday you'll be laying in one of these beds and I can take jabs at you. You must feel awfully safe right now." She looked angry, but something in her eyes gave her away.

Elijah could tell. He'd seen it, but not mentioned it. When she tried to look upset, her eyes would scrunch together too much, and her mouth would terse up unnaturally. When she was *actually* angry, you knew.

"No ma'am. I would never underestimate you. I wouldn't be surprised if you were still packin' heat underneath that lovely, backless hospital dress."

"I just might be. Speaking of which, you better not have snuck a peak down my backless 'dress' as I was being carted around this damn place. If so, have reason to be concerned. I'll check the security tapes," she said, nodding up to the corners of the room.

He laughed. It was strange, but he wholly cared for her. He'd never felt this way about someone and was just beginning to know her. Earlier in the evening, he'd been hysterical on the way to the hospital. He had *needed* to know how she was and could focus on nothing else. He thought back and remembered how he'd just taken the S.W.A.T. chopper. It'd be interesting explaining *that* to Clint.

"I didn't peek. I promise. But if I'm lying, you'll never know," he said with a wink.

He always had such a mischievous look on his face, but she didn't care; she knew he was a good person, somehow. She couldn't describe why she trusted him, but she knew that she did. It had been a long time since she trusted anyone, let alone a man, and looking into the oceans in his eyes, she smiled a bit. "I like you, Elijah Warren. Thanks for not letting me die today. And keep your eyes away from my ass, unless I'm awake to know about it." With that said, she fell back asleep.

It was midnight and Elijah stayed awake with (of course) a coffee, and (of course) a mind that couldn't stop racing. It had been an unprecedented few days.

CHAPTER 24

I n general, Clint Adams didn't travel. He missed his Mom's 60th birthday party because of a late taxi. He missed his nephew's graduation because of a stubbed toe. His late wife had wanted him to go to Argentina. He was still a virgin of that country.

Director Adams walked briskly through the University of Tennessee's hospital. His red-eye flight had put him in just after seven in the morning. His breath was short and his pace fast as he burst into Aurelia's room to find her sleeping in the assigned bed, Elijah perched tediously in a small chair next to it, appendages sprawling the sides like a Great Dane on a Chihuahua's bed.

"Wake up!"

How was Clint's voice always so abrasive?

"You guys look like hell," Adams said, strolling in and over to the foot of the bed.

Elijah opened one eye, noticing the crick in his back and neck, then the other. He closed them again and stretched and nearly squeezed off the chair and onto the floor before replying to the Director. "Holy shit! G-Morning, boss! I didn't think you'd *ever* leave New York!"

Aurelia woke with a suppressed laugh and eyes closed tight, happy that that idiotic and clearly meant to annoy, "G-morning," was *not* just reserved for her. She pretended to stay asleep another moment, then she stretched, yawned, and acted surprised to see Clint, who stood staring down with a terrific annoyance, hands on his hips, lightning bolt vein crashing to the sky from his temples, Elijah continuing, tangled on the chair.

"Boss! You missed your sister's wedding because your suitcase had a rip in it!" Elijah said, now laughing and pulling a sparse, green blanket from the floor, where his shirt, tie, shoes and pants lay.

"Well, yes, idiot. Yes, I did. Now put some damn clothes on. I've found the best lead in this shitstorm thus far, not thanks to the two of you." He paused. "You're welcome," he said evenly, leaning on the foot of the bed. "There was a name carved into our boy at the cabin. We ran it to the Boston PD database, tried and found guilty of vehicular homicide as a kid, pretty messy, but he's been clear since. Current whereabouts, he's been found in Boston's database of missing persons. Disappeared last summertime. Didn't show up to work, and there's no more story."

Elijah and Aurelia listened as he continued, with occasional glances between themselves.

As he spoke, Clint noticed this and couldn't help but think he understood.

Fuck. "The man in the Townsend basement had been there a long while, but not quite *that* long, only six months or so according to the medical examiner. So *he's* still unidentified. We obviously hoped it would be Mario for simplicity's sake, but piss off to simple, goddamn things just never—"

"Got it, Boss," Elijah said, sensing a moment of terse rambling. "So we need to find Mario and still figure out who was in the basement?" Elijah said it through a yawn and stretched his arms and legs from his disarranged position. Light beams from the window lit horizontal stripes on his face, chest, and stomach as he eased back on the chair.

"Mario is our first priority," Clint said. "I've got a plane taking *you* to Boston this afternoon. CSI is still looking into the basement. They know the bear trap set off the bomb, bomb killed the IV. Kid goes kaput."

Ah. The classic Adams charm.

"Odd combination of skills," Aurelia said, "to be rigging explosives and playing nurse for more than six months." She looked up at Clint, but not before noticing Elijah and how little he was wearing. "Adams, I assume *I'll* be staying here since you said 'you' about the flight, and nodded at him?"

"With that said, *I'm* gonna go," Clint said. "Hell hath no wrath. Elijah, Nashville airport at two. Aurelia, keep doin' what you're doin'. You'll be brought a mobile so Elijah can share what he finds and still have your support. I'll be in touch." He paused for a moment and looked back at them. "Yea," he then said. After that, he turned and walked out, already a souring and confused feeling in his stomach.

It took a moment for the door to close, but it was needed. Aurelia broke the brief silence but hadn't quite figured out all she was about to say. Her words spilled; they weren't spoken.

"Who knows what's in Boston, Elijah, or wherever he'll fucking drag you next! I mean look what just happened! How can we even guess what he's doing? This can't happen to—"

She stopped abruptly and no one said anything.

"We'll both be fine, Aurelia. And you know I need your help, so keep your phone on."

"I suppose it *will* be quieter and more civil without you around."

"Yea-yea. I've gotta be at both the coroner's office and the forensics lab before I head north, see if they've found anything else." He pulled on his shirt. "Let me know if you need anything in the meantime." He pulled on his pants. "Hang in there, kid." He tied his shoes and squeezed her hand, pausing for a moment to look at her face. He stayed there as long as he could.

As Elijah walked out of the room, Aurelia had the horrible thought that it may be the last time she would see him. "Be careful, Eli. I really wanna see you when this is done."

He stopped just before the door and turned toward her bed. He walked back, leaned forward and wrapped his fingers behind her neck and up into her hair, and pressed his lips onto hers. It was brief, but she'd never been kissed like that.

It wasn't in her head that they worked together at the Bureau.

Downstairs, a rented Explorer had been left for Elijah at the hospital. Classic Adams.

With two stops for Elijah to make before boarding the plane at two, he sped along the winding roads of the Great Smokies.

CHAPTER 25

Donald Karrow was thirty-two years old, and it was an ordinary day. It was a quarter past seven in the morning, and he sat in a small room surrounded by security monitors. He was security director at the First National Bank Tower. The FNBT was the tallest building in Portland, constructed in 1972. He stared at the monitors and scanned side-to-side, top-to-bottom. He'd been an employee for five years and one of their best since beginning his tenure. He looked from screen-to-screen, searching for what might pose a threat, scanning, scouring for what could be out of place. On this day, that which was out of place was in plain sight.

Slow footsteps entered the bottom floor of the First National Bank Tower.

They walked with purpose, each step moving towards an ugly and inevitable task.

Somebody was going to die.

Donald took a sip of his coffee, then turned to look at the elevators' circuit board. *All green lights.* Exactly what he wanted to see. He turned back to the wall of monitors.

Purposeful monotony kept him grounded in a way.

Elevators were located on one side of the lobby, across from revolving glass doors.

The footsteps moved forward, soon to be going up.

"Didn't need that last beer last night," Donald said out loud. He didn't usually drink on weeknights, but celebrating was necessary. It was his third wedding anniversary. His wife's name was Donna, and she meant everything to him. It took a special kind woman to intently listen to the details of his day, to care. He wasn't exactly a lion tamer, and fun for Donald involved weeding the garden.

Elevator doors opened at the top stop. Feet stepped out and turned toward their final destination. They moved incredulously, easing on with a robotic, sick apprehension. At the end of a thin hallway, a hand reached up and turned a doorknob.

Donald was back to scanning the monitors. He saw, down in the basement, that one of the security lights had gone out in the laundry area. It flickered in senseless strobes.

He'd always a keen eye for the minute. He radioed to the maintenance room and filled out the paperwork for the request. He went back to scanning the monitors, moving progressively up from the bottom. He started at floor one, the first of many horizontal rows, and looked at each camera's view, then moved to the second floor. The FNBT had forty-one floors, standing 546 feet at the top.

The first forty floors passed Donald's inspection (aside from the light), but when he came to the roof, he paused, took a double take and reassessed what he was seeing. A woman wearing a waitress uniform from a nearby café had walked out onto the roof. He picked up his radio and called one of his guards. He watched her on the monitors and waited, wondering exactly what she could be doing.

There was nothing *to* do up there, he thought.

He was sure it was nothing.

He was sure she'd missed the signs, gotten turned around.

He couldn't help but noticing her features, all Italian, it looked, with long dark hair and curves top to bottom.

He looked back at the elevator circuit board and said, "Damn it, red on shaft three." Shaft three was the third of five, and the only elevator that ran to the roof of the building. It had just stopped running. Donald whipped his head back around and watched the young woman walk her last four steps, directly off the roof. All the air in Donald's lungs released with an obscure force. His nonverbal (yet audible) exhalation was followed by an immediate 911 call.

Her body plummeted earthward with murderous intent. Her arms and legs drifted haphazardly around her body, like a strange, aloof marionette. She picked up speed, ripped down by gravity. Her hair blew wildly and she twisted and spun.

"A girl just walked off the roof of First National Bank Tower! Hurry! She would have landed on Fifth Street!" The panic in his voice was an intoxicating symphony, and the 911 operator moved fast to pass on orders.

Priscilla De Luca smashed into the ground after falling forty-one stories to her mortal end. At a height of 546 feet, it took almost six seconds for her to reach terminal velocity, 130 miles per hour. She smashed into the ground a millisecond later. Her head hit and sent a ripple along the cement like a drop of rain in a lake. Her skull shattered into confused bone fragments, ejecting from her skin. Blood and brain met fresh air and oozed from her head and filled in the cracks in the street, eventually spilling onto even ground. Her body remained intact as a scrambled contortionist. It was a tragic day, and to make matters worse, Priscilla's family, back in Wyoming, would find out in a few hours.

It hadn't been long since they'd reported her missing.

CHAPTER 26

E lijah boarded the government issue just after 2:15pm. He was a little late. He'd spent the hitherto hours visiting the coroner's office, as well as the CSI lab analyzing evidence from the cabin. He felt like he was chasing phantoms, a carnival of false flags, left for him to find and be led astray.

As chance would have it, the coroner's office was near the UT hospital where Aurelia was being cared for. It was the first stop. Adams had filled him in on the pertinent details, but he wanted to look for himself. Sometimes he saw things differently. The body was waiting for him on the examination table when he arrived. The dead man bore a shocking resemblance to his "alive" version.

His eyes, which were now closed, had sunk far into his skull. His eye sockets were cavernous circles, his eyes a ghost's gaze when opened. His arms lay at his sides, frail and fading into obscurity. His ribs were blunt rails across his abdomen, and his stomach was a deep depression. His legs were scarcely more than bone. His skin was nearly transparent, due to the absence of light, according to Gerard. His blood-crusted gums were pulled back from his teeth.

"Judging by his molars' wear and tear, the victim was in his late twenties," reported Gerard. "We analyzed the cocktail supplying the IV and the carving in his back. Let me tell you, his back, done with precision. 'Mario Arnold' is carved in like stone." Gerard had been looking down at the name, the letters falling from the back of the unknown man's neck. Then he looked back up at Elijah. "Fucked up how he kept him this way for so long. He was technically alive."

"Could he think?" Elijah said.

"Well not *that* alive. He wasn't healthy enough for full brain activity, but he could dream," the coroner said.

"So he was constantly dreaming? Can't imagine they weren't nightmares," Elijah said, looking down at the fading former man.

"Exactly. This man was literally living in a nightmare. And unfortunately I think he could feel also. Which brings me to my next point. In addition to that constant supply of nutrients, the only substances we found in his system were equal parts methylenedioxy and a severe muscle relaxer."

"Sorry, Doc, I don't know what in the hell methylen...lendixy... whatever...is."

"Ecstasy."

"So he was kept alive on basic nutrients, muscle relaxers, and ecstasy? What's that do to someone?"

"Well, it forces you into your head, and he's made that a pretty terrible place to be. Your mind is racing and your body's senses and nerves are wired. You can feel, but you can't talk, move, or really even rationalize. You exist in a dream that you can't wake from, but you don't feel like you're dreaming. And unfortunately, it's a dream world fueled by X."

"Pretty sure it was a bad dream." Elijah looked at the clear, gelatinous skin of the man from the cabin.

They spoke another few minutes, accomplishing little. After learning all he could and feeling more discouraged than when he arrived, Elijah made his way toward the door.

"Thanks for the rundown. If you come up with anything else, get a hold of me." He left his card on a nearby table and walked away from the Poetic Murderer's latest victory.

It was a three-hour drive to Nashville, from where he was to depart, and also from the forensics lab. The evidence was directed to Nashville due to resources, or lack-there-of. The smaller towns didn't have the people or the technology to be as thorough as needed. He arrived a little after noon and stepped into the elevator of the tall office building. The 13th floor was his exit, the FBI forensics lab; every big city had its own. A doctor named William approached with a large smile upon crossing the threshold of the interior door.

"G-Morning, asshole," Will said with arms held out and a broad smile.

"Ho-ly shit! How do you remember such things? And how did you make it out of St. Louis? Thought you were a lifer."

Elijah didn't have many old friends.

"Too much St. Louie did me in, buddy. Got too old. You seem to be getting there," he said, and tugged on a gray hair behind Elijah's left ear. "Guess I needed something that made more sense. Or at least somethin' I didn't have to try to make sense *of.*"

Elijah was beginning to think he knew *exactly* what Will was talking about. The sense of exhilaration he once felt tracking murderers seemed to be a distant memory.

He shook away the nightmare about Aurelia, and the pervasive feeling of losing the woman he was falling in love with.

"Glad you've found it buddy," Elijah said. "I need to find out how to start slowing down myself. Now, what've you to show me?"

It was a strange coincidence for them both, running into an old friend. William's were mostly dead, and Elijah didn't really have them.

William continued as they walked into the room. "Obviously our best hope was that strand of hair. Good news is, it's a great sample, and if we can ever match it, we'll be in business. Bad news is, we're searching every database and haven't found anything. You know how that goes."

"I'm getting used to that," Elijah said.

"Who knows how long we'll spend trying to find a match? You know the further down the road we get, the more we're fishing for acorns, but we'll keep looking." Elijah nodded his head.

"Now, the rig he built, which was the bear trap, the bomb, and the IV station, was really simple but pretty genius. He was able to keep all of them powered by the heartbeat of the man hooked up to it." William received a look of incredulity so he continued. "Your heartbeat is essentially a small electrical impulse. The killer manufactured it so the IV unit would store those impulses to be used later. It's the same idea as a battery, but a self-sustaining one. So as long as his heart kept beating, the killer's trap remained functional. The impulses were saved over time, and when your partner stepped in that trap, it triggered those saved impulses to act."

"Must be why he stashed him here half a year ago. Bet it's how long it took to store enough power to trigger the bomb." Elijah was thinking out loud.

"Exactly. So when your partner stepped on the trap, it transferred energy between the three components. Trap went off, engaged the charge, which set off the bomb, and the IV turned off."

Elijah didn't respond at first. He simply stood, looking at the ground with wrinkles across his forehead. It happened when he was deep in thought. His old comrade knew it, and William walked across the room to give him a minute to finish the conversation he was having with himself. As expected, Elijah followed behind a bit later.

"How much education would it take to do this, assuming it's just one person?"

"This technology barely exists, let alone in a civilian basement with virtually zero pro-grade materials. Probably requires multiple degrees, plus ingenuity to tweak and connect the different disciplines. Must have been top of the class for them all." William realized this didn't help after he'd said it.

"So what's my saving grace, Will? I assume you're saving it for last?" Elijah hoped he was right. He knew he was wrong.

"I'm afraid I that's all I've got, old friend. No fingerprints. No footprints. The components in his rig were all damn-near impossible to trace."

Elijah's head turned toward the floor. He wondered for a moment if he was wasting his time, his life. They'd made virtually zero progress, and Aurelia was now in the hospital. It seemed the Poetic Murderer was as far away as ever, but always close enough to make them look twice at the obscure shadows outward corners make. The Poetic Murderer was always a step or three ahead.

"Sir, we found a match on that hair sample!" The words came through a proud toddler with a pristinely pressed shirt, straight from the factory, and shoes with no scuffs. They'd never been shined. Elijah almost choked on his tongue as the kid continued. "I…uh…I don't know what to think. It says the hair belongs to someone named Lucas Cullen, but the record it matched was an old death record. Umm, it does say the guy's been dead almost twenty years though. Does this help?"

Elijah's heart sank, and this time deeper into a hole, much deeper and darker than before. For a brief millisecond, when the new guy shot off his mouth, he'd been almost finished, he'd seen a life with Aurelia, one with a mountain cabin, a lake and birds chirping, a lolling mutt sitting by his side and Aurelia in his arms, a fire crackling before them. It had been a good moment, but *this*, was not.

"False positive?" Elijah said.

"Must be," William said. "Thank you, Tom. That'll be all," he said, excusing the man. "I'm sorry, Elijah." They each knew that false positives happened, and for any number of reasons, but it didn't make this one hurt any less. Elijah thanked Will and they exchanged a handshake and a look of understanding.

William opened the door for his old friend and wished that he had better news. A short drive later Elijah arrived at the Nashville airport.

The plane's wheels left the ground just after 2:20 in the afternoon. Elijah had already finished his first Jack Daniels with one more on deck and another in the hole. He spent the remainder of the three-and-a-half-hour flight pondering back and forth between the Poetic Murderer, and his recently discovered, more perplexing interests.

For the past decade or so Elijah knew exactly what his life would be like, even long term. It'd never involved others. And why should it? Relationships end in loss. They end in confusion. They end in regret and they end in the dark and illustrious memories that Aurelia once asked him about. He'd never before known the love he now knew, the love he kept trying to capture when his eyes closed.

As Captain Riff ascended, the darkness in Elijah's fleeting conscious was filled with poetry, tragic and otherwise.

CHAPTER 27

The metropolis of Portland was slow to rise, dreary and somber. Sirens cut through the fog that filled the morning streets, a tumbling blaze strobing blue-red-blue-red in the thick waves of vapor. The fog hung unusually low that morning, trapping the city and its citizens, but from the upper floors of the highest buildings, a swirling white and gray hung below. It wasn't long after the sun began to crest over Mt. Hood that a beautiful Italian woman plummeted forty-one stories through gunmetal sky to her inexplicable end. The 911 call came in at exactly 7:30am. A man named Donald had witnessed it on surveillance monitors from the First National Bank Tower. It was 7:33am when a police cruiser and ambulance were careening to the scene.

A crowd had gathered around Priscilla De Luca. One woman knelt on her knees. She shrieked obscenities. One man stood and stared, tears welling in the corners of kind brown eyes. Groups huddled together, some praying loudly, others just throngs of sadness, sick and still and in disbelief.

Dan and Vince were the first police officers on the scene. They walked quickly but knew not to run. They'd been trained well and knew that running during a crisis only got people more worked up. They were professionals, ready to face the morning. With shoulders back, they navigated the sea of people surrounding Priscilla De Luca, but their pace slowed the closer they neared, then seeing brought a retching horror to their stomachs and their hearts. Their shoulders fell.

The girl's limbs were contorted, each one with a tendon-popped twist. Her head had first landed on the concrete, which splintered around her, spiderwebbing with a radius of about a foot-and-a-half. The impact reduced her head to a pulp, a ravaged pancake of oozing gore. Her shoes had fallen off sometime during the fall, and her feet lay bloodied on the rough concrete.

Vince walked around the body, wincing at each new view of the woman. He couldn't tell that she was once very beautiful. She was a tangled pile of confused body parts and ravaged flesh. Dan had begun clearing the scene of bystanders, and spoke in the firmest voice he could expel. His bottom lip quivered and shook, stiffened with an exaggerated jaw stuck out. On this day, he had broken, despite not yet knowing so. Throughout his career Dan had wondered what might come along that he couldn't bear to look at. What would come along that would change him forever.

Dan had found it.

Sunbeams were beginning to burn through the fog.

Vince circled clockwise. Closely behind Priscilla's feet, he paused. It was hard to tell through the blood, but something was etched there, four tiny lines of text, long ways on the bottom of each foot, impossibly small. He knelt down next to her and read the words out loud.

This living hand, now warm and capable
Of earnest grasping, would, if it were cold
And in the icy silence of the tomb,
So haunt thy days and chill thy dreaming nights

That thou would wish thine own heart dry of blood
So in my veins red life might stream again,
And thou be conscience-calmed—see-here it is
I hold it towards you.

On the opposite side of the country, Elijah had just kissed Aurelia and walked out of the UT hospital. He was headed toward the coroner's office and the CSI lab in Tennessee.

ario Arnold was still missing. The report had come in the summer before. The day had been typical and acquaintances had seen him in passing, assuming that he was on his way to work. People in his building had seen him leaving, but his train pass wasn't used, and no one had seen him since. No surprise, it was at the hands of the Poetic Murderer.

Detectives scrutinized his apartment after he'd gone. They looked for fingerprints, blood and hair. They talked to his neighbors, checked all the messages on his answering machine and asked around at work to see if he had any enemies. They looked into love interests. The list continued with the same result, an incomprehensible lack of evidence. It seemed Mario Arnold had been plucked from this earth with no breadcrumbs to follow.

Elijah's plane landed at five minutes before six in the evening. The date was now March 19th. He'd been lost away in his mind; a distant rumination brought him back to the night he returned home after first reading of the "Indiana Killing." He was excited then. A challenge had been on the horizon and what he felt would demand his full attention had become more of a cancer, not consuming but decaying, eating away at all that remained of what might allow him happiness.

He needed to get back to Aurelia.

He then thought again and cursed Adams, wishing sincerely that the Director had less faith in Aurelia and himself. He was becoming less OK with the assignment. Or maybe he was becoming less OK with the job in general.

The bright and only shining light from his time searching for the Poetic Murderer was what he felt for Aurelia, his partner… his partner at the Federal Bureau of Investigation.

Before Indiana, he'd purposefully kept away from her, and what he noticed in passing surely wasn't positive. He noticed how she was opinionated, domineering, a bitch on wheels at meetings and too hot for her own damn good.

Strange, how a glimpse of time can change everything, now he noticed how she swung her foot when she sat and crossed her legs, how she tossed her hair when she was frustrated, how her toes curled when she dreamt in the hospital bed. He noticed everything, and never wanted to forget any of it.

SHE

WILL

DIE

The disquieting letters flashed in his brain from his nightmare the morning before. He let them scatter and pretended they hadn't been there at all. He stepped off the plane with slight uneasiness from the Jack. He'd consumed three mini bottles before falling asleep three-and-a-half hours earlier. He hated this stage of consumption. He wasn't drunk, just tired and a little clumsy. He wondered to himself if he'd get another Explorer from the rental agency. He enjoyed that his suspicion was proven accurate.

Classic Adams.

As he opened the driver side door, he thought of Aurelia. The last time he'd been on a runway getting into an Explorer, Aurelia had told him she liked him. It was very casual, but he felt something inside of him that he'd only heard called butterflies. He hated the phrase, but whatever. He felt like he was in middle school, excited and utterly compelled by the words "I like you."

It didn't bother him. A remote connection was rare, and this was a far cry from that. There was an idea easing into his mind like a puma in a moonless sky: he wanted a life with Aurelia, a life where they worried not about problems that needn't involve them, a life where they sipped good whiskey and had fires in a soaring stone fireplace, a life that brought them long nights and not early mornings, where they could find happiness, where they could find out who each other truly was and in turn, who they were.

The picture was there, but not visible, known, but not understood, and Elijah could only close the Explorer's door, turn the key, and find the Poetic Murderer.

Mario Arnold had lived in Wilmington, Massachusetts, his parents in a small beach community called Nahant. Nahant is the smallest city in Massachusetts. It sits on a peninsula northeast of Boston. Its total land area amounts to a square mile. The beach community, quaint and beautiful with residential homes accounting for the majority of its architecture, would be just twenty-three minutes from the Boston Logan International Airport. Alvira and Dennis Arnold would be expecting Elijah. Boston PD had contacted them the day before to break the news.

Fuck. The locals always phrased it so positively.

"There's new news on your son's disappearance!"

"A detective from the FBI is now working your son's case!"

"He'd like to talk about some new developments!"

Finding their son's name carved into a starving, tortured man wouldn't be the *best* news.

Elijah abhorred unrealistic expectations.

He felt an overwhelming sense of guilt as he drove. Elijah knew there wasn't much hope for Mario and his family. He'd seen true wickedness, disdain for human kind, and the Poetic Murderer wasn't going to stop. He was clearly headed somewhere, and Elijah knew that Mario had a purpose, a place. He'd be dead soon if he wasn't already, and it wouldn't be pretty.

Elijah spun the radio dial as he crossed onto the bridge connecting the island and the mainland, Nahant Road. The airport was a short few miles behind him. He fumbled with the scan and jabbed it still when he heard 90's grunge rock on a barely existent station. He smiled, and looked out at the sea at his two sides. The sun was setting behind him, to the west, illuminating the water with a golden-orange glow. He loved the world's light at sunrise and sunset. It made him feel sublime. It was a time to sit in awe of the world.

He refocused on the road.

The bridge was a slender four lanes, with the churning ocean ready to swallow it with just a few feet of glacial melt. It spanned two miles. When Elijah reached the island, he made his way through the community, following the directions that Adams had faxed while in flight.

Technology amazed Elijah.

He turned onto Manigola Drive, which spanned the length of the peninsula from east to west. The water was to his left, still and burning in color, and exquisite houses lined the street to his right. The houses were separated by thick groves of mostly deciduous trees. He found himself daydreaming again. He could picture himself sitting on the beach, drinking tropical drinks and reading crime novels. He didn't actually like tropical drinks, or crime novels, but it was a fantasy and things didn't need to add up...

He sure wasn't a detective in his stupid beach reverie.

He drove slowly along the waterfront, enjoying the fast-fleeting moments before his destination was present. He pulled up to the house as the sun had finished its descent behind the horizon. Elijah pulled the car over opposite the water. The house stood back from the street, across a lush, green yard. The lot was striking in a naturally grand sort of way. Elijah walked toward the door with a dash of optimism and a pound of discomfort. He didn't quite understand the discomfort yet. It was new. He remembered a time when he loved every part of an investigation. The thrill of solving crimes had been a high he couldn't find elsewhere. His recent reflecting must have shaken things up.

The house was an old colonial that stood two stories. Elijah walked along a skinny cement path through thick vegetation, through the yard. The prolonged walkway seemed even longer with the weight of circumstance. Weeping willows scattered the lot and intermixed with some towering evergreens and dense red oaks. Some leaves were starting to come back, but most branches were still skeletal frames, bony protrusions jutting and tangling in knots before a red sky.

The yard itself was beautiful; the fact that it led to the ocean made it better. Elijah pondered the property's value. The house was a dark grey with forest-green shutters and a door of the same accenting color. Elijah rapped lightly on it using a heavy brass knocker. A woman came quickly to the door.

"Good evening! Detective Warren, I presume? We were told you'd be stopping by tonight. I'm Alvira," she said all-too pleasantly, all-too excitedly. Elijah again thought about how their situation could only get worse with time and more information.

"Hi, Alvira. Thanks for the warm welcome. Right off the bat I want to pass on that what we've found is minute. I hope it turns a positive course but we can't yet say."

"Of course! Oh, of course. Just come in. But you *did* find something new in Mario's case?"

Fuck. "Well, kind of. There was a situation down south which we feel is maybe connected to Mario's disappearance. As I said, it's definitely not something to be excited about."

Alvira wasn't young, but seemed fit and moved quickly. She ushered him in and through the entryway of the house, then along a slender hallway, indicative of early 18th century colonial architecture. She led him to a cozy living area at the rear of the house. The room had a large fire burning and a man Elijah assumed was Dennis, Mario's father, sat in a leather chair next to it. Across the fire sat a matching chair, which must have been Alvira's. Opposite the fire was a couch made of the same leather. Elijah walked across the dark hardwood floor to shake Dennis' hand.

"Mr. Arnold, thanks for having me tonight." The stern older man said nothing, but nodded his head and extended his hand as he shook Elijah's. Elijah understood his lack of enthusiasm, and he'd seen it a thousand times. The victim's mother is hopeful and optimistic, even after years have passed. The father becomes pessimistic and angry, bitter and sick of those phony fucking phone calls. Elijah understood both sides, but knew he'd end up angry and spiteful if his child were taken from him. The idea in general had a unique significance to him.

Elijah settled into the oversized couch across from the fire, and Alvira sat down in her chair.

"This really will be a brief visit. And I do apologize for bothering you."

"Oh no, Elijah. It's no problem. We would do anything to help our Mario," Alvira said with a too-big smile. Dennis tensed the muscles in his face and looked off into the fire.

Elijah responded, "Ma'am I'm going to be honest. I don't mean to offend you, but I also don't want to give you false hope. Is it possible for me to find Mario? Maybe. It's slim, but maybe." She nodded her head as Dennis continued to stare at tumbling flames. "Now, this is strictly my opinion, but if I find Mario, it won't be good. The things we've been investigating are pretty difficult to stomach. I'm very sorry."

Dennis looked up and straight at Elijah, who was now looking at the floor. Elijah looked up (blue eyes vivid in the firelight) as Dennis spoke his only words of the evening.

"Thank you. I appreciate what you said. I'm sick of the other bullshit."

With that, he rose from his chair, shook Elijah's hand a second time, and walked out of the room.

Alvira looked hurt. "Dennis, don't you want to hear what they've found?" She allowed a single tear to slide down her face. She quickly wiped it away and said, "OK, Mr. Elijah, I'll just show you to his room! That's where everything is."

She hopped up and moved toward the stairs. He followed her to the second floor and explained briefly what they'd found. Alvira smiled and nodded, but was clearly upset about Dennis. After turning right atop the stairs, they arrived at a room at the end of the hall.

CHAPTER 29

This living hand, now warm and capable
*   Of earnest grasping, would, if it were cold*
*   And in the icy silence of the tomb,*
So haunt thy days and chill thy dreaming nights

That thou would wish thine own heart dry of blood
So in my veins red life might stream again,
And thou be conscience-calmed–see-here it is
I hold it towards you.

Director Adams sat, his eyes stuck on the words. He hoped they didn't have anything to do with him, or Elijah, or Aurelia, but he knew better. The situation couldn't have spoken the Poetic Murderer's language more than it did. A gorgeous young woman, full of life according to her friends, family, and acquaintances, walked off the side of the tallest building in Portland. Security tapes at the First National Bank Tower had a plethora of angles eliminating the need for speculation. The girl walked through the building with a phantom's stare. She didn't pause or speed up, and she didn't blink. She didn't make eye contact with a single person and the rooftop cameras showed her willingly walk her way off the building. Then they found an esoteric poem etched into her feet in infinitesimal cursive, razor thin and deep.

Adams shook his head and thought back on his career. This was new ground for him. It felt so different, almost unbelievable like a Hollywood fabrication. He wished that it were. While lost in thought, his morning beverage was ignored and now tepid. His cigar ash was thick and long and had tipped onto his desk. He picked up his office phone and dialed Aurelia's mobile at the hospital.

"Blanc, I'm having some things faxed to the hospital. Get ready to do what you do. I'm also ordering a local to help out. Do what you can. Just don't leave that bed."

Aurelia had enough time to answer with a "hello," and say, "thank you, sir."

Classic Adams.

She wondered if there was a reason for him being so terse, or if years at the bureau wore down his ability to enjoy superfluous human interactions. She liked him no matter the answer, but she *did* wonder. Would *she* someday be like that?

Aurelia was feeling a bit better, but still not ready to leave the hospital. The rusted trap wasn't done with its punishment; she was fighting multiple infections. The traction splint was agonizing. It felt like her bones were being pulled apart, which, in fact, they were. When she was a kid she thought that by 1997 the world would have magic cures for things, at least a remedy that wouldn't hurt more than the injury to begin with. And of course she expected flying cars. So much for those ideas.

She watched an episode of *Friends* while dozing off. She woke off and on and could gather the episode involved leaving a baby on a bus. As much as *that* sounded terrible, she'd have preferred it to what *she* was doing.

At around 11am she was distracted by a timorous knock at the door.

"Good— Good morning, Detective Blanc. I'm Sam Daniels. I was assigned here for the next few days." The door opened and there Sam Daniels stood.

"Good morning to you also, Officer Daniels." The kid looked twelve. He wore navy pants, pressed, a neatly ironed navy shirt. He'd shaved that morning, or his face was yet to grow hair; it was also scrunched and central on his round head. "I appreciate you being willing to help." She said, and watched him ease back and forth on his two feet, going nowhere.

"Actually, ma'am, I'm still in training. Not an officer yet. Just started actually. I'm at the academy."

"I'm very happy to have you here. An extra set of eyes will help immensely. And please, call me Aurelia." She meant that, but wondered why they assigned someone so green.

"OK, Aurelia. Call me Sam."

Aurelia intimidated Sam. She was not only the most beautiful person he'd ever seen, but she had the intelligence to match. *That* was clear. She was in control. Sam thought about what it would be like to be in her shoes, tracking down the Poetic Murderer, caught just days ago in a bear trap and feet away from an explosion that (from what he heard from a friend in S.W.A.T.) blasted open a door onto her and her partner and sent them tumbling down the mountain. She now was in this hospital bed, far away from the case, removed from the investigation, and seemed calm. He respected her. He'd read her file earlier in the day and had been following the story of the Poetic Murderer in the national headlines.

"OK, Sam. First thing I need for you to do is find the administrative offices. Sometime this morning a confidential fax came through addressed to me from a man named Clint Adams at the FBI. Try to track that down and we'll talk after." Her tone was warm, but poised, strong. He began to raise his finger. "Administrative offices," she said. "They'll have the most secure line and anything classified will come through there," she added.

He thanked her for the opportunity and turned to head toward the top floor of the University of Tennessee Hospital. After a few minutes he was on his way back with the documents Director Adams had sent. She thanked him quickly and tore into the envelope. She needed to get her brain working; it'd been stagnant, often toxic and distracted since Elijah left. Her eyes narrowed and met the newest poem. She began to work.

This living hand, now warm and capable
alive-connected-compassion-positive-able
Of earnest grasping
honest-serious-solemn-constricting-contrasts warm from line one?
And in the icy silence of the tomb,
now surrounded-cold-transition-descending positivity-willingness in death?
So haunt thy days and chill thy dreaming nights
afterlife-subconscious-cyclical-haunting or haunted?

She stopped mid thought. "Sam, this will take a while. I'd like for you to head to the library and check out everything you can that has the name John Keats in it, or on it. It'll be a collection of typically oversized, obnoxiously heavy books. Please hurry." He nodded and headed to the

University's library. She turned her attention back to the poem and tried to find the doors to her college philosophy classes. They were down some dark mental hallway that rarely she traveled.

She also wondered how Elijah was doing in Boston. She hadn't heard from him since before he boarded the plane to fly north. She wished she could be there with him, for him. Being stuck in the hospital bed was a cruel punishment. She was emotionally invested in both the case, and Elijah, and she cursed herself for being so stupid, for moving so hastily and not noticing the bear trap. She looked out the window and toward the trees of the Great Smoky Mountains, and a tear fell; she wiped it away.

It was 1:30 in the afternoon when Sam returned. She heard him from down the way, though unknowingly. First she heard a loud crash, like metal on tile. Then, a while later, she heard a trickling of small thuds, each followed by a pause, creaking of tiny wheels, then more thuds.

Sam spilled through the door wheeling a sizable cart, at capacity with stacks of books in leaning piles, haphazard towers heaving with the wheels that turned below. He moved the cart slowly, but books tipped and slid like children from atop a sledding hill. Behind him, Aurelia could see a breadcrumb trail of them leading back toward the elevator, laughing and scattered at the bottom of the hill.

"Detective Blanc, this is all they had. I went to the *public* library also, and I think there's a library in the next county if what you're looking for isn't here."

Aurelia chuckled a little and held her hand over her mouth. "Sam, this is perfect. It'll take forever to find what I'm looking for anyway. I have literally no idea where to find it." She handed him the poem. "And, Sam, call me Aurelia."

She smiled and allowed her gaze to linger on his averted eyes long enough for them to meet hers. "Can I help look?" he said after reading it.

Aurelia grabbed the first book on the stack and tossed it to him.

She then grabbed the next and opened it.

lijah thanked Alvira before she headed back toward the first floor. Mario's bedroom door still remained closed as he stood in front of it. He felt like he was going into battle. In a way he was. He readied himself and walked in.

Mario's high school room existed around him. A poster of Motley Crue was on the wall to his left, Twisted Sister on the right. Elijah had liked both bands when he was in high school. In front of him were two yawning windows with a view of the ocean. A small desk sat under the Motley Crue poster and across the room was his bed. An armchair sat underneath one of the windows with a table beside it. Some shelving around the room displayed high school accomplishments and memories, trophies, music cases, pictures. But Mario's high school memories wouldn't help much with the murders.

A brown trunk rested beneath the other window, leather with golden buttons and fine red stitching running through it. It was where Alvira and Dennis kept what was left of Mario's belongings. The trunk was locked tight, but Alvira had given a small key to Elijah.

He knelt down and placed the key in the lock, turned it, and slowly lifted the lid.

He looked back on the sparse remains of someone's lost life, books and wall hangings, old mail, the remains of a desk, T-shirts and generic business attire, notes from past lovers. Obviously he didn't know what he was looking for, but very few investigations were driven by what was known or sure. He could only pursue what he felt most strongly about, follow intuition from a spur of the moment epiphany, potentially leading nowhere or somewhere undesirable, but occasionally leading to a place of vague promise.

That was a good day.

He picked up item after item, inspecting them carefully. The desk knickknacks were his greatest fixation. He picked up the notepad with a few of Mario's scribbles on it. Nothing really important, reminders and grocery lists. He discarded it then picked up a desktop organizer holding pens, tape, sticky notes and a stapler, pencils, business cards, stationary. Then he picked up a daily calendar where you tear off the days as they pass. He looked through a collection of papers for a mortgage application, a plane ticket and a wedding invitation several months past.

He'd been searching for over an hour and felt silly. It had been a long few months of failure. Were they any closer to the Poetic Murderer than when they started?

An idea struck him like a bolt of lightning. His hunched body went rigid, vertical poise as he began rifling through the pile of already discarded items. He snagged back the daily calendar; it had a scientific fact on each page. One thing had engaged his meticulous brain shortly after putting it down.

November 14, 1996.

Mario Arnold was abducted during the *summer* of '96, the calendar should have reflected the same. No pages should have been turned after that. Elijah felt almost sure he'd found something. The November 14th page on the front of the remaining sheets had nothing written on it. Elijah flipped to the next page and read aloud to himself.

He who makes it, has no need for it.

He who buys it, has no use for it.

He who uses it can neither see nor feel it.

What is it?

He shook his head like a high schooler who'd just been given a test. He was sick of poems and riddles and all the other bullshit. On the next page was yet another cryptic message.

value her shy iris

Elijah looked around the room and held the pages in his hand. He took out his phone.

"Aurelia, I need help. I think I found something, but can't tell what it means."

"Well, hello to you too. Are you only calling because you need help?" She smiled and enjoyed giving him a hard time. "What is it?"

"Maybe. The first thing is a riddle." He retold it to her.

"A coffin," she replied.

"Son of a bitch. You are helpful. How do you know so much random shit?" He thought back over the riddle and put the pieces together for himself. It did make sense.

She'd ignored his question.

"And the second thing?" she said.

"Right. The next thing is just a quote, one sentence that means nothing to me. It says, 'value her shy iris.' No capitals or punctuation. I obviously don't know where to even start."

"Well the iris flower has some symbolic meanings. The name originally referred to the Greek goddess of the rainbow, Iris. It was said that Iris was a messenger to the gods and would ride to and from earth on a rainbow."

"Wow," he said.

"She was the connection between heaven and earth," she continued.

"OK."

"The flower symbolizes good news and good luck," she said. "The three petals symbolize faith, valor and wisdom."

"So… It's a good luck charm?"

"Probably not for us. Whatever the words mean, I'll figure it out. He wouldn't leave this behind for no reason."

"I agree. Thanks for your help, Aurelia. Call me if you need anything."

"OK, Elijah. Be Careful."

They hung up their large mobile phones and went back to what they were doing. Elijah continued searching through Mario's relics, and Aurelia searched for one very specific passage in seas of text. She hoped and thought it was written by John Keats. The words etched into the girl who fell from the Portland skyscraper were cutting across her consciousness like strobe lights in the night sky.

Despite new information, Elijah felt helpless. It had been a very long time since he'd felt truly helpless. The last time had been when he was a child. He closed his mind for a moment and felt darkness, solitude, and he felt truly alone. He opened his eyes and thought back on the first riddle. The one Aurelia had solved within seconds. A coffin. It made sense to him now, just as all riddles after hearing the answer. He wondered its significance.

Aurelia scanned through books of philosophy from the 18th century. Sam, her assistant, did the same. He'd never seen so many confusing words in his life. Aurelia discarded a book she'd finished skimming and wished she had some wine. She picked up a pad of sticky notes. The quote from Elijah in Massachusetts was written on the top one.

"Value her shy iris." She spoke aloud and broke a long silence in the room, which startled Sam. "What does this mean? Value valor? Value faith? Value wisdom? How does this help in any fucking way?"

"Have you ever heard of an anagram?" Sam asked, trying to make conversation after a few loud (yet silent) moments. Without waiting for an answer he continued, "I think Hollywood makes things up. I always see that stuff in movies or shows, but never in real life."

Aurelia started ignoring him.

value her shy iris

She began rearranging the letters.

lijah continued to flip the days of the calendar, tearing off each as he went. The two pages with the Poetic Murderer's flawless cursive were kept separate. Elijah stared at the passing days, one after the next, and found nothing but blank paper and facts about science. After being satisfied that the calendar contained nothing more of interest, he spent another hour with the remaining items. He looked like a sad child playing with inadequate toys, dismayed on the floor with the items strewn around him.

He came up with an absurd idea.

He cleaned up the toys, stood, looked around the room one last time, and left.

He took the relevant pages of the calendar back down the stairs. He again thanked Alvira, who was sitting in front of the still blazing fire, and asked for plastic bags to hold the calendar pages. She pointed him in the right direction and thanked him for his help. Her face was solemn and she kept her gaze averted from Elijah's.

Elijah drove along the road. The view to his right was now dark and less interesting than the waning sunlight and ocean a few hours prior. He was in route to the Federal Bureau of Investigation's crime lab in downtown Boston. On his way out of the Arnold's home, he phoned Adams to make sure there would be a technician awaiting him. The tech would most likely be pissed because of the hour of the night, call him crazy, reserve him a spot at the asylum with nice white and padded walls.

Such is life.

Aurelia hadn't made any progress. At least that's how *she* felt. She'd rearranged the letters in every way possible and come up with nothing logical. Some options thus far were, *sir veil hush year* and *ye rule his ravish*. Frustrated with her lack of progress, she kept on.

It reminded her of school. Back in Wisconsin they'd give her riddles, things to solve when she would inevitably complete her work hours before the others. Aurelia was bright and exhausted her teachers with esoteric queries that they'd usually no answer for. When she was thirteen she began to answer her own questions. Why be disregarded or be made to feel as if wonderment, the pursuit of knowledge, was a bad thing? In hindsight, she didn't blame them. The states' school system rarely could accommodate the highly precocious or the fallen behind.

Aurelia knew how many possible combinations there were for the anagram, if, in fact, that's what the phrase was. She tossed the idea to the side, flustered, and grabbed a cup of cold coffee sitting beside her. She'd been stagnant all day, and it was killing her.

Sam quietly turned the pages of John Keats' work. He'd been at it for ten hours without complaint. The opportunity to work with Detective Blanc was his motivation, and he did his best to observe and understand her process. He'd been watching her (hopefully not creepily) work and couldn't fathom what she was doing in that brain of hers. She'd be stone still and silent for hours, staring at the fifteen letters, moving naught but surely busy. Then she'd come back to life, easing in sometimes with a quiet anecdote and sometimes with a brusque realization or question.

Sam was currently leafing through a book called *The Complete Works of John Keats,* and thinking about the inaccuracy of its title. There were (at least) twenty or thirty books strewn and stacked around the hospital room with text that wasn't included in, *The Complete Works.*

He didn't understand *why* he was looking for the poem, but it didn't really matter.

He was there to do a job.

Elijah stepped out of the car and walked toward the FBI's crime lab, the calendar pages burning in his pocket. A small office building housed the lab on the western outskirts of Boston. A man named Tony met him at the door. Tony looked to be in his late fifties, and was not tall but stout with broad shoulders. Tony was not happy. *That* was clear. He opened the door.

"I'm Elijah. I really do apologize for getting you called in."

"Thanks," Tony kind of mumbled.

They walked next to each other through the building and exchanged names.

Then there was the overwhelming white of a lab surrounded them.

Tony was tapping his foot and leaning against a table with cold chrome finish.

"I'd like to have this looked into," Elijah said and handed him the two plastic bags.

. . .

"Yea... So, the ink is what I'm interested in. Can you see if there's anything unusual about it?"

"I can do it, but I haven't before. I can at least cross-reference it with a typical pen. See exactly what's in it." Tony said nothing for another moment then said, "Maybe talk to an ink connoisseur or something."

"Those people exist?"

"I don't know. But aside from its makeup, I can't help."

Tony took the bags of leaflets and walked to the other side of the room.

"This won't take long," came quietly over his shoulder. He was almost to the opposite corner.

Elijah looked this way and that, propped up on one arm on one of the chrome tables. A cylindrical container bumped his elbow and came sputtered out and almost off, but he grabbed it. Luckily, it was empty, and he readjusted his stance. The lab was foreign and spotless with a bunch of stuff he didn't recognize. He thought about how he should have paid more attention in high school science class. A microscope was about all he could identify.

After a few minutes, Tony wandered back to Elijah.

"This is a pen from our office, made up of petroleum, linseed oil, soybean oil, mineral oil and a dye made from carbon. I tested a different one. Different, but same. Yours was *very* different."

Elijah's heart thudded in his chest.

Tony continued.

"Primary component is Egyptian pine bark, followed by corroded bronze, a unique ground vinegar, gallnut, which are insect deposits found in the oak trees of Egypt, and iron sulfate. One final component is what looks like blood. Minus the blood, it resembles ancient tattoo ink. It's interesting that these components took to paper as nicely as they did." Tony kept his gaze at his report, looked like he was about to say something, but the air remained noiseless.

Elijah had been listening carefully. The obscure list meant little to him, but he knew rare meant easy to track. He thanked Tony profusely and asked him to fax Director Adams. Clint would get the info to Aurelia. Elijah needed *her* mind working on it. He walked out of the crime lab and began incredulously thinking about how he was about to attempt to find an "ink connoisseur."

Aurelia stared at the fifteen letters in front of her. She had cut out each one and was scrambling them around on a swiveling hospital table meant for eating. Her brain hurt. It was late and she'd just thanked Sam for his time. He insisted that he stay, but she assured him he'd done more than enough.

"Hurry," she near-shouted. She'd re-composed the letters. She hadn't yet seen that particular word she kept those squares together. She began to work faster and the letters began to rise up at her, assembling themselves. They began to shape a sentence. Her arms dropped to her sides.

She read the words aloud.

"Hurry. She is alive."

CHAPTER 32

E lijah drove slowly toward his hotel, lights of the city streaming past the Explorer's windows. Night shapes occupied the streets of Boston, wavering silhouettes and figures that hunched against buildings, hoards that stood stagnant in lines under neon signs, thumping music in waves as doors were tossed open and fell back shut. The neon sign chasers could have that kind of fun, though Elijah wondered if he knew how to have fun at all anymore.

What he really wanted was to see Aurelia, but he'd have to settle for gin and dinner.

Or gin *for* dinner.

Driving, he found himself lost in what he'd discovered minutes earlier. The ink may have been the first puzzle piece that the Poetic Murderer didn't set him up to find. Or maybe he had, but the fact was Elijah *had* found it, and it couldn't hurt. Right? There was a sick sense of doubt that he did his best to keep at bay, a lingering suspicion, a troubling concern that he was just a puppy following along a trail of attractive promises, following to trouble or into a trap. He didn't know why, but it all felt wrong somehow.

This sentiment stayed at the fringe of his consciousness.

His phone began to vibrate and pulled him from his reverie.

"Elijah! I found something!" Aurelia's voice said through the phone.

"About the Portland girl?" he said, a little out of it.

"Unfortunately not. Still nothing there. My new assistant and I literally searched all day to match that poem on her feet. Maybe it's not even Keats. But listen! That sentence that was written on the third calendar page, I think it was an anagram!"

"I don't know if I know what an anagram is..."

"It means that in order for the message to be read as intended, the letters must be arranged in a specific order." She read the words through the phone, "Value her shy iris, once arranged properly, becomes, hurry she is alive."

His excitement matched hers. "That's great, Aurelia! But who's alive? Where do we go to save her?" he said, now rambling a bit. "Also, I might be getting somewhere with the ink! Whether he meant for us to look into it or not, the notes were written in a very rare ink that we may be able to track."

Aurelia began to think. "Elijah, the two notes connect to each other. No way he leaves the two together arbitrarily. Especially now that we know the ink's unique. We need to get this figured out tonight. If 'she' is still alive, we need to find her, and fast. What are you doing next about the ink?"

"I *was* planning on drinking gin and eating a burger, but I guess that isn't an option now. I don't know exactly *what* to do. The less than thrilled lab analyst suggested that I find an, 'ink pen connoisseur,' or something like that," he said with air quotes.

"Don't be such a shit. He may not have been literally serious, but take his advice."

"Ink pen connoisseur?"

"No, donkey. Not necessarily that phrasing. But if you find someone who specializes in antique pens, or rare books or something like that, they may know something about the ink. Like if I wanted to find out how old was Lane Staley when Alice in Chains made the Dirt album, I might find an idiot that's spent his life listening to their music."

He knew she was right. "Who in their right mind gave you an assistant?"

"Don't start. I'm stuck in this hospital and Adams sent a kid from the academy to help with things. He actually was the one who mentioned the possibility of an anagram. See, if I was as pessimistic as you, I'd have dismissed him."

"Fine. I hear you. So I'll go look for ink pen connoisseurs in the yellow pages?"

"I'd say start with antique shops in the city, and have Adams run a search for who owns them. Once you have contact info I think home visits will be in your immediate future. Get ready to piss some people off."

"I hope I don't get stabbed in the middle of the night. Hope no one lives in Southie."

"I wouldn't worry, Elijah. I'm sure you'll fit right in on the south side. You've been lookin' a bit rough lately." She was having fun and laughing to herself.

"I'll keep you in the loop. Better luck with the Portland girl." She began to say goodbye when he blurted something and interrupted her. "Do you wanna get a drink when I'm back? Er— A dinner— When— Um— When we're back home— Eh— In New York... City...?"

She smiled all her teeth.

"Detective Warren, I've never heard you struggle so much to get words out. I would love to have a drink— Er— A dinner— With you. Who knows when it'll be, but I can't wait."

Elijah was certain that this had been the best day he had had in a very long time. Now he needed a phone book. He wished there was some invention that he could just type in a question and immediately have an answer. This was going to be tedious.

A scratchy voice answered the phone. It was 1am. "Yes?"

"Adams. It's Elijah."

"I know, Elijah. Who else calls me at this hour? Warren, what in the hell do you want?"

"I've got some names for you to look up. Well, obviously not for *you* to look up, but names for you to have someone *else* look up."

Elijah then explained the circumstances and the reason for the expedited nature of the request. Somewhere, some woman was in a coffin, probably buried, and it'd already taken him a couple hours to scour the Boston phone book for five antique shops within the downtown limits.

One of shops was *Old World Literature,* and he figured it was as good a place to start as any. Elijah hung up the phone and kicked feet up on the small hotel room desk to wait for an address. He'd been working there since he found the phone book. His foot tapped impatiently as the minutes ticked by, glancing down at his watch every couple. He knew the bureau wouldn't take long to generate a list of addresses and phone numbers, but it felt like eternity.

He wanted to sleep. His brain wouldn't let him. He was wired with the excitement of possibility. He wondered what the Poetic Murderer was doing at that exact moment. He wondered if the Poetic Murderer knew what *he* was doing and thinking about. He didn't care either way. He had faith that he would soon be knocking on the serial killer's door, be it physically or figuratively. Elijah Warren could feel the winds changing, and for once, felt maybe they would gust in his favor.

t was after 1am and Aurelia continued her search for the John Keats poem. She'd been at it since 7am the previous morning. With no sleep, the work was taking its toll. She caught herself spacing out, musing colorfully about a mountain getaway. She could see rocky hills, evergreen trees and a blanket of thick, white snow. She could hear a crackling fire, taste wine; a sunset was through the window. She had warm socks and a blanket to curl into. She loved her distraction. Her lack of good sleep was easing her into semi-conscious naps, near-lucid dreaming that felt so real she could touch Elijah's face, see the wrinkles beside his eyes when he smiled. She felt his rough hands in hers as he looked into her eyes. Then she'd ease back to the reality of the Poetic Murderer, the elusiveness of John Keats' writing.

In 1848, John Keats published a series of letters. They were written to his brother, and contained a plethora of things: theories, commentaries, questions, answers, and of course poetry.

One of those poems was called, "This Living Hand."

Aurelia had found it. It was 2:06am and her adrenaline pumped and thumped, enlivening her, just as it had during the shootout with Elijah and Charles Larson during that cold winter's morning in January, three months before. Before she'd remembered the work of John Keats, before she'd been caught in the bear trap, before Colorado, before Indiana and before she was falling in love with Elijah. She couldn't yet see that for herself, but she felt it, and it scared her more than she could ever explain.

After finding the poem, Aurelia ignored her fatigue and dove headfirst into research.

In the year 1818, Keats was engaged to a woman named Fanny Brawne. She was, "beautiful and elegant, graceful, silly, fashionable and strange."

The quote was found in a letter Keats wrote to his brother on the eve of his and Fanny's first meeting. Despite euphoric disposition, tuberculosis was consuming his lungs. The bacteria showed no signs of stopping. Shortly after learning of his condition, "This Living Hand" was written spur of the moment, and as a distraction from a different poem, which he couldn't quite finish. "The Cape and the Bells," which satirized a particular courtroom trial about a politician and his mistress, was longer, substantial, and carried the weight of expectation. Keats encountered writer's block and gave up work on, "The Bells" before it was finished, and "This Living Hand" was written in the margin.

One of Aurelia's first thoughts after picking up "This Living Hand," was that it was self-centered. As she read it for the hundredth time, she spoke out loud her interpretation.

That thou wouldst wish thine own heart dry of blood
So in my veins red life might stream again

"The poem's subject is hoping the 'other' will be willing to sacrifice their own life."

Aurelia then thought to herself about how Keats may have been thinking about his own hand being, *warm and capable,* and how it would soon be, *cold and in the icy silence of the tomb.*

"He was trying to deal with death," she said. She moved onto her next thought. Each anecdote was being recorded furiously on a yellow legal pad. She dissected each part of the seven-line poem. She wondered if maybe the 'other' in the poem was Fanny. The timeframe worked. Did Keats question her loyalty? Her devotion? She knew it had to mean something, the subtleties and the nuances that could be *easily* ignored. *They* would be the key.

She ended her analysis with the final line of the poem, *I hold it towards you,* she thought, and paused for a moment. Her eyes dropped off to the side of the bed and she ran her hand through her hair, a subconscious tick when she thought.

"He's expecting it. No, demanding it. Maybe he's finally accepting his death." She pondered exactly why the hand was held forward. The hand represented must have been Keats'. As more lights were extinguished around the hospital, Aurelia kept working, thinking, trying to figure out how to end the mess she was in. It was late when she fell into a restless slumber.

Several hours later, she shot up in her bed.

"The killer is expecting to skirt blame. He's holding it towards someone. It's an opportunity. The killer is dying. He wants us to catch him."

She rambled thoughts until sleep fell back over her.

CHAPTER 34

A fter talking with Director Adams a second time, it was late, or early, depending on one's definition. Elijah had just hung up the phone and had the addresses and landline numbers for the owners of the prospective stores. *Old World Literature* seemed the best option, and was owned by a man named Ezekial Vincent.

Ezekial's house was at the junction of Pond Street and Lockhead Avenue, a picturesque corner surrounded by trees, sprawling houses and plush lawns, a view of the lake. His home was a part of the Jamaica Plain neighborhood, or JP, southwest of downtown Boston. Mr. Vincent had made a lot of money somewhere or another.

Before getting into the car, Elijah had first tried the landline, called twice and listened agonizingly to each late night ring. Now, he was on his way to try in person. He could fathom the reception he'd receive. *Hostile,* he thought as he walked towards the house.

The house was illuminated by vivid light, cameras, a small hexagonal sign that reported a security company's name. Elijah found a bit of ironic comedy in moving to a posh neighborhood just to be followed by the urge to overprotect. To Elijah, it seemed a waste of resources. Then again, someone could break into *his* house and he might not notice. He *might* notice if they stole the gin. *Maybe* if they took his bed. He then pondered his capacity to have an opinion on the concept of home.

The sprawling house stood tall and grand, a beacon of bright in the dark of night. Elijah walked up to the door, looking around as he did. Several light raps on it, followed by a ring of the doorbell, did the trick. Through the window and out of his peripherals, Elijah noticed a light ignite from somewhere inside. He also heard deep, guttural grumblings that sounded less than welcoming.

The door rocked forward as a man from inside lurched against it.

The peephole darkened.

"It's almost two in the damn morning. Who are you, and what the shit do you want?"

The voice came through the door with what sounded like a Turkish accent.

"Mr. Vincent, my name's Elijah Warren. I'm with the FBI and would be very appreciative if I could share a few minutes of your time. I understand the late hour, but if it wasn't a matter of life and death, I wouldn't be here."

Ezekial pondered for a second. Then came the click of a lock, and the heavy slab of wood arced inward. Elijah stood face-to-face with Ezekial Vincent. He had a slight frame and a head of grey hair. It stood up on end and he had square glasses below. Rivulets ran in his face, and he slouched forward and onto a cane. The most pertinent information regarding Ezekial was that he had a large pistol in his cane-less hand. It was held toward Elijah.

"Mr. Warren, I can't fathom what in the fuck *I* can do to help, but, I'm lonely and bored. I'm also crass, so if you can deal with that, I have nothing better to do than humor you, even at two in the fucking morning." He started to cane away. "You better not be yankin' my chain," he said over his shoulder. Then he said, "I'll put on some coffee," and disappeared around a corner.

Elijah liked the old man and followed him.

Ezekial and Elijah sat facing one another in a covered outdoor area at the back of the house. They weren't any longer looking at the pond, but soaring evergreens created a sense of distinct solitude. Space heaters kept them warm, and stone and pillars surrounded them. The fifteen-foot ceilings were lit with recessed lighting, angled towards that most worthy, the seating areas, the sprawling grille, the bar and the hammock. Ezekial's home spoke an elegant language. Elijah began to talk shortly after Ezekial brought him his coffee.

"Ezekial, I'll get right to it. I found a rare type of ink that may be linked to a serial killer the media have been calling, the 'Poetic Murderer.' I was wondering if you could tell me what kind of ink it is and help me track the person that purchased it. One thing I must disclose is that a woman's life depends on whether or not we arrive at the right conclusion."

Ezekial laughed a subtle laugh. "No pressure. Right?" Then he said, "Elijah, I'm willing to bet I can help. I've dedicated my life to understanding languages and ultimately, the recording of information. This just sounds damn interesting, and an old man like me needs some excitement in his life once in a while."

Elijah smiled and looked into the man's enlivened eyes. Could he get so lucky that the first listed house would disclose an answer? "Well, Ezekial, if just *that* sounds interesting, I think I've got something for you."

He gave him the Reader's Digest version of the past three months, The Poetic Murderer's heretofore legacy, and handed over the recorded calendar pages, as well as the report created by the angry Italian at the Boston crime lab.

Ezekial adjusted in his chair, each movement slow and deliberate. His eyes moved over the pages. Elijah watched the old man's reactions as he studied. After a few minutes of silence, Ezekial finished with the documents. He put down the file and looked up at Elijah.

"Elijah, I may have good news for you."

"I hope so, sir."

"The ingredients definitely aren't common, and the technique used to create the ink is relevant in ancient forms of tattooing, mainly in Egypt. I'd assume that's why you have components found and exported strictly from there. A Roman physician named Aetius originally created the technique. Now, it's known more in novelty than practice. We've developed safer inks." He paused and looked out into the dark yard. "It's interesting. Your killer has altered the technique to be used on paper and not skin." He kept his gaze to the yard.

"I'm sorry, Ezekial. What's my good news?"

"Right. Few people practice this type of ink making, and it comes at a serious cost. Even if the killer's not known for this, the Egyptian ingredients can be ordered only through a select few dealers. I'll be right back, Elijah. I have a phone number you'll be interested in."

Ezekial caned away, and Elijah waited.

CHAPTER 35

E lijah woke with the sound of thunder. It rumbled from a distance, came upon the city with crashes and quakes. It was 6:35am, and he was hazy-headed and tangled in the sheets. Sipping coffee at Ezekial's house just hours before, the milieu had been different, the stone walls and pillars, the cobbled floor, the expansive bar and the hammock, replaced now by the chipping paint of the hotel, not a forest green and not seafoam, but a stale avocado, wood paneling along the bottom half of the room, and muddled brown carpet with a plethora of organic stains. Pictures of fruit, now rotten from fading and withering, hung askew above two beds. The phone had black tar fingerprints along its shaft and the clock blinked a strobing time that doesn't exist.

He fumbled into the bathroom at around 6:40am, and a square, frosted window lit up with a brilliant flash of white, followed by a rumbling that shook the dilapidated walls. Several small, blue tiles fell from the walls onto the sink and floor. He stood before the toilet with a tripod hand pressed behind it. He was exhausted, but feeling the same sensation of intrigue that he'd felt in the dead night's hours. He was getting somewhere, and the further he got, the closer he was to getting that drink with Aurelia.

Speaking of Aurelia, he had called her while driving back to the hotel, shared what he'd learned from Ezekial. Through the phone, she couldn't hide her excitement, and despite the horrendous time, she'd been awake. One thing Elijah didn't know was that Aurelia was ready for the case to be through. She could barely care anymore about John Keats or the Poetic Murderer, though her day *had* been successful. She had still been full tilt, absorbed in the work, but it felt stale, soft around the edges, and her focus was shifting to something else entirely.

After hearing about Ezekial, Aurelia had shared what she'd been reading, thinking, and though it was a different type of news, Elijah was excited to hear what she'd theorized, the potential leads she'd dug up.

It had been a good day all around.

They'd hung up slowly, wanting hearts and minds restive on each side of the line.

Elijah flushed the toilet and wavered back to the bed. He flopped back down. In the back of his mind he still knew a trip to Portland was necessary. The First Financial Bank Tower incident had obviously made it to national news, and the press was having a field day. Somehow, it'd taken more than a week for roasted Marcus Felway at the farmhouse to make it, but it'd only been twenty-four hours since Priscilla walked off the tower.

She was now famous.

Elijah realized at that moment that he'd barely thought of Priscilla, and wondered how: the hospital with Aurelia, the coroner's office in Tennessee, the CSI lab in Nashville with his long-removed friend from St. Louis, the Arnold's house near the beach, the CSI lab in Boston with the bitter Italian, his hotel room to study the phone book, then Ezekial's house and back to the hotel.

It had been a long day.

It had been a long few months.

After his morning shower, he was off to the diner. Coffee, food, and a phone call to a man named Dominic Glass would be next. Dominic owned a shop in New York City.

Elijah shook his head as he thought about that. He'd traveled from Tennessee to Boston to contact a man back home in New York.

Ezekial had advised him to wait for a decent hour. Apparently Dominic was less open to untimely botherings than his friend Ezekial Vincent. Therefore, Elijah planned on taking full advantage of what he liked most about the morning. He hoped it wouldn't cost a woman her life. Not far from Elijah's hotel was the breakfast place he'd eagle-eyed the night before.

Elijah sat at his table and looked out the window. His coffee warmed his hands, and sitting there made him feel right. The young staff moved about in circles around tables. An elderly couple was talking about things they "just didn't get" about what they were reading in the newspaper, the same one Elijah was reading; young boys talked about the girls at the table four down from them; the girls giggled back and tossed their hair. Several men and women in suits and pressed skirts sat and ate quickly, though plenty of those came and left, some with crumbs falling off their face as muffins were smashed in, some sitting and doing makeup in a tiny mirror with a latte and some hash browns. The wet floor by the door squeaked and shrieked with the rubber of feet.

Elijah recalled discussing his morning routine with Aurelia a few days or weeks earlier. He couldn't really remember. Time had begun to run and each day was a bit more confusing than the one before. Clint could even tell something was up. Each time they talked, Elijah felt like he was probing, walking the fringe of questions he couldn't quite ask. Clint had never *not* trusted him, and the feeling of wonder was unsettling. What could be on his mind?

He read the newspaper without reading it before looking back to the window. The morning kept its dark rage. Rain was pummeling the streets. Wind blew droplets in horizontal beams. Elijah couldn't decide which way the wind was actually blowing and finally settled on the fact that it came ubiquitously. The paper had told him that the high for the day was forty, and the storms weren't to stop.

He thought back to Colorado.

Three hundred days of sun.

His mind wandered some more and finally landed on the Arnold family. Alvira and Dennis were very much affected by the Poetic Murderer's work. He felt a heavy debt unto each of them, but for different reasons. Alvira seemed sad. She wanted her son back clearly, desperately. She had no signs of hope and was still optimistic, *willing* to hope. Dennis on the other hand was angry, vengeful and spiteful. Elijah thought about being in Dennis' shoes, and was scared to know that he himself would do *anything* to kill a man who'd taken his son.

The Hollywood detective stereotype gained the attention of a waitress as he sat deep in thought at the diner. She couldn't help thinking how he'd been ripped from the movies, the deep, pondering eyes, the rough exterior and the scruff on his face. His loosened tie hung down a button or two and she could see the gun holstered under his arm. A long overcoat sat on the booth next to him. The girl wondered what in his mind could keep him so consumed.

She wanted it to be her. She was lucky to not know.

After spending more than an hour at the diner, Elijah paid in cash and headed out to brave the weather. Although the diner was just down from his hotel, the storm persuaded him to drive. He was in a rented Explorer and on his way back to a lonely room.

The strobing clock flashed the same haphazard time as he reread the documents from the Poetic Murderer's file. They were strewn haphazardly across the small desk in the corner of the room. They were strewn on the bed, and they were spread across the floor, a confused puzzle that he was beginning to resent.

He missed having his life figured out.

He hadn't minded his solitude. He looked forward to his job. How was he now so fed up with work? How could he not keep from wandering back to Aurelia? From feeling so lonely?

Finally, he made a call to Dominic Glass. It was just before nine in the morning.

"Grehhh," answered a sound from the other end.

Elijah introduced himself and explained both the situation and how he'd gotten the phone number. After the brief, but luckily effective explanation, Dominic responded.

Dominic seemed nice enough, but *wasn't* friendly, and kept talking in gruff mumbles. It lessened as he woke but never went away. Dominic had worked for Imperial Imports for nine years, and whether you want fine art or rare chemicals, you contact them.

"One order for Egyptian pine bark and gall nut. About a year ago," he grumbled.

Elijah could feel his heart speed up. He began to sweat, and then he began to cringe, thinking about the hotel shower and the molding crust along its floor, its sides and the fucking showerhead itself.

His foot bounced off the brown carpet, and his fingers tapped. He held the phone as far from his face as possible and strained to hear. Rain battered the window and wind howled past in gusts that rattled the thin panes of glass.

"It'll take time to sort through records, but I should have his name. Books are a mess, but I remember *him*. Creepy as hell. Ya know? One you can't forget."

Elijah's eyes yawned and he focused on what Dominic was saying.

"I was here when he came in. Looked up when he should've been here at the counter, but he's barely inside. It took him a whole minute to make it. He was in black boots, black pants, a black coat. Had his hood up. Didn't like the guy. Made it here and spoke like he walked. Words came out pokin'. No doubt he was smarter'n me, but fuck. He was weird. He ordered those two things, paid cash, and left."

Elijah scribbled what Dominic mumbled.

"Do you remember what he looked like?" Elijah asked.

"Yea. Prolly six feet. Real green eyes and black hair. Thirty-ish. Like a real evil version of that X-Files guy."

Elijah laughed inside.

"Dominic, I can't thank you enough. I'll try to never call you this early again."

"Yea. I'll have a name and shipping address by the afternoon."

After scheduling a time to meet at Dominic's shop, Elijah thanked the ill-spoken imports dealer, then called Aurelia and Adams.

A name and an address couldn't have sounded better. They had finally found something concrete. Elijah packed his things, feeling that he'd done all he could in Boston.

He was excited to meet Dominic Glass later that afternoon.

Elijah walked out to the Explorer with a thin smile on his face.

And he didn't care that he was drenched.

CHAPTER 36

As Elijah went to breakfast in Boston, Aurelia sat up in her bed, doing her best to decipher her prior day's notes on the Keats poetry. Motive can be paramount in solving serial murder cases, and she hoped her research would help expose one. She felt she was getting closer, but something kept her thoroughly dissatisfied: Priscilla De Luca. She'd been re-reviewing the details of *that* incident. She'd been reading background dossiers of employees at the tower. She'd been looking into Priscilla's prior life. She'd been going over the security tapes. She couldn't count the number of times she'd watched Priscilla walk off the First National Bank Tower. After a while, she set aside the laptop computer that Adams had sent for the security footage, as well as the files and photos.

Aurelia was doing *alright*, aside from the romantic confusion, the agonizing pain of the traction splint, the infection, and the stitches. At least she could think. Her mind was most important, and if she could keep focused, she'd be able to skirt stir craziness. She'd be able to figure things out.

Her assistant, Sam, was back at work for his second day. His face was turned down and into a book amongst books, focused, a Styrofoam cup steaming beside him. He was at a small, circular table across the room from Aurelia.

Priscilla's case file hadn't been out of the ordinary, at least by the Poetic Murderer's standards, and though Aurelia figured it was a long shot to find a connection between Priscilla and another of the victims, she asked Adams to look into it anyway. The victims appeared to be entirely random, an arbitrary collection of people from equally arbitrary situations. Aurelia adjusted in the bed as she reframed the information before her. Maybe the arbitrary nature of the victims was, in fact, the pattern, a lack thereof. They're similar because they're all different.

Aurelia sat still and processed.

Despite the *former* atrocities, De Luca's situation seemed almost the strangest of them. It didn't appear part of the grand plan. Nothing was showy or shocking. Nothing was complex. There was no six or three month or near-year setup. The girl just walked off the building, and technically, by choice.

She *did* walk through the building. She *did* walk off the roof.

The whole thing just seemed different, fundamentally different than the rest of the deaths.

Aurelia quickly turned to the phone. When Elijah had called and told her about Dominic Glass, the imports dealer, it planted the seed of an idea that just blossomed.

"Adams, get the Portland authorities back to that diner. Re-interview the staff now that we have his physical description. See if anyone remembers this fucker. From what Elijah described, he's pretty striking. If he was there, I bet someone remembers him."

Adams made the necessary phone calls and eleven minutes later an officer named Pam stepped through the doors of the Riverside Café in Portland.

Aurelia worked for a few hours before her phone rang.

It interrupted her and Sam's noiseless scouring.

"Aurelia! The flowerbeds! Remember the ones by the walkway at Peak Lane? The house in Tennessee! Weren't those just recently dug?"

She wasn't expecting it to be Elijah. Caught off guard, she responded.

"Yea. I guess so. I *think* so. I didn't recognize it at the time, but I think so."

"The address where the ink's ingredients were sent was *that* address, and before the anagram was solved, it talked about iris'. Maybe both forms of the message had meaning. I bet she's buried in front of that house. And listen! The name on the address was Mario Arnold."

CHAPTER 37

Pam had spoken with six of the seven total employees from the café. None could recall an attractive, yet peculiar man, dressed in all black and at a table of Priscilla's. The seventh employee had different information. It had been a couple days, but the busboy, Dan, remembered him vividly. Pam's description matched Dan's memory, and the man at the table had taken an immediate interest in Priscilla. He spoke to her gently throughout his meal. He leaned forward on his elbows each round she made. He watched her back to the kitchen. Yes, the man wearing black was interested.

Dan had taken the bill and some cash after clearing the green eyed man's plate. Dan had heard the man ask Priscilla to meet him for dinner, and Priscilla had been smitten.

Dan sat and thought, and his memory bounced, a pinball in a pinball machine. He couldn't remember what restaurant the man had named.

"Portland Manor," Dan finally blurted. "That's where he was staying. I remember they could meet *there* and walk. Still can't remember the restaurant. I'm sorry."

The Portland Manor wasn't far from First National Bank Tower.

Pam continued through the questions Aurelia had given Director Adams.

Meanwhile, Elijah was on a plane and heading south toward the cabin in Tennessee. Captain Riff had been blabbing about a Portuguese "lassie" that he'd met on the beach a few weeks back. Her name was Paula, and she had dark hair that curled in waves down her back. She had round hips and a thick...

Elijah sat silently in the back of the plane, tapping his foot, vexed and trying to envisage the forthcoming days as the Captain kept chattering away up front.

It'd been at least a minute since Elijah stopped listening.

Elijah wondered how close they were.

He still couldn't see any big picture to the deaths, but knew there had to be one.

Elijah sipped a gin and tonic. He looked down to find an air telephone attached to the table next to his seat. He reached back, pulled a wrinkled piece of paper from his pocket, and dialed the number on it.

"Alvira, this is Elijah with the FBI. We may have found something else in the case. I can't promise good news, but I think we're getting closer. Please let Dennis know as well."

"Thank you, Mr. Elijah. I hope you get him."

Elijah's ears caught something.

"Alvira, is everything OK? I'm sorry to ask, but…"

Tears were pulled back; breath was caught, and Elijah didn't finish his sentence.

"Yes. Yes things are, Mr. Elijah. I'll let Dennis know when I see him."

"Alvira, really. Is everything OK? You seem upset."

"*Yes*. Elijah. I'm fine. And thank you. Please keep trying to catch him."

With that, Alvira hung up the phone.

Wispy cirrus clouds fluttered past the windows of the plane as it propelled into Tennessee airspace. Elijah wanted to fast forward. He wanted to be there.

Hell. If he *was* fast forwarding, he'd fast forward to the end. He'd fast forward to a life with Aurelia and a cabin all their own. As a kid, he used to play self-contained games of *is it worth it*? He would think about skipping portions of time, chunks of his life, deciding if the skip forward, assuming the penalty was completely blank memories from that time, would be worth it.

Would it be now?

The local officers were almost to the cabin, armed with shovels, axes, and crowbars, along with an ambulance and medical team. The officers were usually prepared with a different set of tools. It was an odd day, heading out with shovels, ready to unearth a potential vic' from semi-frozen earth.

An incessant, nagging idea, a dead woman buried alive, kept them silent, uneasy.

An officer named Laura swallowed hard and closed her eyes to avoid what was real. She was scared, but not for her life.

"T-minus twenty minutes everyone," spoke the team leader.

Laura again tried to swallow the knot in her throat, to clear her head. The sixteen-passenger van moved precariously along the winding mountain roads that led to the cabin. The view out the windows didn't gain any attention. Eyes were poised. Air was void of talk.

Elijah poked into the cockpit to see how long until they were to land. Riff replied with, "not a minute before or after I intend to."

Elijah at least knew *where* they'd be arriving, the T. Milton County Airstrip, an 800-foot length of cement that could barely serve as a place to take off and land. It generally lacked the essentials of an airport. There was no tower, no one monitoring the area, no building, and no aircrafts. It was a tree-surrounded field with a strip of spidering concrete. It was deserted, and its only relevance geographically was that it was near the Great Smoky Mountains; most National Park visitors don't fly on private jets.

Aurelia sat in her bed thinking hard about the following minutes and hours. She looked across the room at Sam, still stuck in the slew of books he'd collected for her. He'd been running through police databases for descriptions matching the one Dominic Glass had given Elijah. He'd seen more criminal pictures and profiles than he ever thought he would, despite his career choice. He was happy with the recent shift in record keeping, a transition from file cabinets to Internet databases.

Sam sat with a bulky laptop, scanning profiles and thinking about how much more tedious the work would be if he had had to do it with hard files in a police station basement. Those were always dingy, dusty and damp, reeking of mold and past horrors.

Aurelia spun a pen through her fingers. At the particular moment, she couldn't focus on anything but the cabin in the mountains and the woman they hoped was buried there.

The van pulled up and officers burst out the doors. They went to the flowerbeds that lined the sides of the walkway. The first three began digging in the left bed; the next three took the opposing one. The dirt was hard from the cold, but they appreciated that they were in Tennessee where the winter was rarely too harsh. If they were in Alaska, the tomb would have been cemented following the first freeze of the year.

Piles of dirt began to heave from the ground around those digging. The officers encouraged each other and moved with speed and purpose. Who knew how long the woman had been down there? Who knew how long she had to live? Who knew if she was there at all?

"Fifteen minutes, asshole." Riff's updates were (in general) equal parts information and belligerence. Elijah stared from the window of the four-seater plane. He wished a request for Riff to hurry wasn't futile and irrational. The plane was flying hundreds of miles per hour and taking him to a near-non-existent airstrip within miles of the cabin. How could he ask for much more?

"I've got something!" shouted an officer digging in the flowerbed on the right side of the walkway. "It's wooden. Hurry up!" He clanked the tip of his shovel down into it.

The team excavating the other bed shifted over and kept digging. They worked as quickly as they could. The hole was now six feet deep, four feet across and eight feet long. They'd been digging thirty-five minutes and sweat dripped off faces.

"Almost there," someone shouted. They were in the right place. Clear as day, a coffin began to reveal itself beneath the pounds of dirt that had been exhumed.

"Crowbar!" yelled one of the men. The largest of the group, a down-home boy from Townsend, ran back to the van to grab his.

A *CRACK* filled the air as he chopped down into it.

The crowbar crashed into the coffin and reverberated in waves in the winter air.

Splintered wood shavings helicoptered as the metal connected.

CRACK

Another blow connected with the coffin. The lid began separating from the base.

CRACK

The man had worked halfway around the box with the crowbar.

CRACK

The final blow needed entered the coffin's lid. It was an awkward space in which to work, down below the earth's crest. People lay on their stomachs and reached downward to help pull the lid up and out of the hole.

The lid finally was removed.

Elijah's Explorer had been waiting for him. He thought about what a nightmare it was for Adams to arrange his rental cars. Obscure and often last minute requests had been the standard over the past couple months.

On the way to the cabin, his driving was far hastier than it was on the same drive a few days earlier. The roar of the Explorer's engine peaked and shifted as the roads wound upward.

The Explorer red lined its RPMs as it shifted into top gear, racing underneath the tunnels of barren trees. The tires bounced haphazardly, and the car moved across the terrain at dangerous speeds, its roof leaning out and over the steep drops waiting beside the road.

The wooden lid was tossed aside as Elijah's vehicle howled to a stop in the driveway. His gaze met the hole, the mounds of dirt, then the lid. He still couldn't see what was beneath the earth. His heart pounded and he was out of the car almost before it stopped moving. He ran to the excavated area and looked inside.

A woman, tattered clothes and with an oxygen mask, lay curled inside the coffin at the bottom of the hole. The team stepped back to allow the medical staff to take over. Elijah kept his gaze down to see if the woman was alive. He couldn't tell. The medics dropped a backboard into the hole to strap her down and raise her out. Elijah circled like a dog trying to retrieve a toy he couldn't reach. When the woman was on ground level, Elijah stared at the outline of her chest. It was barely moving, but it was rising and falling. She was alive.

Her eyes suddenly opened. The mask was on her face and she tore if off and tossed it aside. Her breath escaped in a brash lurch, and the EMT began checking her vitals. The woman was thin and clearly malnourished. The oxygen tank couldn't have had much air in it. Elijah had overheard that the tank, when new, could sustain someone for a few days in the confined space, assuming unstressed respirations.

Elijah followed behind as she was carried to the ambulance. He flashed his credentials and climbed into the back. As he pulled the door shut, he heard a faint voice from behind him.

"Thank you, Elijah." The woman's eyes closed, and she looked content.

Elijah was also, though he couldn't place why the woman had known his name.

CHAPTER 38

E lijah was walking briskly toward Aurelia's room at the UT hospital. They'd not spoken since his race to the cabin, and it'd been several hours. Adams had called her though, given a quick summary of the day once it was all said and done. She'd celebrated silently in a lonely room. Sam was already gone; she'd sent him home, trying to keep his schedule reasonable. She was exhausted and *knew* he had to be. Her eyes hurt and her brain felt like it was sagging. She'd been reading nonstop, almost.

During her breaks in studying, simulated laughs filled the stagnant air, and the television's reruns were memorized, wired in, heard even before they came crackling from the TV, circa 1983.

She smiled a bit at Seinfeld and let her eyes waver shut. She was pleased with what they'd done in the past days, and though it hadn't been physical, the work was exhausting. She wanted cold wine and the crackling of a fire.

Her eyes shot open and toward the door when a knock came.

Her "come in" was a hopeful one.

"You shouldn't just invite people in. You should ask who it is first. It's safer. Ya know?"

"Why do you *always* give me a hard time, Elijah Warren?"

"I apologize, Ms. Blanc. It won't happen again." He smiled that thin smile. "How do you feel?"

"Physically, fine. Mentally, cheese is sliding. I need to be out of this room. There's an infection they can't quite keep quiet. It isn't serious, as long as I'm here, but they need to keep an eye on it. Goddamn bear trap."

Elijah liked her so much. She said things to catch him off guard. "Well, at least it's still attached. Gotta put that in the win column. You heard we found the girl?"

"Yea! That's great Eli. Adams called right after. How is *she*?"

"Stable, but not ready to talk. She was pretty malnourished. Doc said tomorrow morning we can speak to her. She's downstairs. It's lucky that our boy in black is courteous enough to attack people in a central location. That way I can combine visits."

"Absolutely. I like that you're lookin' on the bright side, Warren. Didn't think ya had it in ya."

They laughed and felt exactly why time together was so nice and time apart so hard. Elijah sat at the small chair beside her bed and they continued to talk.

At around eleven, he was asleep. Aurelia fell shortly after.

They'd had long days and needed it, but the slumber wasn't voluntary.

They'd have talked all night if they could have stayed awake.

CHAPTER 39

Acadia National Park consists of 47,450 beautiful acres of forests, mountains, shorelines, and wildlife. Along the shores of the park, cliffs explode from the sea, towers of granite with waves crashing at the base. It is here, in Acadia, that the sun first touches the United States each morning.

Cadillac Mountain is that place, named for the French explorer Antoine de Cadillac, a man given more than a thousand acres of land along the North Atlantic Coast for a French settlement in 1688, only to abandon it; he later founded the city of Detroit, and a car company came after and bore his name. In the process, Cadillac ran from the law, created aliases, cheated and stole and made money exploiting local tribes. People who encountered him reported him a liar, a nasty son of a bitch. Now, one of the most beautiful places in North America has his name on it.

Funny world.

It was a picturesque morning and the man wearing black was slowly hiking down from the top of Cadillac Mountain. The sun was yet to crest over endless ocean to the east. The night stars were still vivid and seemed close enough to pick. He was pleased for it to be Acadia's off-season; otherwise his plan couldn't have included the park. Hordes of tourists would have made what he'd just done impossible.

Left, right. Left, right.

The man wearing black loved Acadia and the panoramic view from the North Atlantic's highest point. He loved looking down at Bar Harbor and the Cranberry Islands, little worlds all their own. He thought about the people below. He thought about how long it'd take them to find the latest piece to his puzzle. He knew it wouldn't be *too* long, but couldn't wait. His smile reflected the morning's success.

Anita and Larry Holzin were on their first vacation in years. Anita, an office secretary, rarely got time off. Larry owned a lawn care business and could leave as often as he wanted. Though, with the business in only its third year, it wasn't fully established and could barely spare its owner, even for a few days. Their daughter, Melanie, was seventeen and had spent the two prior days of their trip complaining about bugs and the lack of cute boys in Bar Harbor. Their thirteen-year-old son, Lawrence II, wasn't complaining, but was constantly trying to cause himself harm, eating caterpillars, running full tilt downslope or climbing up rock faces that bottomed out in peril. The Holzins had their hands full.

They'd planned an early morning, and it'd been like pulling teeth to get the kids out of bed. They were going to hike the highest peak in the park and watch the sunrise from there. At less than a mile, they could arrive in a half hour or so, and from the summit, be the first people in North America to see the sun for the day. It sounded unforgettable. A memory they'd always cherish.

At least to Anita and Larry.

The kids were less enthused, as kids many times are.

The family enjoyed solitude on their way up, except for a man wearing all black; he was on his way down and came out of the darkness like a phantom. They encountered him halfway to the summit. He was hiking with a small backpack and didn't make eye contact. He moved at a snail's pace and made the Holzins feel pretty good about how fast *they* were moving. After passing the man, he uttered something slowly, quietly, but surely, and Anita felt gooseflesh on the back of her neck.

"Enjoy the view. It's more spectacular than usual this morning."

As the Holzins neared the end of their hike, dawn's glow lit the mountains and forests of Acadia. They hoped the horizon would remain flat, and that they wouldn't be too late to see the sun crest up from past the ocean. Melanie was complaining about her boyfriend and his friends being in Panama City for spring break. Larry thanked god that his young daughter wasn't in Panama City for spring break and hoped she'd one day understand his concern. Larry II ran ahead of the family to climb a large boulder beside the trail, and his mother scolded him back down.

"Lawrence, we can't carry your body down this mountain! Keep yourself not dead!"

Thirty-eight minutes after they began, the Holzins reached Cadillac's summit, and it was exactly as the parents had hoped. The view was indescribable, a fiery torch rising from the ocean, radiant beams shimmering and bouncing off the rippling waves, sprawling across the trees in the rolling hills and the town and the bay. As Anita looked, tears filled her eyes. She grasped Larry's hand, and ignored the upset coming from the two children. She then turned around and took in the rest of the mountain's crest.

Her eyes fell upon something ripped from nightmare.

She screamed and collapsed to the ground.

CHAPTER 40

The Poetic Murderer sat alone at a local Bar Harbor restaurant. He was waiting for his breakfast, watching out the window toward the harbor, toward the sails and the sterns and the bows. The sun was just visible from town, and the day was turning out precisely as he'd hoped. Despite this contentment, he scribbled chaotic thoughts in a black and white notebook, a custom he'd always practiced. He reflected on the morning.

What does it mean to deserve? Who deserves new cars? Nice TVs? Decapitation? Who deserves a home wrecked by disaster? Who deserves cancer? Who gets private school and who's shoved into an overcrowded, underfunded classroom? These questions matter naught, for the answers will polarize. Decision makers. Leaders. The mighty officials and the self-promoting tyrants. This country. The next. Everywhere the same thing. Distant decisions brought down to the masses. Commandments disseminated to choiceless followers.

This makes more sense than any of that. Novelty is, in the end, how we continue, how we flourish. It's quintessential, can be passed on as easy as blame, and is necessary in the perpetuation of beauty. Necessary in finding true happiness.

I won't stand for a lack of what's novel.

After my initial assessment, it was clear. The Becky girl was the one. She spoke apathetically, attended college but handed the opportunity, floundering in major, living an unfocused life. She was floating, a balloon blown where the world might blow her, and she was the perfect target.

Becky had been sitting quietly behind a window at Tito's Coffee, lolling her head in bulky headphones attached to a portable CD player, obvious disappointment on her face, etched into her posture. It plagued her, the concern of how she should look versus how she wanted to look, a head constantly swiveling, cataloguing, deciding how she should be. She was lit in vague uniformity amongst the other University of Maine students, a standard duckling following the louder ones.

Offering an alternative to idle sitting was all it took to garner her company.

Carrying her and the supplies to the top of Cadillac was a challenge, and after more than an hour driving from the college, I was sluggish, tired, but ready. I knew she would be worth every minute. The hike and the drive had at least allowed time to fantasize, play it over in my head, to muse on the sights, the smells, and the sounds of the simmering act I was about to perform.

When Becky and I reached the summit, the sun was still another hour from breaking the seaward horizon. I carried her to a flat spot of granite and laid her down on the rock, cold from the night's darkness. There were no hikers. Scattered peaks of the park were all around and beautiful, though sightseeing wasn't why I was there. I pulled out a drill from my pack, drilled two holes and fastened I-bolts, just like in Colorado with Serena. I then tied Gordian knots around her wrists, attached the other ends of the rope to the I-bolts, then drilled twice more into the rock near her feet.

When she was secure, it was time to work. I walked back to my pack and unloaded a smaller case from within. The case was lined with insulation, dense insulation. Sustaining temperature was important on such a brisk morning. I stood above Becky Fairchild and looked at her naked body; nothing could stop me, but I knew that.

I first took out a blade, just three inches but razor sharp. I slit her stomach left to right. The sensitive flesh filleted open exposing gory insides. The smiling wound breathed steam into the morning air in captivating little puffs.

As I watched silently, I wanted to tell her to calm herself. People suffer, and nothing makes it fair. It's simple. I looked into Becky's eyes as I gathered that which would transform her life. I grabbed two coals from the insulated chamber. They were scalding hot and sizzling. Thick gloves helped exclude me from the pain. The coals billowed steam, and I held them for a moment in my hands and looked out at the view.

Dawn was beginning to fill the world, and there I stood with a burning orb glowing hot in each hand. The morning sky glistened reds, yellows and the deep blues of night. The ocean reflected the colors and skewed them into an abstractionist's work.

I then placed the coals inside Becky Fairchild's waiting stomach. The coals seared and scorched her soft tissue and forced her to madness. Wild screams and shrieks came from her as she writhed in the chains. I could hear her insides sizzling, popping like sauce on a burner. I smelled her flesh char as the fringes of her wound melted away. Her eyes moved wildly in their sockets. The drug that kept her docile hadn't affected her pain receptors. That'd be too easy. It was a bad day for Becky, but a beautiful day for me. I even enjoyed the hike down, more so after seeing a family on their way up. They were in for quite a surprise.

CHAPTER 41

Aurelia woke at 8:18am, easing in from a dream world of bright colors, the sights of spring, the smells of grass and the sound of birds chirp-chirping away. It took her a minute to rise out of it, to let her eyes take in what was the real world, and to see what had woken her to begin with.

Steam lifted from two cups of coffee on a table opposite the bed. She hadn't noticed a table there before. Wait, of course she had, but it'd been filled with books, books and an assistant. Now, the assistant and the books had been replaced, and when she squinted groggy eyes she could see two plates, each with heaping scrambled eggs, sausage, golden-crisp hash browns; fresh pineapple and strawberries were in a bowl between the plates and coffees.

She wiped the sleep from her eyes and finally met Elijah's gaze.

He'd just finished setting things down and hadn't noticed her waking.

"G-morning, Doc. I heard you're allowed some activity today. Time to celebrate. Want to sit at the big kid table?" She stared at his smile and into his face as he closed the distance between them.

"I would *love* to sit at the big kid table! I'm so sick of being in bed."

"Then let's get you over here. I figured we could start with this and ignore what we'll need to do later."

Aurelia agreed.

Because before long, they'd be questioning the woman downstairs, the one excavated from the coffin at the cabin. The moment was bittersweet. On one hand, they were getting closer to the Poetic Murderer. On the other, they were about to crash headlong into their first survivor. She'd been through a lot. Not many people have been buried alive. *Could* she help? How much harm was done, mental or physical? What could she recall at all?

Those questions were put aside.

"I know you never settle on one thing," Elijah said. "So I wasn't sure what to get you to eat. Since *I* always get some variation of the same thing, I ordered two. If you don't like it, that's why there's fruit. If you don't like fruit, then I'll grab you some gourmet eats from the hospital cafeteria."

"Hospital food *does* sound tempting, but this will have to do. I don't want to walk all the way down there," she said, smiling big. "How long have you been awake, Elijah Warren?"

"Not too long. With that chair as a bed, it's hard to sleep in," he said. "I saw a breakfast place when I drove in last night, so I figured I could surprise you." As he spoke, he was helping her from bed and into one of the two chairs at the table. She hadn't weighted her foot in days, and it throbbed. Thankfully, Elijah had scooped her up, had her cradled in his arms, which were wrapped under her, hers wrapped around his neck. He set her down in the chair across from his.

"Thanks for doing all this. By the way, do you have some sort of breakfast establishment radar? And are you always this kind to the women in your life?"

Elijah laughed softly and said, "I don't have any women in my life."

"I'll bet Mom gets something special on Mother's Day."

A silence existed for a moment.

"My mom actually passed when I was a kid. But if she *was* around, she would *for sure* get something special on Mother's Day."

He said these words strangely, like they weren't his words, like they weren't being spoken, but like they were easing out of him unconsciously. Aurelia could figure this sentiment only as saddened nostalgia, a thick blanket of it that took his voice and his words away and out of him and into the world.

"I'm sorry, Elijah."

She paused before asking a question that she couldn't decide if she should ask.

"Did something happen?"

Another small silence existed.

"An accident. Kind of. I'd prefer to continue in the direction of eggs and sausage, and fruit, and coffee…and celebrating you getting out of bed." He smiled a bit and looked at her past his paper coffee cup, taking a long drink from it.

"I'm sorry, Elijah."

She didn't push the issue.

She'd buried her own tumultuous childhood. It'd been nearly fifteen years since she'd mentioned either of *her* parents, and she changed the subject.

"Holy shit this coffee is good," she said taking a drink. "It's interesting how coffee can incite feeling. I always *feel* better after my first drink of coffee in the morning."

Elijah nodded his head and took a bite of eggs. "Me too. As you know, I over-enjoy my mornings, so I definitely understand. It's weird that taste or smell can do that."

They talked and enjoyed every minute. They took their time. They knew the next thing on the agenda wouldn't be pleasant, even if it *did* provide the next step in the case.

As they were finishing, Elijah sat back in his chair and folded his hands behind his head. He stared around the room, looking up and past the ceiling, past the sky and the stars and into what was beyond. At least that's how it looked. Aurelia had seen him do it before.

She wondered what was going on in that mind of his.

She then got lost in herself, thinking about how they'd ended up in the hospital room having breakfast. Not long ago, Elijah Warren had been a guy from work that annoyed the hell out of her. She didn't like his sarcastic tone or aloof disposition. She didn't understand how a man so astute could be so indifferent, such a blunt ass. They'd worked within a hundred feet of each other but rarely (if ever) spoke. They'd been barely acquaintances, fueled by mutual dislike, at least mutual disquiet, and now she could only think of him being by her side.

She wondered exactly when her opinion of him turned around.

It took a moment's thought, but she had an answer. It was that winter's night north of New York City, the night in Grand View On Hudson, the snowstorm and the shootout with Charles Larson. Whatever had gone on that night had begun to open her eyes, show her some things that were different about Elijah Warren. His aloof confidence was sexy, his sarcasm somehow funny. Plus, he was less of an asshole than she thought. She saw through his disposition, past the standoffish neutrality, and found why it existed. At least she was beginning to think so.

She thought about how their *partnership* would end if they started a *relationship*.

She didn't quite understand it, but she didn't care.

And she didn't care that she didn't care. *That* was foreign to her.

Crazy what can happen in three months.

Elijah's eyes kept about the room, looking at nothing in particular but thinking of Aurelia. She sat across from him after a bedridden few days, still gorgeous as hell. How had he never (until recently) recognized how attracted he was to her? He looked across the table, gazed into her brown eyes, and thought back to their kiss in Colorado.

It had happened quickly and he never even got to mention it to her. He remembered standing idly outside his room after she had entered hers. He hadn't known what to think, but was happy, maybe for the first time since he was a kid. He knew, sitting in that hospital chair, that as long as he had anything to say about it, Aurelia *wasn't* walking out of his life.

His mind flashed back to the dream he'd had a few days before on his flight.

SHE

WILL

DIE

He pushed the words from his mind and refocused himself. He was suddenly back in detective mode. He knew he needed to catch the Poetic Murderer before something happened to Aurelia. Just a dream or not, Elijah had a bad feeling about the puzzle becoming more personal than it already had.

He worried further that with each passing minute another person was going to be found, cut up or skinned or whatever was planned next.

He got his attention back to Aurelia. After talking about their game plan, Elijah went for a walk, and Aurelia showered and changed out of her hospital-issue "dress." Even if she wasn't *leaving* the hospital, she wanted to get back to normalcy in all the ways she could.

Adams had called Elijah while on his walk; he'd informed him of the girl's name, Gina Lowbank. He'd said he was happy about them still being alive. He said they needed to, "hurry your asses up and find this prick." His voice wavered in a way Elijah had never heard.

Elijah returned and found Aurelia in one of her usual outfits. The crutches beneath each arm were the lone difference. As he stood before her, looking at her from the doorway, he felt something, a peregrine wholeness. He'd started to feel it in the past months, but having her back was something consuming, something that changed the way he stood and felt and the way he saw the world. He held the door open for her to exit and couldn't muster words until she'd passed.

"You look nice," he said a bit too loudly, his voice echoing down the hall, turning heads.

She said, "Thank you," and smiled at him from the middle of the hallway.

Eli and Aurelia crutched and walked the hospital toward Gina Lowbank's room. They knocked on Gina's door and waited for her to invite them in.

"Good morning, Gina." Elijah spoke first.

"Good morning, sir." She responded with words but barely spoke them.

Gina looked like she'd been in a street fight triathlon.

Elijah thought this, then thought about how strange his mind was.

Although better than the day before, Gina was malnourished and dehydrated. Her eyelids hung and her shoulders touched her waist. As Aurelia made eye contact with her for the first time, she couldn't *not* feel a connection. One thing was certain. The Poetic Murderer left quite a particular mark.

"Hi, Gina. I'm Aurelia Blanc, and this is my partner Elijah Warren. We're detectives with the FBI and are working this case." She reached out her hand to shake Gina's.

The girl immediately found comfort in Aurelia and shook her hand. She couldn't explain the sentiment, but felt connected to her.

"We've got some questions if it's OK?" Aurelia continued.

Gina uttered nothing, but nodded two faint nods. Elijah wondered what she was like prior to the abduction. Was she equally timorous, or was it compliments of the Poetic Murderer?

"Gina, we're both so sorry that you're here dealing with this. We truly are," Elijah said. "And we understand that this will be difficult to recall. However, any information you can give might help us catch the man who did this. Believe me, *when* we catch him, he's gonna answer for everything." Gina looked into Elijah's deep eyes and found comfort somewhere. She believed him. She could see that he desperately wanted to catch the man who wore black.

After a long pause, she began slowly. "I was driving to work. I manage a local fast food place. I saw him on the road with his car's hood up. I had a couple minutes so I stopped. I didn't have it in park and he was moving to my window. I rolled it down he was really nice, but spoke really slowly. I guess creepy in hindsight."

"What did he say?" asked Aurelia

"He asked if I had jumper cables, which I didn't. Then he asked me for a ride to town so he could call a tow truck. I know I shouldn't have let him in. I was trying to do the right thing." Tears welled up in the nineteen-year-old's eyes. She kept her chin on her chest and her gaze toward the floor.

"Gina, you didn't do anything wrong. You were just trying to help. Unfortunately, the world is a place where people prey on kindness," Elijah said. "What happened next?"

"I let him in. He didn't seem dangerous. He was in his late twenties or early thirties. He had really green eyes, black hair. I was attracted to him." Her words muffled and faded as she began to cry. The detectives waited patiently. "Our drive to town was fifteen minutes, but after a mile or so he started talking. He'd been silent up to that p-p-point."

Gina was tormented recalling the event's incipience, and it was far from over.

"Take your time, Gina. We're not going anywhere unless you want us to," Aurelia said.

"He told me my life was about to change. I was part of something bigger than myself and what I was before. Then he told me that if I didn't do exactly as he said he was going to carve out my eyes, kill me, then kill my family." She stopped suddenly as the tears began to spill faster.

Aurelia thought about the girl from Portland, and her hypothesis on why she might have killed herself. Gina's story corroborated.

"Your family is safe now, Gina. And so are you," Aurelia said. "We have two officers at your parents' house. Elijah requested our boss make the arrangements when they spoke this morning."

"Thank you," she whispered. "So I told him I would do whatever he wanted. I didn't want them to get hurt. He told me I wasn't meant to die. Well, he said it wasn't in his hands. He said it was in yours."

Elijah and Aurelia looked up from scribbling in notepads, replying their confusion in unison.

"He told me that two people named Elijah and Aurelia were the only ones who could decide if I lived or died."

Elijah suddenly understood how she'd known his name back in the helicopter.

"He said he'd be 'fascinated' to see what happened. I was so scared. I've never met anyone like him. He seemed smart, almost eccentric. Half the time I couldn't even understand him. It was too abstract, too far-fetched. He kept talking about a lack of novelty in the world, about 'congruence in humanity.' He talked like people didn't matter."

"How much more time were you together?" asked Elijah.

"He told me to turn toward the Smokies, and after we got out of town he asked me to pull over. He said that I'd be temporarily knocked out. He told me I'd be unconscious several hours. I'll never forget what he said next.

"'Listen carefully and you may make it through this alive. You will wake up beneath the ground. You will be in a coffin with a tank to support your breathing. The harder you breathe, the faster you die. If you remain calm, you live longer, and if you stay alive long enough, you may find yourself back amongst the living.' " Elijah scribbled feverishly.

"All I could do was nod my head," Gina said. "I remember every word he said. How could anyone forget? He seemed to choose them so carefully. I didn't know what else to do. I don't even know how he drugged me."

"Did he say anything else?" Aurelia said. "Anything that might hint at where he was going next?"

"Yes. Before I was knocked out he had me memorize something to tell you."

The detectives looked at one another, then back to Gina.

"What was it?" Elijah said.

"A riddle. I don't know the answer. He just told me to remember it. I wrote it down when I got to the hospital last night." Gina pulled a small piece of paper from her bedside table and passed it to them. They each read it twice, then looked up from esoteric stanzas.

Storm clouds collide
Injustice...Arise
The path to righteousness
A son's nightmare
A family's despair
Self-given purpose parts the seas of logic and reason
Not as it seems
Requiem of dreams
Find the connection that brings you to me

"Like I said, I don't know what it means. I'm sorry," Gina said through more tears.

Elijah sat, again frustrated. He hadn't any idea what to say, but spoke his last words to Gina.

"You don't have to be sorry, Gina. We've been chasing him for months and are just as confused as you. If you think of anything else, here is my number. If you'd prefer to speak with Detective Blanc, her room is up on the fourth floor. Contact us anytime."

Elijah turned and left.

Aurelia looked at the Gina, still weeping. Before crutching out of the room Aurelia leaned down to give her a hug. As she did, she spoke.

"Gina, we're getting the man who did these things to us. I'm going to be here in this hospital with you, and Elijah is going to find him. He's very good at his job, and I know he's getting close."

When Gina heard "us," she looked into Aurelia's eyes, and they spoke without speaking. Gina hadn't realized the crutches were from the Poetic Murderer. As much as Gina didn't wish ill upon people, she was relieved to have someone she trusted in the same shoes she was in. She thanked her and Aurelia stood and followed behind Elijah.

CHAPTER 42

Elijah had one trip to make that day. He hoped Portland wouldn't occupy much time.

Thanks to Aurelia, the local police had re-questioned the café employees, and Elijah had new information.

He felt he needed to find something in Portland. He didn't know what, but he needed to find *something*. Afterward, he planned on flying back to Tennessee to check on Aurelia.

He would shortly discover that divergent plans had been made for him.

Elijah had never been to Portland. Upon arrival, Riff shook him awake with a bundle of laughter and a mouth full of whiskey.

Elijah had been dreaming of a simpler life.

Elijah looked out upon the city and the surrounding mountain peaks. Mt. Hood stood, as always, just east of the city. Its unique form caught his attention as he walked down the aircraft's stairs. He was appreciative that he gained three hours between Tennessee and Portland. It was only 10am. He loved traveling from east to west. He always had thought about how days should be longer. Twenty-four hours just didn't seem like enough.

He arrived at the police station almost without noticing. He'd spaced out and just gone through the motions. The phenomenon of driving, only to find you were on autopilot, is a strange and uncomfortable sensation. He shook it off, but logged away that he needed a break, time off.

Upon Elijah's arrival at the station, everyone had been pleasant, and a squirrelly little man led him to where he could talk with Pam, a woman in her forties who'd been with the Portland police department almost twenty years. She was absent at first, but after a literal minute of waiting, she arrived with two cups of black coffee.

Across the conference table sat Pam. Elijah was appreciative for the coffee and made small talk about the city. After they'd settled into the familiar, albeit uncomfortable, police station conference chairs, he began asking about the witness from the café. Pam retold what she'd been told.

"The busboy, Dan, was who recognized him. He remembered seeing him at Priscilla's table. He described him word-for-word as Aurelia said someone might. Handsome, green eyes, black hair, a rugged demeanor. He said that he spoke painfully slow, seemed creepy to him. He said Priscilla was intrigued, really wanted him. She kept walking back to the kitchen talking about him. How interesting he was. Apparently Dan was the only coherent one working. No one else recognized him."

"Did he overhear anything else?" Elijah said.

"Apparently he heard about their evening plans. He didn't remember where they were going for dinner, but he could remember where he was staying. The Portland Manor. It's a hotel not far from First National Bank Tower. That's where she jumped."

Elijah sat, listening carefully. He couldn't gather much from what he was being told. He knew that the man wearing black wouldn't pay with a credit card, and he knew he wouldn't have left prints anywhere. Elijah kept on, looking for the single detail that would connect things. After an hour with Pam, he gave up and figured he'd exhausted what the busboy had to tell. Someone saw him, could describe him, but little more. The hotel was promising, and he hoped he'd find something there, but feared it would be the same ambiguous search he'd been part of for the past months. After leaving the police station he planned on investigating both the Portland Manor and Priscilla's apartment. He decided to start with the hotel.

Of course the front desk agent recognized the description.

"Real strange guy? Dressed in black? Moved real slow? Yep. He was here."

Unfortunately, this information was followed by irrelevance, useless silence that helped no one. The killer had not spoken a word more than needed and had paid in cash upon arrival. He hadn't left a name.

Elijah inspected the building and the Poetic Murderer's room. He'd not shifted the covers on the bed and hadn't turned on the shower. Elijah was disappointed, but almost expected it. Finding nothing of interest, he headed to Priscilla De Luca's apartment across town.

Priscilla clearly wasn't making much at the diner. She lived on the southeast side of the city, across the river from where she worked. These neighborhoods had the highest property crime rates in the city, and topping the list for the country. It boils down to one out of every two people affected, astounding for a city of generally good safety. No one chooses this neighborhood if it's not due to economics.

Elijah drove through the Buckman neighborhoods, scanning addresses as he went. For the area's reputation, it didn't look dangerous. Elijah thought to himself how an area notorious for property crimes typically looked different than an area notorious for violent crimes. Property crimes meant people wanted to steal or vandalize. Violence created a whole different atmosphere. One trip to Cabrini Green on Chicago's north side exposed that reality.

Now, he was south of the Buchman neighborhoods, and quaint streets were lined with matured trees; unique little houses sat at the turns. The Explorer rolled slowly to a stop in front of an old Victorian, turned apartments just a few years ago. It had a big front porch with no furniture. The shutters hung haphazardly to the sides of mismatched windows. To the left of the porch was a large bay window, and on the second floor above, the same. Above that, stood a small cupola, a tower typical of Victorian architecture. He stood scanning it, taking it all in. Dark blue paint was chipping away; pieces fluttered to the ground like leaves as the wind blew across.

He'd procured the key from Pam at the local PD. The front door to the building was unlocked and led into a tall atrium that gave access to both the upstairs apartments and the ones on the ground floor. He began his ascent to floor two.

The rickety staircase showed the home's age, matched the paint on its outside. Each ascending footstep created a new moan or groan from the misshapen stairs. Uneven heating and cooling had warped the wood to the point of necessary replacement. At the top, he continued forward down the short hallway. Only four apartments existed, two on each side of the hall. He walked to the end and turned left, the crime scene tape still slung across the door. The rusted lock took a bit of manipulation to permit the key's entry. The door swung in. He squeezed his way underneath the vibrant tape and closed the door behind him.

The apartment was homey. It only consisted of a small living space that spilled into a kitchen, and a bedroom was beyond that through a small door. The living area was well put together, simple and tasteful. The furnishings seemed refurbished antiques, but based on what Elijah knew of Priscilla, he assumed they were well-searched thrift store finds. Resilient looking could pay off at those places.

The kitchen had only a tiny table with one place setting. The living room had no TV, but books sat on a beautiful bookshelf. Ornate lion heads guarded the top two corners of the shelf. A fleur-de-lis was carved into the middle, directly between the two lions. Mostly classics lined the shelves.

Elijah mumbled to himself as he scanned the titles, then turned back from the shelf and continued through the apartment. The kitchen cupboards were nearly empty, as was the refrigerator. Elijah checked each drawer and cabinet. He moved to the bedroom and looked through the closet, then through unimpressive dressers and underneath the bed.

Priscilla seemed reserved. Her clothes were conservative, as were the pictures that hung on the walls. He left the bedroom without success. He stood in the doorway, looking out toward the living and cooking areas.

"What am I missing?" His words trailed off as he contemplated. His forehead crinkled forward and his eyebrows turned down towards the middle of his face.

"What the fuck am I missing?" His patience dwindled. He looked toward the entryway.

To the side of the door sat a picture frame on the floor. Elijah approached it and found that a mirror was inside. *Curious.* It looked pristine, new, out of place. *Why is it on the ground?* He held it in his hands, looking at his reflection as he thought. His face slowly tilted upwards and toward the blank wall directly in front of him.

A lone nail was obscurely pounded into the wall. It wasn't centered. It wasn't level with anything. Elijah turned and looked at the other pictures hung throughout the apartment. Each of them was hung carefully and systematically. Why was this one nailed so haphazardly? Elijah hung the mirror and was again looking back into his own blue eyes. He looked past his reflection and saw exactly what the mirror was meant for him to see: the ornate bookshelf. He whirled around.

"Of course!"

The craftsmanship was analogous with that of the chair from the Indiana farmhouse.

He moved toward it and began examining more carefully.

He suddenly felt cold and nervous.

Had he missed things like this at the other crime scenes?

He pushed the thought from his mind. It couldn't help now.

He ran his fingers around the bookshelf. He leaned around the corners and peered behind it. He finally sat down in front of it; the lions stared into him as if determining his fate. He scanned the books lining the shelves. The bookcase rose three feet in height and spanned four in width. Elijah read the names of the books out loud. He stopped suddenly. Every book pressed lightly against the back of the bookcase, except one.

"Acadia National Park." He spoke the name of the book again after removing it. He opened it and began flipping the pages. On page thirty-seven, he stopped. The heading at the top read "Cadillac Mountain." Halfway down the page were three lines of text forming a haiku. The traditional Japanese poetry was generally themed in nature, the first line having five syllables, the middle having seven, and the final matching the first, with five. It was written in immaculate cursive, and was written in dark black ink, off to the side of the printed text.

Where the sun first hits
Back to where it all began
One more to be found

Elijah read the page about Cadillac Mountain.

"'Where the sun first hits,'" Elijah said out loud. He quickly learned that this particular mountain was the first place in the US that the sun touches each morning. His heart pounded in vivacious bursts. He could hear it echoing in his ears, feel it in his wrists. He retrieved his mobile phone and dialed Adams. Riff was prompted and prepared for departure. Elijah took the book and headed toward the door. After another phone call, Pam had a team ready to search the bookcase and its contents more scrupulously.

The wheels of Riff's plane left the ground at 1:18pm with a heading for Maine and Acadia National Park.

CHAPTER 43

A t around 10am Tennessee time, Gina, the woman buried alive, ventured to Aurelia's hospital room. It had been a long morning of self-reflection since the detectives left. Their questions had gotten her imagination working, and she went back over all she'd been through. She thought back on every word the Poetic Murderer spoke. She was over-thinking things and could hardly know *what* to think. She knocked hesitantly on Aurelia's door, and a soft voice ushered her in. Aurelia sat at a circular table, dressed as she was hours earlier, papers scattered haphazardly around. When Gina gained her view, they each smiled gently.

"Ms. Blanc, may I come in?"

"Gina, I'm Aurelia, and of course you can. How are you feeling?"

"I'm OK. Just going over everything in my head. You know? Everything he said to me and everything about everything. I can't stop obsessing over it. I can't help but feel like if I can remember something new, or think of something in a different way, it may matter."

Gina lingered in the doorway.

"I know the feeling," Aurelia answered. "That's exactly what Elijah and I have been doing. It's been since early this year. Starts to own you, doesn't it?"

"Apparently so. I guess I was just wondering if I could sit with you, or talk with you? I don't think being alone with my thoughts is doing me any good. I guess I don't know what I'm wondering."

"I understand completely. The worst case scenario is we think all day and then drown away sorrows in wine," Aurelia said.

Gina laughed and wondered how Aurelia could have such a positive view on life. Who tracks down serial killers for a living and remains so compassionate, so realistic? Gina didn't have answers to these questions. Nor did Aurelia, if the questions would have been asked.

"So, what are you doing?" Gina finally said as she sat down opposite her at the table.

"I'm going through all the case files, looking at some different books that may relate to what he's doing, ripping my hair out, and trying not to become an alcoholic."

Gina's eyes loosened up and her face relaxed.

Aurelia smiled when she realized her joke had landed.

"Elijah is in Portland following up another lead, and since I can't move from this hospital, I'm doing research. When you're dealing with a killer as intelligent as this guy, you can't underestimate what you may find in a book."

Time passed. Gina sat and Aurelia read through the case files, through the Keats literature. Gina observed. Aurelia didn't mind, and it seemed that having company was improving Gina's mood. Occasionally they'd make small talk about one thing or another.

Aurelia kept reassuring herself that progress was being made, despite not feeling so.

She recalled successes from past days to keep motivated.

She'd already solved the anagram left at Mario's parents' house, figured out the coffin riddle, found all the different Keats poems and developed theories on why they were left, reconnected Pam with the witnesses at the café in Portland and was now continuing the ostensibly never ending search.

Although not satisfied, she was proud of what she'd achieved from her hospital room, disconnected from it all. She hadn't heard from Elijah yet and hoped he was finding something worthwhile in Portland. At 4:18pm Tennessee time, her mobile phone rang. It was Director Adams with new information.

CHAPTER 44

W hile flying to Acadia, Elijah contacted the Bar Harbor police department. He informed them of a possible murder near Cadillac Mountain. They informed *him* that he was late to the party. Earlier that morning, before daybreak, a woman was found dead at the summit. She'd suffered a full-width laceration across the belly, and burning coals had been placed inside her.

A family had seen the young woman first.

The father rushed back down the mountain.

Composure, even in the strongest men and women, didn't stand a chance against the expression left on the woman's face. It spoke her anguish, screamed her pain, and obliterated the first responder's composure. A fifth year officer keeled forward as he came up and into the sun atop the mountain peak. The woman's mouth lay open, her eyes bulging and fiery with blood-red veins. A gaping void hung open across her stomach, still smoldering and sizzling as the coals began to cool. The edges of the wound had peeled back away from the mess, white and black and charred and still melting. Small pops and a perpetual simmering emanated from the large gap. It was grotesque, like looking into hell's violent mouth, dripping flesh and liquefying ribbons of large and small intestine, liver and lungs, piles of gore, glowing hot and oozing, dripping from the bottom of the yawning slit. It was something the responding officers and the Holzin family would never forget.

Elijah's head dropped with hearing the news. He had made progress, just not fast enough. Briefly losing composure, a primordial scream escaped his lips and filled the plane as it rocketed overtop the Great Lakes. The Poetic Murderer was again at least one step ahead.

Elijah picked the phone back up and redialed his contact at the Bar Harbor PD.

"If you ID the girl, contact me immediately. I want to know where she lived! I need to know right fucking now, because if she isn't from Bar Harbor, I'm going somewhere else."

The officer acknowledged the detective's wishes and apologized for not yet knowing.

Elijah's anger wasn't with the PD, but his sentiment was clear, even over the phone.

A whiskey emptied itself into Elijah.

The local officer called back just a moment after hanging up.

"Warren," he said answering the aircraft's phone.

"Detective Warren, I just had a thought. The girl's wearing earrings with the University of Maine's logo. I bet she goes there. Even if we don't know who she is, that may be where you want to start."

Captain Riff sent the plane lurching southward, what Elijah assumed would have been a *small* adjustment, and they were headed toward the University's private landing strip. Elijah thought of the college kids that flew home on their mommy and daddy's private planes. He ignored that distraction, and hoped that by the time he arrived at the University he'd have an ID on the girl.

He ruminated, and an idea struck him like lightning.

He picked the phone back up.

Shortly after, he had record of the missing persons currently enrolled at the University of Maine. The most recent was listed a few hours former, and not yet official. The buffer period was yet to pass, but a woman named Becky Fairchild hadn't made it back to her apartment the night before; she was last seen leaving a fraternity party.

Elijah's heart thudded in his chest. He requested that the information be sent to the on-scene officers for confirmation. He may have been too late to save Becky Fairchild, but if it *was* her he was closer behind than ever before. He hoped that his hunch was right.

He allowed himself to doze as the airplane continued toward the University of Maine.

CHAPTER 45

"This is Warren."

His words were groggy from an in-flight nap.

"It's her. It's Becky Fairchild. We've got her address."

Elijah dropped the phone and felt adrenaline begin coursing. His intuition had been correct. He looked out the window and saw that they were descending. He picked back up the phone, wrote down the relevant information and hung up after thanking the officer. He didn't know what to expect, but every sense was firing. He knew that he was close, close behind the Poetic Murderer.

Another idea came to him.

The man wearing black *had* to be staging clues after the murders. It couldn't be the other way around. Could it? He reflected back. It was nearing the end of March and the weeks prior had been a whirlwind.

He and Aurelia began working the case three months ago. Their success tracking down Charles Larson had culminated in Aurelia saving his life, and ultimately, a partnership. After the Larson job, they began work on the farmhouse killing. After the stay in Nashville, they returned home to New York with intrigue and frustration. Many weeks passed with nothing new, and then out of nowhere, they were called to Ouray to continue like no time had passed. That brought them to the cabin in Tennessee, then to the hospital and to Maine and Portland for Elijah.

Elijah wondered how long the Poetic Murderer had been calculating. It had to be a year or two in the making; the timeline for the victims was still hazy; it gnarled, and the disparate locations didn't help. It was extraordinarily well thought out, yet arbitrary and chaotic. Some things made sense, others not at all. He still couldn't see the big picture.

On the plane, he had written down an address.

He was racing toward it.

An Explorer's tires squealed as they skidded around another corner. He didn't quite know *why* he was in such a hurry, but he hadn't yet felt close enough to rush *anywhere*.

Presently, he *knew* he needed to. He could feel it.

The address ran through his head like a stock market update.

4299 Garver Street… 4299 Garver Street… 4299 Garver Street…

A mundane apartment building approached from the left as the vehicle slowed. Elijah parked and felt inside his jacket, reassuring himself with the presence of his firearm. He looked down the street, behind his own car then back to the front past the hood. He ran his eyes over the building before getting out. The red brick was worn, typical for most college housing. It stood three stories high and was narrow, sprawling back away from the street. Judging by the windows, Elijah guessed it had sixty rooms per floor, thirty per side. As he approached, he noticed two stairwells, one at each end of the building, close and far from the street. They allowed access to the halls.

The final part of the address was committed to memory.

Apartment 322.

He assumed this would lead him to the third floor.

He approached the building, eyes scanning. He turned to scale the nearest set of stairs, which were accessed from the sidewalk. Using the handrail, he whipped himself through the turns. He reached the third floor and continued through an open doorway and toward apartment 322. The hallway induced vertigo, and loomed before him.

He took note of the first door's number, printed on a worn golden plate: 370.

Sixty wasn't a bad guess.

He headed toward the other end of the building. As he paced forward, he noticed a man heading in *his* direction from the far end of the hall.

But it barely got his attention. He was focused on what he'd do when he got to the door.

Kick it in?

Knock?

He didn't really know. He hadn't been able to get keys from the locals yet.

After pondering his options, he noticed again the man walking toward him. He'd hardly moved, and Elijah had covered a quarter of the hall.

Elijah's eyes widened as he studied the man wearing black opposite him. As he reached for his gun, a bullet went whickering by his ear and penetrated the stairwell's wall behind him.

The Poetic Murderer turned and ran quickly away down the hall. He moved like a sprinter. Or maybe it was just regular speed. Was it the contrast that made the difference?

Elijah crashed to the ground and fired his Glock twice, bullets slicing the air of the hallway, the Poetic Murderer retreating to the stairs as a bullet tears through his arm. He stumbled into the wall but kept his pace swift.

"Son of a bitch!" Elijah shouted and pushed himself up from the floor. He headed in the direction of the staircase from which he'd come. His heart was pounding and his eyes were focused. He had been waiting for this.

He swung his head into the second floor's hallway, then continued.

Beginning down the last set of stairs, he slowed his speed. He checked the lowest hallway then moved toward the building's exit. He eased open the door and looked around the corner. The opposite end of the building ended in dense trees. The man wearing black couldn't have made it to the street before Elijah made it down the stairs. He had to be in the woods. Elijah covered the distance using parked cars and the structures of the building as intermediate cover. His .40 caliber pistol was firmly settled in the grasp of his right hand. His finger hovered steadily above the trigger, knowing that it'd only need to travel twelve millimeters to put a hole in that piece of shit.

He *couldn't* be far behind.

When he approached the woods he scanned the best he could. The trees were dense, but he found small droplets of blood. He tried to pull back his view, to almost *unfocus* his eyes, and survey things generally.

He caught a glimpse of movement.

He moved quietly, thinking only about killing the Poetic Murderer.

Elijah didn't know how hidden he was. His feet moved silently (he thought) through the vegetation. He used the trees as cover and tried to remain unseen. Looking ahead, he caught glimpses of the black clothed figure skating in and out of view.

A bullet burst into the tree beside Elijah, splinters somersaulting from the back of it. Two more bullets followed, skimming over Elijah's head as he dove down and behind a fallen tree. As he lay prone on the earth, he looked into the woods to relocate the man wearing black.

He noticed a subtle shift in some brush across a sloping ravine.

He fired the Glock into the dense foliage and heard snapping twigs.

The man emerged with a jolt.

Elijah adjusted his aim and fired again.

Fuck!

The man gained cover and moved out of sight.

Elijah pursued the Poetic Murderer for another quarter mile before the trees ended in concrete.

Elijah stood tall and looked at six lanes of highway, sprawling in each direction.

The man wearing black had gotten away.

CHAPTER 46

After calling Adams from his mobile, which he'd left in the car because of its weight and size, Elijah headed back into the apartment building. Adams called in a search crew to scour the surrounding area, a helicopter as well as dogs and a S.W.A.T. unit. The crime scene team arrived within minutes as well.

The look on Elijah's face kept people from speaking to him.

It was the angriest Elijah Warren had been in a very long time, maybe since childhood. He hadn't yet put his gun back into its holster. He held it at his side and squeezed the life out of it, walked his way back to the apartment from the Explorer. Cruisers were pulling up alongside ambulances and other emergency vehicles. The afternoon sky was filled with blues and reds, and Elijah was an orb of anger as he broke through the crowds.

Elijah walked up the stairs.

He moved easily, each step exact and quickly gaining ground.

This time, when he approached the door, he knew *exactly* what he was going to do.

With one powerful kick the door smashed against the inside wall of the apartment and ripped from its hinges. It hung askance.

Elijah glared around the apartment. He noticed an elegant desk, carved from dark wood, in front of the window opposite the door.

He walked to it and began his search.

The drawers were empty, but carved into the top, in plain sight, was another haiku.

Where we all must go
Where the ocean meets the sky
I'll be welcomed home

His rage was fueled. The killer had left his next clue in plain view, as if to taunt. He knew he'd need Aurelia's help, especially after the day's events. His thinking wasn't logical enough to start solving another riddle.

Killing the man wearing black was solely on his mind.

He memorized the traditional Japanese poem and called Aurelia.

"Aurelia, I've got a new poem."

"Elijah, what's wrong? Are you OK?"

"I'm in Maine. He just got away, Aurelia. I fucking let him get away."

"Elijah, I'm sure you didn't *let* him get away. Are you OK though? Are you hurt?"

"No. But I fucking shot him. We'll at least have a good blood sample. Maybe we'll have more luck than we did with the hair sample."

"So what happened?" she asked.

"I got an ID on the latest vic' and found out where she lived. I was walking toward the girl's apartment and he was walking toward me. It was a long hallway. I saw him coming and didn't look closely enough to realize it was him. I was just thinking about what to do when I got there. I looked up and realized. He shot at me and took off."

"Wait, Elijah. Are you telling me that the slowest murderer in the world outran you?"

"Shut it, lady. And not exactly. I shot him in the arm as he headed down the stairs. I followed him into the woods behind the apartment, and we exchanged a few more bullets. I lost him there, maybe to the highway, maybe in the trees. I don't know."

"Elijah, this is huge. We have another DNA sample *and* another poem. Who knows what else we'll find in that apartment. Or maybe the chopper will pick him up! Really, who knows! I'm proud of you, Elijah."

"Thanks. I hope you're right. So now I need your help with this poem. You're better at this stuff."

She could hear his frustration; it came pouring through the phone line.

"Elijah Warren, has being shot at made you nicer?"

"I doubt it…highly."

"Doesn't hurt to ask, though I didn't figure."

Per usual, they laughed, despite the circumstances. He was immediately feeling better about how the day had unfolded. Aurelia was right. He may not have gotten him, but the Poetic Murderer was closer than ever.

lijah took the red eye, commercial, despite his vivid objections.

Aurelia stared at the information he had collected over the past days. She was up to speed on everything that happened both in Portland, and in Maine. The specifics of the Cadillac Mountain incident had rocked her to the core. She didn't think the Poetic Murderer could do much else to shock her, to twist her insides. She had underestimated.

Why go to such lengths to make someone suffer?

She thought back to each of the murders and answered her own question.

It's his method. Whatever he's trying to prove, ultra-violence serves a purpose. She didn't yet know the purpose, but in the late hours of the night, she studied the haikus found in the latest victims' homes.

Where the sun first hits
Back to where it all began
One more to be found

Where we all must go
Where the ocean meets the sky
I'll be welcomed home

She was feeling the same frustration that Elijah had felt the day before in Portland, the frustration of ambiguity, a tangled quest with a conclusion that seemed out of reach. She again had no idea what to look for. She was sick of arbitrary looking. At the late hour, she was beginning to feel the effects of reading case files since morning. Her eyes hung low and were kept open by rigid willpower.

Elijah was still wired from his day as he boarded the miserable jet along with the other hundred passengers. He cursed Director Adams for making him take the flight.

Perfect departure time or not, it isn't worth the saved money. Where in the hell is Riff? He cursed and walked to his seat, glaring ubiquitously. He at least was sitting by a window, which he preferred, but his neighbors needed three seats, despite only purchasing two. As he squeezed the armrest down between him and the large man to his side, he ordered a double whiskey from the passing stewardess.

After its quick descent, Elijah went careening into much needed sleep.

Aurelia finally moved from the table to the bed. Her body was giving up for the day.

Not long after she fell asleep, a man wearing a brand new black jacket walked into the University of Tennessee's hospital. He walked slowly in the direction of Aurelia's room. He nodded easily to the workers.

His face mirrored Elijah's earlier that day: pure hatred. His eyes were fixed in front of him and he didn't bother to blink. He stood in the elevator and gazed outward as the door closed, then opened to the fourth floor. The Poetic Murderer smiled. He stepped off and turned toward the room at the end of the hall.

He could see that the light was off. He opened the door slowly and saw Aurelia sleeping on the bed. He smiled again, and took the time to enjoy it. He stood in the doorway of her room, the hallway's light spilling around his body, an ominous silhouette. He stepped into the room and closed the door behind him. He took five equally spaced steps to her bed and looked down at her.

SHE

WILL

DIE

His voice filled his head, and his eyes glowed fiery green in the sparse lights from the street. He raised a serrated blade above his head and brought it back down. It ripped into Aurelia's body just above her heart and pierced straight through. A loud gasp escaped her mouth and her back arched violently off the bed. The Poetic Murderer's hands held the knife's blade firmly in her chest, lodged into her heart directly between the left and right atrium. As Aurelia's eyes closed, her body slowly went limp.

A tear fell from one of her eyes as the last bit of life left her body.

CHAPTER 48

The sun was just coming up and Elijah's plane landed safely in Knoxville, Tennessee.

The morning was beautiful, and he awoke as the wheels touched down.

He'd get to see Aurelia within the hour.

This was his first thought, and his second was pain, an electrifying pain from his lower back. The large man beside him had put up the armrest while Elijah was asleep. Elijah now occupied only half of his commercial-class window seat and was curled into the wall of the plane in a half-realized fetal position.

His back was screaming. His neck felt horrible.

He held in frustration and hoped he'd make it through the day without firing his gun. Besides, they'd be off the plane momentarily.

Forty-five minutes later, Elijah settled into his rental. He drove the car toward the hospital and fidgeted in his seat. He was uncomfortable, and he couldn't decide if it was simply his seating arrangement, or if dreams had kept him tensing his limbs, grinding his teeth. It wouldn't be the first time. He often woke with headaches, aches in obscure places, sweat soaked into his collar and armpits. It could have been the nightmares, but the big guy wasn't off the hook yet.

He dropped the subject.

Besides, he rarely remembered his dreams. It'd be a waste to try.

He looked out the window.

He cursed commercial travel again, but since it was early, kept a positive attitude.

The morning light bathed still barren trees and rolling hills in its warmth.

The quick drive ended and Elijah walked into the hospital and to the elevator. He saw no one, except the lone desk employee. The early morning shift was the slowest of the day. After exiting the elevator, he walked toward the end of the hallway. Aurelia's light was still off, which was weird. She was usually up by that time. He opened the door quietly so to not wake her. The room was dark and he walked to the bed.

He stopped abruptly.

She was stunning as ever. She looked peaceful, on her side with one arm and a leg wrapped around a pillow. Elijah didn't figure he looked quite like that when he slept. The discomfort in his neck and his back made him think again about nightmares.

Then he remembered.

He could see the man wearing black's face, his green eyes ablaze as he brought down the knife.

He exhaled a thankful breath as he leaned down and whispered softly.

"Good morning, Aurelia Blanc."

He cast off the memory of his nightmare.

CHAPTER 49

A urelia stirred as he spoke.

He leaned down once more and whispered something that she'd never know.

She curled up in her blanket and pulled the pillow tight with her arms. She was still asleep, but a smile crept over her face. Elijah took her subconscious hint and headed back out to have coffee. It would be good for him. He missed his NY diner and could use some time to himself. Historically, while working murder investigations, time to himself ate away at his consciousness. He'd felt he could be doing more, or was bound to miss something. He knew it wasn't healthy, but he was consumed. He could only think of how to keep working, keep solving. His mind couldn't shut off. Somehow, something was changing.

At just before six in the morning he was seated at a table at the Southern Belle, a five-minute walk from the hospital.

The hostess had been attracted to Elijah. His stature and bright blue eyes had gotten her attention. And his smile, it caught her off guard; she didn't know why, but it captured her and took away her words and her eloquence.

She seated him and wished him, "a good breakfast time."

She shook her head at herself as she returned to the front.

Elijah had requested a window seat.

The glow of morning was still vivid and basking the early spring world. It was too soon for flowers and trees to be in bloom, but it was days like this that made Elijah look forward to the blossoming of a new year. Everything came back to life, got a fresh start. He liked that idea, starting over. He liked the idea of having a reset button or a logical place to begin again and reevaluate.

He sipped slowly and looked out the window at an empty parking lot, an empty backcountry road and the forests beyond. He thought about the evening before and the misfortune of the Poetic Murderer's escape. He'd been right there, looking him in the eyes. How could he let him get away?

His consciousness fought, but he knew Aurelia was right. They *had* made progress, just not enough to satisfy.

He moved on and thought about the conversation on the phone after the man wearing black had gotten away. Somehow, Aurelia knew how to calm him down, and she barely knew him.

It was a peculiar sensation, feeling comfort in a relationship after swearing them off for so long. He thought about what their "relationship" actually was. At best it was a fling from middle school. He hadn't mentioned his feelings to her. They'd barely kissed. They sometimes talked on the phone. It wasn't much but that didn't matter. What he felt for Aurelia was real, and he didn't need to understand it. Each day, he knew he wanted her more by his side. She could make him laugh, which happened rarely. She instilled in him a sense of calm.

With another drink of coffee, an idea snuck up on him. When Adams had asked where his flight was to go after Maine, he immediately said Tennessee. His home was New York. Tennessee was not his home. The only thing in Tennessee was Aurelia. He suddenly noticed that being with her in the hospital made him feel more at home than his apartment in the city ever had, more at home than *anything* ever had.

Elijah's waiter approached for the second time, refilled a coffee, and wrote down the order for both he and Aurelia. This time Elijah mixed it up and ordered blueberry pancakes, a move that stemmed outside his egg and breakfast meat comfort zone.

It was a short walk through the air of the south to arrive back at the hospital.

He closed the distance along the fourth floor hallway and noticed the light in Aurelia's room was on.

"Oh, Mr. Blanc," said a doctor approaching from the opposite direction. "Mr. Blanc, good news about your wife."

Elijah looked around a bit, holding the breakfast, and took too long to realize what was happening. *A case of mistaken identity, albeit a pleasant one.*

"G-morning, doctor. I'm actually just her work partner, Elijah Warren. But great that there's good news! What's going on?"

"Really? Just partners? The way she talks— I mean— I never would have thought. Um." He stopped and looked embarrassed. "So anyway, the good news. As of this morning, Aurelia performed well enough on her range of motion tests to be released. Nothing strenuous and nothing more than ten minutes up at a time, but she can go. The stitches should hold."

"That is great news, doc. Does she know yet?"

"I figured I'd save the news for her husb— Er... Her partner to pass on."

Elijah laughed a little.

"Thanks for taking such good care of her."

She was sitting up in her bed when he got there, stretching and yawning. Elijah paused a moment and looked through the window, trying to gather his thoughts. Was it crazy to think that he was in love with this woman? They hadn't even been on a real date. The entire time he'd been interested they'd been tracking a serial killer. Elijah discredited this hesitation and just went with it. He reached out and twisted the handle.

Aurelia turned; dark hair trailed and tumbled perfectly around her face and over her shoulders. "Good morning, Detective. Should I get used to this breakfast in bed thing?"

"G-morning back at ya. And maybe you should. Apparently I'm getting used to bringing it to you. I stopped in a half hour or so ago. You were out cold and drooling like a St. Bernard."

"Shut it! Although it doesn't surprise me. And that stupid, 'G-morning,' is that ever going away?"

"I doubt it. So let's just have breakfast. Guess what?"

"Oh. I don't like this game. Is the question rhetorical, or do you actually want me to guess?"

"I actually want you to guess," Elijah said.

"I guess that, you ordered the same food as always?"

"Actually no!" He set their food on the table. "I got us blueberry pancakes."

"Elijah Warren, you're stepping out of your comfort zone. I'm proud of you! And I love blueberry pancakes. Thank you so much!"

"You're very welcome. But that actually isn't my news. We… Um… You get to go home today."

"Really? Holy crap! That is good news. I can't wait to be out of here. Who told you? Adams?"

"Nope. Actually, it was your doctor. He called me 'Mr. Blanc.'"

"No he didn't!" she said with a bellowing laugh. Then she gulped some coffee.

Elijah couldn't get enough of hearing her talk to him. When did all this happen?

They worked their way to the table.

"Well, at least he thinks I have good taste in men," Aurelia said.

Elijah found some comfort in her response. He had at once an idea he could not set aside.

"I know we're making progress on the case, but I thought, tonight, maybe we could go out and celebrate you being better? When we get back to New York? Maybe drinks and dinner?"

"Eli, I've wanted that since Colorado."

He was suddenly distracted. His mother used to call him Eli.

"Elijah, what's wrong?" she questioned after seeing a subtle change.

"It's nothing. I promise. It was just a thought I had. No one's called me Eli since I was a kid. I like hearing it from you."

"Oh. OK. Well, if it bothers you, let me know."

"No. I promise it doesn't. It's just— My mom used to call me that."

"Elijah, do you mind me asking what happened to your parents? I don't want to overstep my boundaries, but I'm curious."

His mind flashed back to childhood. He closed his eyes and silence hung between them. He began to speak very quietly. His words were void of their usual confidence.

"My parents didn't get along very well. We lived in Pittsburgh until I was ten. Dad worked at one of the automotive plants. Mom stayed at home with me. Pretty typical family. I loved her, and Dad too. I was young and didn't realize how serious some of the things I saw were. You know how kids get used to things because they don't see anything different?" Aurelia nodded her head and listened intently with kind eyes, sipping her coffee as he spoke.

"On my ninth birthday, I came home from school to find Dad's car in the driveway. He usually worked late. I was excited and thought, because it was my birthday, he'd come home early. Turns out, he'd been laid off. Dad never dealt with anger well. Factories had been shutting down since American car production started being sent overseas, and apparently it was our turn. I walked in the front door and found him standing over Mom. His hands were around her throat. I remember, when I opened the door, she was blue in the face, eyes almost popping out of her head. I screamed and ran over to Dad. I was clawing and punching and kicking him. He was strong and obviously I was a kid. He knocked me down and I watched him until he was shaking a lifeless face. He made sure she was dead and I was there on the kitchen floor. I watched him make sure."

The room was again silent. Elijah stared down at his plate. He hadn't told the story since he was a child and had to testify in court as to what he'd seen.

"Dad went to jail, and I moved on," he finally said as he picked his fork back up.

"I'm so sorry, Elijah. I know there isn't anything I can say but, thanks for telling me about it. This may be unbelievable, but I do understand."

She could see the story pained him. He hadn't made eye contact with her since he mentioned fingers around his mother's neck. She could tell he was ashamed.

"Elijah, you know that you're very different from him. Right?"

He paused and had a bite of his pancakes, mulling the thought over in his head. "I guess I just always tried to stay out of relationships. I never wanted to be like him. I didn't even want the chance to be."

"Elijah, I can tell you for sure. You and your father are very different people. I didn't know him, but I know you. Take my word on that."

She then leaned across the table and ran her fingers along his neck and into the hair on his head. She pulled him forward and pressed her lips onto his. Elijah threaded his fingers into her open hand and kissed her back. He'd wanted it, and despite the conversation, it seemed perfect.

Once settled back into her chair, she looked back up. He stared back and they enjoyed that moment. It had been a great day, and was to only get better.

A celebration in New York was soon to come.

CHAPTER 50

A plane was descending through the skies of Tennessee, and Riff looked out its front and towards the earth. He was humming and tossing Cheetos into his mouth, crumbs spilling at the corners. Then he almost choked. What he was seeing below on the tarmac took him by surprise.

"I don't mean to be nosy," Captain Riff said, standing in the open door of the plane and atop the foldable stairs. "But did I see you assholes makin' out as I landed this buggy?"

"Riff, you absolutely *do* mean to be nosy," Elijah said on his way past and toward the fridge. "But yes, you did."

"So don't look at my ass this time through," Aurelia said, following behind. "I'm clearly taken."

She kicked the fridge shut.

"Jesus! What am I? An animal? Anyway, don't worry. You're a little old for me, Blanc."

"You're almost twice my age, Riff!"

"Yes."

"Gross."

"Anyway," Riff said back. Then he thumbed another Cheeto into his mouth and wiped the orange residue onto his famous Hawaiian shirt as he rambled on.

"Well. Suppose I'll get to it. We'll be back on the ground in a while. I'll keep ya in the loop with frequent updates about altitude, speed, my own personal thoughts on life, Thai food, or whatever."

He continued on through another mouthful of Cheetos and sauntered back into the cockpit.

"I like him."

195

"Elijah, you have to be kidding?"

They were talking at just above a whisper, and Riff had begun audibly humming from behind the controls, "Never Gonna Give You Up," by Rick Astley, and didn't seem to be paying attention anymore.

"How can you not?"

"Maybe he's a *little* funny, in an idiotic way. But he *couldn't* be around for more than a flight! We'd kill him!"

"I bet he'd grow on you."

"Lobster dinner and overpriced wine says he wouldn't," Aurelia said with a leer.

Elijah thought momentarily.

"If the situation arises, the deal's on," he agreed.

Aurelia knew very well that the middle-aged, chauvinistic, barely scraping handsome, "Captain Riff," with his moronic Hawaiian shirts, sandals and sexist jokes, *would* grow on her.

They decided a while later to spend time on the case before making it to the city.

The newest poems were situated in front of Aurelia. She stared hard at them. There was something that didn't sit right with her. The poems' themes weren't cohesive. Why?

Elijah was looking at the evidence files that focused on the victims. He couldn't help but think how each death was so minutely orchestrated.

The first was Marcus Felway, melted over a pit of fire, his bones then put on display. Serena Miller was second, hung below a waterfall and frozen for the winter. Next was the man in the basement, Tyler Bromville, they came to find out, abducted, starved, but kept alive for half a year, just to be taken off life support. The name on his back, Mario Arnold, was a hollow promise. He was still missing. Neither Elijah nor Aurelia had any idea where, or if, he would turn up. Then Priscilla De Luca, a beautiful woman who walked off the tallest building in Portland. Then Becky Fairchild, a woman whose stomach was slashed open and filled with burning coals. The sole survivor, Gina Lowbank, was abducted and buried at the cabin amid the Great Smoky Mountains with intent to be found.

It wasn't the body count that made the Poetic Murderer different; it was his method. As Aurelia had mentioned in the days prior, the imaginative brutality *had* to serve a purpose.

Aurelia was still staring at the two poems. She'd not moved in several minutes, though it didn't mean she wasn't busy. Finally, she grabbed a pair of scissors from her briefcase and separated each line of the two poems. She had six different lines of text scrambled before her. She began to rearrange the prose in different ways. She knew that six lines could produce 720 possible outcomes. She'd always had a mind for math. She closed her eyes and the possible arrangements coalesced in her mind, assembling, then dispersing and fading to the corners of her brain. After each mental arrangement, she would open her eyes and arrange the physical strips on the table. After thirty minutes of rearranging and pondering, opening and closing her eyes, she gasped.

"Elijah, look at this."

Elijah looked up from an awkward nap and looked at the poems. Aurelia had switched two of the lines. They now read like this…

Where we all must go
Back to where it all began
I'll be welcomed home

Where the sun first hits
Where the ocean meets the sky
One more to be found

Elijah looked over the words; the poems made more sense with the new arrangement.

"Holy shit, Aurelia! They're perfect. There's someone else on Cadillac Mountain."

Thoughts escaped his mouth in bursts.

"Mario!"

He thought of Alvira and Dennis Arnold.

"What does the other poem mean?"

"I'm not sure," she said. "I guess where it all started was Indiana, but I don't know how being 'welcomed home' has anything to do with anything…"

Her words tapered to an infinitesimal whisper as revelation fell over her face. She began rifling through the pages spread about on the table. She was picking them up and disregarding them wildly, a hurricane of murder files. Up to that point, they'd been kept quite organized. Files flew and she was almost frantic as Elijah watched her, completely blank as to what she was searching for.

She'd been staring at those files for days, and could rehearse the majority.

It was about to pay off.

"What were names of the people that owned the farmhouse in Indiana?" she blurted.

"Aurelia…I obviously have no idea."

"Hold on!" She was focused to the point of possession. "Here it is! Hold on! I need one more thing! Where's the report from the Townsend cabin? The one with the hair sample?"

Elijah knew she wasn't asking, just thinking out loud.

She finally had the two documents together, and her expression displayed what she'd found. Her mouth dropped, and the two sheets of paper fluttered from her hands and down onto the rest of the mess.

can't settle on how this might end. I know how it should, but not how it will. It wouldn't be right if I had complete control. And the outcome is less significant than the process of which I've kept true to, the overall picture to be seen when people step back. The outcome will be less important than the detectives' search for truth. Less important than the victims' pain and suffering.

The gravitational pull of reason will still keep many from understanding what I've done. This work will be lost on the masses, the fucking conformists, the puppets dancing about for the masters that tell them how. Those who look, however, will understand, will praise me, will forever be changed by this. Because of my vision, their minds will be opened, boundless and unhindered. They will realize unrestricted reality, and many will be left behind.

Because what one person sees is not sure to be the same as another.

One person swears miracle.

Another shouts tragedy.

If people can view the exact event differently, how can truth exist at all? How can we trust opinion or perception? How can objectivity exist if its foundation is subjective and flawed?

The answer is this.

It cannot.

Perception becomes certainty. Opinion becomes fact, and we accept the opinions of the people speaking loudest, or those with the greatest resources, or those with the easiest message to digest. We allow governments or celebrities or even strangers to decide for us, to tell us where to drive our cars and how to talk to people and what clothes to wear and what is worth our time.

We spend our lives building metaphorical palaces of information.

We categorize.

We list.

We judge.

We must tear down these palaces.

We are not free until we free ourselves from prior knowledge and impression, from fabrication and deceit. Even plain truth has nuance, and though this is all but plain, my point will emerge from the blood and flesh. People will wonder, marvel, despise and question. They will seek truth and find enigma. People will resort back to what they know to explain this, but what they know cannot.

These schemas, these judgments, take place of moral evaluation, of unique interpretation. Can no one think? Can no one appraise for themselves when the moment is new, decide for themselves what is right or wrong or beautiful or ugly when they're faced with it? If all new experiences are categorized with preprogrammed ideas, how can we accept novelty? How can we accept creativity? How can we truly experience something when we've already a supposition of how it will be?

People may look at what I've done negatively. Say it was an atrocity. Say I was monstrous, or evil, or some other fucking vindication. No matter how it is explained, people will, with time, understand what I've done.

But first, they will be shocked.

Sometimes that's exactly what people need.

History, if nothing else, has proven this.

The Poetic Murderer looked into his rearview and deliberated his journey and its implications. He'd been ranting in the depths of his mind for nearly five hours. He was driving somewhere very special and with a very unusual passenger in the backseat.

And they were almost there.

CHAPTER 52

The plane adjusted its trajectory away from New York. Aurelia was now pacing through the aircraft, describing what they'd found, despite Elijah staring at the same information.

"'Where we all must go

Back to where it all began

I'll be welcomed home'

I can't believe this, Eli. How did I miss it?"

"Aurelia, how could you *not* miss it? It was two arbitrary names on two very separate documents. It makes less sense that you remembered at all!"

"Shut it! I'm serious! The owners of the farmhouse in Indiana, Beth and Martin Cullen. The DNA match from the hair sample, Lucas Cullen. It must be the son. We've had his information this entire time. Those are two huge pieces! Those are two huge pieces to miss!"

"Aurelia, sit and calm yourself down. You are one of a whole lot of people who missed it, myself included. So if you want to continue berating yourself, consider me offended and hurt."

"Elijah Warren, you shit. Don't do that me." She hated how he always knew how to get his way, and placed her hands on her hips.

"And besides, it still doesn't make sense! When you have a death record, you don't have much reason to question it!" he said.

She knew he was right.

"Fine. But I'm still not happy about it taking me this long. Is Adams looking into them? He is right? You called him about the Cullens?"

"Yes, yes, and yes. And that's fair to be upset about how long it took. But even still, how does it explain how he has a death record? How could it explain how he's flown under the radar all these years? We can't be sure that it's Lucas Cullen."

"Elijah, we know how smart this guy is! And the poem says, 'I'll be welcomed home.' It's got to be him. I don't know how, but it is! I just know it!"

A short while later a blaring fax arrived from Adams, the result of an extensive FBI search on the Cullen family. They tore into it and were consumed…

"Can we go through it one more time? Just to make sure we didn't miss anything! It's just all so strange!"

Elijah laughed and of course gave in. "Yes, ma'am. Whenever you're ready."

Aurelia began pacing again.

"So, Beth and Martin were activists jumping from cause to cause. They lived in Birmingham and did research for the Brown V. Board case in Topeka, culminating in school desegregation in '54. Then they moved to Dallas, Texas until just after Kennedy was shot. They moved again and ended up in Cambodia just after the US invaded in 1970."

"I don't understand why, as an American, you would move to where America has just gone to war," Elijah said.

Aurelia didn't seem to notice his comment and continued.

"Then they move back to D.C. as the Watergate Scandal starts swirling around. Then they move again on August 9, 1974."

"Wasn't that the day after Nixon was impeached?"

"Right you are, dear Elijah. Watergate's loose ends are tied up. Then they move to—"

"Can we Reader's Digest this thing? We're in the mid-70's and need to be in the mid-90's."

"Not exactly. We can skip ahead to April 30, 1975."

"Fall of Saigon. Vietnam War ended. Got it."

"Smart ass. You know, not everyone would know that off the top of their head," she said. "So a year *after* the war ends, Beth and Martin moved to Son La, Vietnam with their eight-year-old son, Lucas. After living there a few months, a gang of locals tossed an extremely volatile, homemade explosive through their window, destroying the house and killing the family."

"Right. But it still doesn't explain how Lucas survived and why he has gone on a serial murdering spree in the United fucking States."

"I know, Elijah, but it all makes sense otherwise. What a perfect alibi. He doesn't exist on paper. There is no means of tracking him. You and I both know it's him whether we understand it or not."

"I hope so. But I can't stop wondering. Something's not right. How are we putting together these pieces? The details seem implausible, like it's all a set up."

Aurelia knew exactly what he was talking about. She'd been obsessing over and questioning what they knew for months, but after this breakthrough, logical or not, she was completely sure of what they'd find.

Lucas Cullen was the murderer, and he was waiting for them in that farmhouse.

Though one thing still gnawed at her. What did the killer mean by, *where we all must go*? She focused on the word *we*. She wondered who *we* might include.

They spent the rest of the trip in silence, each consumed in the same focus: finish the case and keep the other alive. It was now seven in the evening and Riff was on course to the airstrip nearest Nashville, Indiana.

CHAPTER 53

The plane landed on a decrepit tarmac at Brown County's airstrip. Elijah and Aurelia were wired. They didn't nap or finish their drinks. They were restless with the idea of ending the case of the Poetic Murderer. An Explorer awaited them steps from the plane. They were a few minutes from town, but another twenty from the farmhouse. They wasted no time.

The car stormed toward its destination, the people inside ready for a fight. Aurelia ran her fingers over the engrained ridges in the handle of her Smith and Wesson. The .45-cal pistol was big and obnoxious, but she'd never been interested in little girly guns. She wanted a cannon. The pistol was holstered underneath her left arm. She was ready to use it, and for once, kind of hoped she would get to.

Elijah's gaze stayed straight, unflinching. He looked out the windshield, and his imagination filled the infinite complexity of the night. He couldn't stop thinking about the subject of his worst nightmares.

SHE

WILL

DIE

He turned off his brain. His thoughts were getting the best of him.

The Explorer's lights cut through dense fog, reminding Elijah and Aurelia of the night they caught Charles Larson. The circumstances had been similar, and déjà vu crept up their spines.

"Why can't I ever have déjà vu at nice moments?" Elijah said.

Aurelia looked at the man driving and said nothing, but smiled. She knew in her heart that she was falling in love with Elijah and had spent the majority of the drive pushing thoughts of losing him from her head. She knew how dangerous the man wearing black was, and she wasn't going to underestimate him. Her fingers were still moving gently across the handgun. She finally said something.

"Eli, I think we need an overall change of scenery."

It was the last they spoke before arriving at the farmhouse.

Brake lights ignited and the vehicle turned slowly onto the dirt driveway. Large oak trees still loomed on both sides of the path and directed their way. Halfway along, their tires (unknowingly) rolled over a security buzzer.

When the house came into view, gooseflesh pulled up on the back of Aurelia's neck. It was just as she remembered, weathered and worn and paint chipping away, shudders banging loosely in the night's wind, a rotting corpse peeking out from the fog.

An old Bronco was parked in the drive.

Their Explorer slowed.

Elijah and Aurelia looked at each other.

Then the porch light came on.

"Are you fucking kidding me?" Elijah said.

"What do we do?" Aurelia whispered.

"I don't know. Do we just knock?"

Aurelia didn't know if he was being serious, but a raid on the house didn't make any more sense than knocking.

"Maybe so, Eli. He obviously knows we're here. He obviously *wants* us here. Maybe we just knock? Spraying bullets isn't exactly his style, and I don't think he'd let it end so messily. He wants something from us."

Elijah agreed.

They emerged from the car with their eyes fixed, guns ready. They approached the front door and recognized a small silver speaker had been installed to its left.

Then they heard the Poetic Murderer's voice for the first time.

It came into the night like a phantom, slow and filled with horror, each syllable crawling.

"Good evening, Detectives. I will say these words once. If you listen, things will work out in your favor."

A pause existed and the detectives said nothing.

"I will be sitting in a rocking chair in the living room. There are two more waiting. I am unarmed and do not plan on hurting anyone else, especially the two of you. I am willing to answer all your questions, and the time is now. I will never speak again once our conversation is finished."

Elijah and Aurelia were puzzled once again. Aurelia shook her head subtly side-to-side before deciding what to say.

"Elijah, I think we have to listen. He's got an agenda, and if he says he won't talk to us after this, I'm sure he means it. This may be our only shot for a confession, or answers in general."

He knew she was right and responded through the silver box.

"Lucas, we understand, but make sure you're being honest. I'm sure you know, but I'm looking hard for an excuse to fucking kill you. If we suspect something, this ends in a way you aren't OK with."

"Elijah, I don't mean to be uncouth, but you don't have any idea how I am, 'OK,' with this ending. The threats aren't necessary. I haven't lied once and don't plan on starting now. Please come in."

Hatred boiled inside Elijah Warren. His mouth came together and his brows angled in. Aurelia slipped her hand into his. She looked up and into his enraged blue eyes and said, "Hope you're not too hungry. At the speed *he* talks we'll never go on that date."

Stress eased from Elijah's body, and he allowed himself a small grin. He was surely in love with Aurelia Blanc. She always knew what to say, even at the worst times. She opened the door and led him inside.

The couple stood in the entryway, hands knotted together, ready for some answers.

Then their hands fell apart. With guns drawn, they descended the hallway to the living room where Marcus Felway was burned alive. They turned the corner.

The Poetic Murderer sat in the very same rocking chair they'd examined in January. He rocked leisurely. Each swoop of the chair creaked the floorboards.

"Welcome to my home, Detectives. Please, have a seat."

They looked at the man with a million questions. Aurelia couldn't help but find him attractive. She hated him in her heart, but he was *very* handsome. She began to understand how it was so easy to lead people astray. The detectives went to the chairs, but moved them so that they faced Lucas and the entryway from which they'd come. It was the only exit to the room. They sat down.

Directly before them sat the Poetic Murderer, calm and poised. Elijah squeezed his pistol, which sat in his hands across his lap. Aurelia put one hand over Elijah's, but kept the other firm with her pistol toward Lucas.

"Where do we start, Lucas?" Aurelia asked.

"Detectives, I figured you would take the reins. This is my first interrogation."

"How do you feel about being caught?" said Elijah.

"Have I been?"

"Have you not?" Elijah said.

"I suppose, Detective. I am sitting in front of you. I allowed you to walk into my home. I guess I just see things differently."

"That's fucking clear," Elijah said.

"You are quite a unique soul, Elijah. Are you upset that you have been changed by this?" Each syllable crawling.

Elijah's chest filled with a long breath, and he gritted his teeth.

"I am exceedingly impressed, to be honest. Each murder held a secret, and you discovered most all of them. You see, I have been at this a long time, detectives, and these were the *first* of my codes to be deciphered. Think how empty it was, all the effort I commit to my work to have it dismissed almost immediately, the evidence unseen. It was *exciting* for me to have found the two of you." Each syllable crawling.

Elijah tongued at his teeth. He could not take his eyes from Lucas Cullen.

"Does that mean there are more victims? More bodies to be found? When did it start?" Aurelia asked.

"*Many* other bodies, but they have all been found. Like I said, it took a long time to find the two of you. Do you know how many murders go unsolved each year in the US?! Or the world?!"

His composure seemed to slip, but just for a second, and his voice evened back out to its crawling drawl.

"Wait, have you found Mario yet? If not, you'll find him on the north side of Cadillac Mountain. Now," he paused and made a sweeping motion with his hands. "There are no more bodies to be found."

"What did you do to Mario?"

"Do you really want to know, Detective Warren?"

Elijah said nothing and kept his eyes on the Poetic Murderer.

"If you wish. I drugged him and dragged his body down an alley in Boston. I tossed him into an old Bronco and drove him to a small residence outside of Acadia. He was a pathetic man, so willing to give in and give up. I loathed him the moment I met him."

The Poetic Murderer adjusted his weight, the chair still creaking with each rock forward and back.

"Mario was lying on his back, bound to the floor by his wrists and ankles. He begged. He was screaming before I began. I'd brought a tool with me in the form of a cement block and first focused on his hands and feet. Who knows how many blows it took, but the bones turned to powder. The joints dislodged and hung limply. His toes and fingers popped like popcorn and the restraints slid off through the mangled gore. Then I turned to his head. His screams began to muddle as the block came down on his face, each blow confusing his features until there was a puddle of carnage that melted away from his shoulders. You should have seen the cement, the blood and the bits of skin, majestic pools and splatters of flesh and bits of brain swimming in the blood. I stood him up and the negative space was a work of art. He bled out down there and decomposed in the months following. He was there until just a few days ago when I hung what was left of him from a tree on Cadillac Mountain."

Elijah's fingers clenched, some on his pistol, the others in a fist, and his eyes narrowed further in the direction of Lucas Cullen. All he could think of was Dennis and Alvira Arnold. He could keep his thoughts quiet no more.

"Have you thought of how this affects people? Like, real people? People that feel and love and give a fuck about others! People who care about empathy! About humanity! How can you stomach yourself? How can you live with this? Have you thought about the families? The parents?"

Elijah was now shouting.

A tiny laugh erupted from within Lucas. He nearly repressed it and continued, keeping his tongue slow and calm.

"I actually *have* thought of those things, Detective. Quite a lot, actually. I had a point to prove, but I believe in balance and retribution. Everything is connected. You will soon see."

Elijah scoffed and Aurelia spoke up, giving him a sharp glance.

"Maybe we're getting ahead of ourselves, Lucas. Let's start from the beginning. Tell us about your parents."

He nodded his head a bit.

"They were activists, as I'm sure you have found by now. You personally should look more into them. They were fascinating. I didn't get to know them very well, but I loved my mother and my father. They were very busy, and after a move to Vietnam a group of local thugs threw an explosive device through our window. I learned this long after, of course. My dad rushed to the bomb, and my mom grabbed me and rushed me into a fallout shelter. I wasn't aware of its existence until that moment. I was confused and scared. I remember looking into her eyes as she closed the hatch door. She had mesmerizing green eyes. I watched her burn as the door locked shut."

"You aren't getting sympathy from me," Elijah pointed out evenly.

"Detective Warren, weren't you just talking about how *I* lack empathy?"

"Ignore him, Elijah," Aurelia interjected.

Elijah again tensed his fingers around his pistol, now so hard he could feel the gun's heartbeat.

"Continue, Lucas," Aurelia said.

"I spent the next minutes crying in a corner of the room. It was ubiquitously black, and I could see nothing. When I gathered myself, I explored. As mentioned prior, I didn't know exactly where I was. I ended up finding a lifetime's worth of canned food, batteries for a flashlight, and endless books and candles. Apparently knowledge was all Mom and Dad revered. Now, I'm glad they did."

"How long were you down there?" Aurelia asked.

"The bomb went off on October 11th, 1976. I was eight. Our house lay as a pile of rubble for the better portion of twenty years before someone bothered to clean it up. Apparently, when Americans die in Vietnam, investigations don't account for much. Just another unsolved murder." Lucas closed his eyes for a moment, then continued. "A family opened the hatch on January 4th, 1991. They had bought the lot."

Elijah and Aurelia dropped their jaws. Lucas Cullen had been alone in his parents' fallout shelter for fifteen years.

"So what did you do down there, Lucas?" Aurelia continued.

"I read. I learned all I could. I had enough literature to last me five lifetimes and plenty of topics to intrigue me. I memorized almost all of the thousands of books. I dreamt about the beauty of the world, about nature, about seeing the sunrise and sunset. I thought about the human existence and the way people lived in this world. I didn't hate being there. I began hating the world outside. I began to understand what was wrong with humanity. I began to understand what needed to change if I ever got out."

"So what are you trying to change, Lucas? What do you consider this appalling mess?" Elijah asked.

"Maybe I can begin to answer your question with a question, Elijah. What makes this an appalling mess? What makes what I'm doing different from anything happening in the Middle East? Or any war really? People are suffering at the hands of others. Is what I'm doing worse than the genocide in Rwanda?" Each syllable crawling.

"Yes. It is fucking different than war. And I don't see a purpose in comparing one atrocity to another. Rwanda was an appalling mess, caused by horrible people. This is an appalling mess, caused by a horrible person. Wars are not senseless shock value violence. That's the difference. Wars are fought for a reason."

"Can you really say that, Detective? In 1991, we sent troops into Somalia to retrieve a few American soldiers. *Thousands* of innocent Somalians were killed that day. Our government decided that those lives were worth just *a few* of our soldiers. Mind you, we weren't *invited* to Somalia. And we were in *their* country, Elijah. You see, murder isn't wrong as long as it serves a purpose we appreciate. And different people appreciate different things. I guarantee the families of those Somalians would say what the US did that evening was an, 'appalling mess.'"

"So what you're doing is just? Because horrible things happen, that makes this OK? I don't agree," Elijah said.

"Well, Detective, the beauty of this world is that you don't have to agree. By the way, how are you two enjoying John Keats?"

Lucas Cullen's tone continued to crawl underneath Elijah's skin. Aurelia responded to Lucas' question.

"You know, Lucas, I think Keats was a great writer. I wish you hadn't ruined his work for me. I think you've taken his writing very differently than he intended."

"Detective Blanc, I disagree. With the first John Keats poem I led you to his theory of negative capability. It explains what I've done quite well. You are analytical, exacting, grounded in logic and reason. And you, Elijah. I knew that it would take people like you to begin piecing my puzzle together.

"What I have done is pure and beautiful, each victim completely random…well except Priscilla. Each murder was new, different, something the world has never experienced. You and I have been in perpetual opposition. I on the side of beauty and a lack of reason, you yourselves on the side of logic, rationale, a truth for things that had no truth."

Elijah interjected. "So has our logic and reason triumphed, Lucas? You are here in front of us. We've found you. Does this show that we have reasoned through your beautiful masterpiece?"

"Parts of truth, Detective. There are parts of truth in that. You have accomplished what I thought no one would. Fuck, it's been since '91." Each syllable crawling.

Aurelia swallowed hard. For six years the murders were going unsolved.

"But there are pieces still missing, Detectives. You'll soon see. What I want to prove is that the way we live is flawed. We humans build up experience and presuppositions so we don't have to think later. Why? Why can we not rethink things at every opportunity? Why must we be set in our ways with nothing but prior knowledge to make our decisions? We cannot truly understand the world until we discard how we log what is true. Until we view each day anew, each moment fresh, with no assumptions or predetermined knowledge, we cannot be free. Then and only then will our society find truth, and in turn, find that sometimes, truth cannot exist because things cannot be explained."

He looked patiently back and forth between Aurelia and Elijah, reading their expressions with undisclosed elation.

"That is the ultimate goal, for society to understand that no matter how comfortable it is to understand, to recall, there will always be things that cannot be understood. There will always be experiences that cannot be compared to prior ones. We cannot reach our potential, if we are not willing to fully think for ourselves."

Trying to gain some trust, Aurelia spoke back up.

"Lucas, I understand what you're saying. I really do. If humans are constantly referring back to prior experiences to deal with the new ones, how do we ever experience anything new? How do we ever give someone different from us a chance if we assume things about them? I get it, but why this? Why approach it this way?"

"Because the world needed to be shocked. Humanity needed something that couldn't be categorized, something that couldn't be classified in some file. I wanted to do something the world could not ignore. The drones of the earth needed to wake up, to look around for once without being told how to look or what to look at. Detectives, the world is desensitized, and that is not my fault. But I wanted change, and I had to go to drastic measures to achieve it. I had to go beyond the desensitization of society."

Elijah stared with hatred. He hated every word that the Poetic Murderer said. He hated his reasons and his justification. He hated the blank expression on his face. He hated him with every ounce of his being.

"What more would you like to know, Detectives?"

Elijah thought momentarily. He'd dreamt about it for long enough that he had an answer posthaste. He raised his Glock directly toward Lucas Cullen, the man wearing black, the Poetic Murderer.

"Do you believe in hell, Lucas?"

"Elijah, don't!"

Lucas Cullen closed his eyes and smiled. Then he lowered his chin to his chest and answered Elijah's question.

"Yes. I do."

The deafening crack of a pistol filled the room. A lead bullet pierced Lucas Cullen's temple and ripped through the frontal cortex of his brain, exiting on the other side. It blew out the right side of his head and brain matter and skull fragments showered onto the dilapidated wooden floor. His body collapsed onto it and the rocking chair toppled to its side. Aurelia jumped up from her chair and sprinted into the kitchen. Elijah followed behind, baffled, wondering who had beaten him to the trigger.

As he turned the corner, he looked into the familiar eyes of Lucas Cullen's murderer.

CHAPTER 54

D ennis Arnold was pinned to the ground with Aurelia fastening handcuffs around his wrists. An antique Colt pistol spun idly on the dirty linoleum. Elijah stood above them in disbelief. What was going on? How was Mario Arnold's father suddenly in Indiana?

Aurelia lifted Dennis to his feet then moved him to sit against a wall.

Dennis seemed satisfied. Elijah and Aurelia again had a million questions, but for someone new.

"What in the hell are you doing here, Dennis?" Elijah almost stammered.

"I'm sorry, Elijah. I know you wanted to catch him. I know you wanted to catch him," he repeated. "And to be frank, you did. You and Aurelia were exactly the people he was looking for. You were as big a piece of this as he was!" Elijah clenched his teeth. "He said it was the two of you who were meant to do this. He said that this was your story and not his. He said it would be the start of something much bigger for you. He said something about how, even when things can't be classified, people still need to understand why things happen. It was his plan to be caught, but you *did* catch him. He needed it for his 'masterpiece' to be complete."

This information was a bit much to consider.

"So then I ask again," Elijah growled. "What the fuck are you doing here, Dennis?"

"Not long after you left our house, I got a phone call from Lucas. He explained who he was, and what he had done to our Mario. He told me that he wanted to give me an opportunity. He told me he wanted me to kill him." Dennis' eyes began to tear up. "I couldn't say no, Elijah. Mario was everything to us. Don't tell me you can't understand! I didn't care why he wanted me to kill him! I just wanted it! I needed to do it!" Dennis was now screaming, tears streaming from his eyes. "Don't you tell me you wouldn't have done the same, Elijah!"

This was true, and Elijah thought back a few days; he had had an identical conversation within himself on the way to the Arnold's house, and knew that if someone had taken and torturously murdered his child, he would fight to the end of the earth to kill that person.

Aurelia spoke next.

"Dennis, we both understand wanting revenge, but do you know what this means for you?"

"Yes. My wife is going to kill me." They noticed it was a joke and laughed a small laugh with Dennis. He was well aware that he was going to jail and clearly OK with it.

"Did she know?" Aurelia asked.

He began to cry again and lowered his gaze from theirs. "She didn't," he said. "After the phone call from Lucas I told her I needed a break. I said goodbye and left the house, met him at a train station outside Jersey. He brought me here. He told me the time would come. I had to promise to wait. It had to be in front of the two of you, and it had to be after you'd talked. Those were his only conditions."

"Why did you listen? I mean, why did you wait?" Elijah asked, and Dennis laughed.

"Detective, have you forgotten who Lucas Cullen *was*? After knowing what he's done, I wasn't going to ruin my chance. I knew that I wanted to kill him, and I believed that he was going to give me the opportunity. So I waited. I was unarmed until you showed up. He walked upstairs to where I've been sleeping and told me that it was time. He handed me the pistol and said to wait until after you'd come into the living room. Then I could come downstairs and hide in the kitchen. He told me I could shoot him after your conversation was done. He said he'd close his eyes and put his chin to his chest. Then I'd know he was ready."

The pieces were starting to fit together, despite their obscure shapes. They all stayed silent after that. When S.W.A.T. arrived, the detectives passed the responsibility onto them. They said goodbye to Dennis and wished him good luck, then walked out of the house. Halfway to the Explorer, they turned and looked back at the weathered paint, the flapping shudders.

"Back to where it all began," Elijah said with a small laugh. "Well, he said he'd never speak again when our conversation was done. I guess he was being more literal than we thought. How do you feel about havin' some beers back in town? I know this lovely little place called Hoosiers."

"Elijah Warren, you and I both know that 'lovely' doesn't describe that place, but I don't care. I would absolutely love to."

Elijah and Aurelia drove back toward Nashville with fingers intertwined. Aurelia thought back one more time to the John Keats poem. She thought about the hand being held forward and her theories on what it could mean. Never did she think about the killer offering his own hand forward to sacrifice himself, but that was the truth. It was the final act of beautiful madness, the final act of disregard towards human nature, the final piece to the puzzle that the world might never understand, that is, unless *they* talked about it.

Elijah wondered if in some crazy way, Lucas was right. Maybe Lucas' masterpiece *had* opened his eyes. Maybe he was seeing the world clearly for the first time. He obviously saw life differently than before the case. Maybe the Poetic Murderer's unhindered, calculated violence and novel approach had him feeling a way he'd never before. He wasn't sure *what* to think, or *how* to feel, but he did know that he was in love with Aurelia Blanc and was going to make some changes in his life. Had it been the unexplainable brutality that helped him find what he felt was beautiful in the world?

Who knew?

But maybe.

Aurelia smiled as she stared from the window and into the darkness of the Midwestern sky. It was the happiest she ever remembered being. It was an odd time to feel so euphoric, but that didn't matter to her. She turned her head toward Elijah and watched him until he turned his blue eyes to her.

"Thanks, Elijah." The words slipped from her mouth and he laughed.

"For what, Aurelia?"

"I don't know, Eli. My life is just better now that I know you. And I'm glad we finally get to go on that date."

Elijah smiled and stopped the car in the middle of the deserted road, in the middle of the sprawling black of night and underneath the billions of stars above. The fog had subsided. He leaned and turned her head, just enough to kiss her deeply.

Shortly after, they walked into Hoosiers.

And for once, they didn't envy the other patrons.

Kevin Cady lives in Colorado Springs with his girlfriend and their pets. He teaches various courses at a local high school and earned degrees from Miami University, a bachelor's in rhetoric, and Colorado College, a master's in education. He is a routesetter at a rock climbing gym and spends most of his time (when he's not writing) climbing in the mountains that lay just west of his front door. The books of The Warren Files are his first novels.

Many people have contributed to *The Warren Files*. My parents and brother, Sue, Steve, and Matt, have supported my every endeavor, and this maybe is the craziest. Thank you to them for their unfathomable support. Mom, thanks for reading through the books more times than any human ever should. I want to thank my girlfriend, Danielle, for being able to keep me positive, for countless nights talking about characters and plotlines, for reading it out loud and for keeping me sane when pieces of text went missing. Thanks to Lynn Booker for her watchful eye and ideas. Finally, thanks to the many others who have read, discussed, criticized and helped improve. *The Warren Files* simply would not be if I had been alone in this.

The Warren Files

Book One: A Solitary Awakening
Book Two: Crooked Principles
Book Three: Truth's Illusion

Available at any online retailer and at…
www.kevincadyauthor.com